Goodbyes &
Second Chances

T.I. LOWE

DEDICATION

To the younger me, Tonya, aka Rooster. You had to say goodbye to much at an early age, but your second chance gave you   so   much   more.

ACKNOWLEDGMENTS

A special thank you to my fabulous readers for appreciating my imperfect Bleu Family. You get what I'm trying to do with them and that just makes my day!

My Lowe family, thank you for your unwavering support. Much love and appreciation. My beta readers, Trina Cooke, Lynn Edge, and Jennifer Strickland. You girls help me keep the story on track. Y'all rock!

Lastly, but always firstly, my Heavenly Father. You are a good, good father. Thank you for loving me and accepting my flaws. And also for allowing me the epic opportunity of sharing your incredible love with the world.

WHITE TRASH

White trash is not a choice. Just like any other social status, you are born into it. You can take as many bleach baths as you want, but the stigma is embedded in your pores. Trust-fund babies are born with a silver spoon in their million-dollar mouths, while white-trash babies are born with a rusty fork, with missing prongs, in their poor mouths. But hey, you learn to take what you can get.

In the brutal life of white trash, you grow up in tired, worn-out houses that continue to be punished with the build-up of way past-due bills and beyond-neglected chores. No one wants to take responsibility for any of it. It is always someone else's fault and someone else's responsibility. And you're lucky if it's a house. Normally, you move a lot and see the inside of too many ramshackle motel rooms and mildew-recking trailers.

Beer bottle fights over women, emergency room visits for stitches, and police reports for domestic violence are a given. A white-trash family responds to their disputes with fists or any object they can get their hands on. There seems to be a lot of underlying anger—for what? Maybe past disappointments? Or life struggles? Or instabilities? Most likely, it's a combination of all. There's never a break to be had. Never...

I have tried to push this stigma off and dress in normal wear. But no matter, I feel that I will always wear my white-trash badge whether I like it or not. It's part of my roots even though I have groomed myself to blossom into something better.

PART ONE
GOODBYES

The Young and the Stupid

ONE

Sometime in the late '90s...

In the great state of Georgia, you are tried as an adult at the ripe ole age of *seventeen*. Even though I'm the correct age by law to be incarcerated, I'm really a decent young lady who should not be old enough to go to jail. Yet, here I sit. It's just that unfair situations always seem to find me. Tonight's foolishness is no different.

Oh, to be born on the other side of Shimmer Lakes, where everything glitters with wealth and prestige. This dumb incident would have certainly been laughed off on that side. Instead, I am from the wrong side of the *water tracks*, and this is why the pad of each finger is smudged from being booked. My attempt at wiping the evidence of my guilt off onto my jeans is unsuccessful. The ink seems imbedded. I try again with a little more force until my skin begins to burn.

Even though the oval-shaped lake has mirrored shores, the reflection is nowhere near similar. Although we share the same body of water with those people, many levels of social status separate us.

The other side is dotted with expansive lakeshore homes, resorts, high-rise condos, and the million-dollar marina. To live on that side, bank accounts have to range in the six to seven figures.

My side of the lake's reflection is tarnished with tin-can trailers that smell like mildew, modest vehicles dressed in rust, and a weathered dock. Most struggle to even make it into the five figures.

It's not that this side doesn't try. It's because most of us have been born into it and seem unable to figure out how to better ourselves. Once you've been deemed a nobody, society struggles to see you in any other light. Not many opportunities present themselves, so the hopeless cycle of poverty continues.

I scratch my head. *How in the world did I get myself in this mess...again?*

My eyes narrow and shoot daggers at my cohorts as the officer ticks off the long list of charges. He's already told us our offenses once, but now he is repeating them for Aunt Evie.

"Arson, unlicensed use of pyrotechnics, operating a powerboat without a valid license..." Blah, blah, blah... In other words, we've screwed up. *Again.*

Aunt Evie's nightgown peeks from underneath her long coat as she wraps it a little tighter around her thin frame. She trains her tired eyes on the officer, nodding with understanding, while a nervous hand works on tucking a few wayward strands of her long silver hair back into the lopsided bun. It's well past midnight, and her day will begin too soon. Thief might as well be added to my list of crimes for stealing this poor woman's much-needed sleep.

Good grief, this has been one long night. There are only three guilty parties present in this station. The other three were lucky enough to get away unnoticed. They are faster runners, and it's my fault that the three of us sit here now. I'm short and slow, and these two wouldn't leave me. For that I'm thankful. Really, who wants to get handcuffed and hauled off to jail alone? No one, that's who! This is one of those situations that is most definitely better with a buddy.

The officer finishes the spiel of charges, and Aunt Evie cuts her eyes so sharply at me that I can feel the sting straight through. The guilt eating at me makes it hard to swallow. This was stupid. Just plain stupid. I'm the oldest, so the blame will be solely placed on me.

"Do you have anything to say for yourself?" Aunt Evie directs her words toward me as if on cue.

"Nothing. All I can think about is a nice, hot shower and dry, clean clothes. We've been sitting here for hours with the air conditioner blasting on us!" I snap off that last part in the direction of the officer, but he ignores me while shuffling through a stack of forms.

Without offering a towel or blanket, he assigned us seats right underneath the air conditioning unit. It's felt like some type of war torture tactic, but we've managed to keep a tight lid on tonight's incident.

"Young lady," Aunt Evie warns in a low voice.

And that's all it takes for me to cower down. "Sorry." I slouch further down in the plastic chair, causing my soggy shoes to squeak against the tile floor.

One of my cohorts lets out a subtle cough, but I don't care to look to see where it came from. I can hardly care past wanting to get out of these constricting jeans and my wrinkled T-shirt, both still holding tightly to the lake water they sucked up earlier. It's beyond uncomfortable. I'm beginning to wish they had offered us orange jumpsuits. Wearing dry prisoner attire has to be better than sitting here wet and freezing.

"What you reckon is gonna happen to these young'uns?" Aunt Evie looks over each one of us as though she is trying to decipher where we keep our stupid buttons, in hopes of turning those suckers off.

"Since it's their first offense, they will probably get slapped with a fine for the damage caused and sentenced to community service."

I hear a quiet chuckle and look over to find Dillon smirking at the first offense statement. I cut my eyes at him again, glaring with all my might. Those charges against me last year were dropped, and he knows it—not enough evidence to pin me with that stupid choice.

I glance between Kyle and Dillon—both lanky, shaggy-headed troublemakers fighting to hold back teasing smiles. *It might be time to start keeping different company.*

"So, I can take Jillian and Kyle home now?" Aunt

Evie signs the document to verify she gets how stupid we were tonight.

"Yes, ma'am." The officer accepts her check, which is automatically added to my I-Owe-Aunt-Evie list. *Sigh.*

"Are you sure I can't take Dillon home, too?" We look toward the man-child in question as he scratches at the five-o'clock shadow on his chin. He's the same age as my brother Kyle, fifteen, but Dillon's features are closer to that of a twenty-year-old.

It would be easier to believe his mother lied about his birthdate had we not grown up together, but I've witnessed him hitting those overly-anxious growth spurts. Dillon claims it's the Italian in him. Whatever the cause, it doesn't seem natural... or fair.

"Cora is working... I don't mind one bit to take him off your hands. Surely, you've had your fill of these young'uns for the night." There's a polite plea in her weary voice as she glances at the black-haired punk who's way too handsome for his own good.

Dillon flashes the only thing boyish about him—a deep set of dimples—while training those deep-blue eyes in the direction of the officer, looking way too hopeful about Aunt Evie's request.

Put the charm away, Dimples. It ain't gonna help you this time. I roll my eyes at him, but he misses it. Those dimples he's nicknamed after disappear as the officer shakes his head.

"Sorry, ma'am. He has to be picked up by a guardian." The officer's sorry, but sounds like he couldn't care less. He has the audacity to begin playing on his computer as Aunt Evie pleads with him. I bet he's playing solitaire. I can't see the screen from where I'm sitting, but I just bet...

"Well, I'm on his school forms as an approved person to pick him up. Ain't that good enough?" She's trying to stay calm, but her tone is tightening and the polite smile slips to a frown.

Now, here is another perfect example of the type of issue caused by being from the wrong side of town. This wouldn't be a problem for the other side of good and plenty. No, sir. This thick, bloated officer would be slapping the pick-up person on the back, having a good laugh at the expense of the rich kids' stupid prank gone bad, while telling them to put their fat wallets away and pretend the incident didn't really happen. The pick-up person would promise a lunch date soon at the marina and haul the whole lot home without question. But poor white trash doesn't get such breaks. We are already deemed a nuisance to society, and they seem to take seriously the charge to keep us in our place.

"Sorry, ma'am," the officer repeats again, without even looking away from the computer screen. The mouse clicks and clicks and clicks. Yep. The jerk is playing solitaire.

Aunt Evie walks over to Dillon. He has soot smeared across his forehead, and she tries unsuccessfully to rub it off. I watch as he plays into her pity for him—lips slightly puckered and eyes solemn. It's not that he is on board to be pitied, but he has no qualms of playing into it with adults to get his

11

way. I narrow my eyes at him to convey my not pitying him. A smile twitches from the corners of his wicked mouth, but he controls it in front of my aunt.

Dillon was exiled to the Shimmer Lakes Trailer Park and Campground a little before me and Kyle. His dad was killed while serving our country the same year Dillon was born to a seventeen-year-old Cora, who was not allowed to marry Dawson Bleu before his deployment. He left behind a brokenhearted girlfriend who wasn't legally his widow, so the death benefits were directed to his family instead.

The only things left behind that Cora got to claim were his newborn son and his Gibson electric-blue acoustic guitar. Dillon laid claim to the guitar before he could walk and plays that thing like it is his life's purpose. The boy is crazy talented and can play any instrument placed in his hands. I've never seen anything like it anywhere. He brings an instrument to life like it's some divine calling. I would be jealous if I wasn't in such awe of his talent.

There's nothing divine and awe inspiring about his mother, except for her strong work ethic. Cora waitresses to make ends meet, so Aunt Evie has helped her care for Dillon over the years ever since Cora stumbled into the trailer park, flat broke and devastated. That feisty woman busts her butt in hopes of making a better life for Dillon one day. Neither side of her family wanted her after they found out she was unwed and pregnant—another example of judging someone due to their circumstance. Cora has spent many a night on our small porch, crying on Aunt Evie's shoulder. I really do feel sorry for her until she starts in on Dillon. She rides that boy something hard. Cora has voiced repeatedly over the years how she hates the path her life has taken and hates that she dragged Dillon down with her. She also has no qualms about letting it be known how much she hates me. For some reason, I'm not good enough to be her son's friend.

Kyle and I fall into the trash from birth category, so maybe that's why...

Our parents were into the gypsy lifestyle, so we've lived in a variety of places—anywhere from trashy roach motels and campgrounds to squatting in a few abandoned homes. They fall into the category of parents mindlessly spitting young'uns out into this world and having no clue as to what to do with them. Aunt Evie, being childless, offered to take us in after the authorities hauled us away.

"It's okay, Aunt Evie." Dillon's deep voice booms around the small police station, dragging me out of those depressing thoughts.

Aunt Evie shakes her head. "Son—"

"Y'all head home. No worries." Dillon pushes his hand through his long hair, unearthing the blue streak tucked in the front of the dark locks.

I notice he's mindful not to push it too far back, keeping the guitar silhouette tattoo with his dad's initials concealed. He claims he had it inked behind his right ear as a reminder to always be listening for his dad. I personally know he tucked it there to hide it from his mother. She would beat him silly if she knew he got a tattoo behind her back.

Aunt Evie places her hand somberly on Dillon's shoulder, as though he is the victim and not a conspirator in tonight's fiasco. "I'll find Cora and get her here as quick as I can, sweetheart." She hugs him and then motions for me and Kyle to follow her.

"Aunt Evie, we can't just leave him here." My voice breaks. *I don't pity him... Okay... Maybe I do a little.*

"Well, we wouldn't even have to worry about this if you would act your age. Jillian, you are almost eighteen. You know how to make better decisions than this. I depend on you to be more responsible. Now look at the mess you have gone an' gotten your brother and Dillon into."

Dillon has a stoic expression painted on his aggravating face. When Aunt Evie turns toward me, that manly face transforms into a mischievous brat with dimples popping out full force. Jerk. *I take it back. I don't pity him one bit.*

"Me?" I jab my finger toward him and Kyle. "It was their idea!"

"Don't even blame those boys for your decision. You're older!" She's full of vinegar, and I can't blame her. She has the trailer park to manage and will be dead on her feet in a few hours when she is expected to get to work.

"I... I'm sorry, but I don't feel right leaving Dillon here."

"We'll stay until Cora arrives." Aunt Evie relents

and settles into a chair beside me.

The boys have muttered only a handful of words since we were brought in, so I decide it's in my best interest to follow suit. I look over at Kyle with envy. He seems to not have a care in the world, nodding off to sleep with his dark-blond hair flopping over his eyes. It's all frizzy from our unexpected plunge in the lake. I brush my hair in the identical hue over my shoulder and twist it in a long braid to try to tame it for the time being until I can get access to a shower and a gallon of conditioner.

Time sluggishly moves by until Cora storms into the station at three in the morning, wearing her food-smudged uniform, with her dark auburn hair slipping from her ponytail. Bags are prominent under her eyes, and her mouth is set in a severe sneer.

Oh boy, is she ticked.

Her whole body trembles with anger as she marches over to a sleeping Dillon and lands a slap across his face, causing him to almost fall out of the chair. The severity of the hit is evident as the sound bounces off the cement walls and has both me and Kyle flinching. The red handprint instantly blooms across his face. I try catching his attention, but he won't even meet my gaze. Just hangs his head and stands behind his witch of a mother.

"I'm s—" Dillon begins to mutter, but hushes when she lets out a sharp hiss.

Cora shoots me a look that sends the message loud and clear—*it's all your fault.* She doesn't say a word to anyone as she signs the required documents and storms toward the door.

I'm about to give Cora a piece of my mind, but I catch sight of Aunt Evie shaking her head sternly at me as she points us to the exit. Out of respect for my aunt, I bite my tongue and file out of the police station behind her. Aunt Evie gets ahold of us without using her hands or making cutting remarks, so I see no need in Cora handling Dillon that way.

"She ain't got any business laying a hand on him like that," I whisper toward my aunt's back, with her nodding her head in agreement.

I may be young and stupid, but I already see this woman coming to regret how she's treated her incredible son one of these days.

TWO

The bleak truth reflects against the glassy surface of the lake, revealing the burnt remains of our boat and a charred dock. They were the victims of a poorly-executed stunt. Another charred piece unceremoniously plops into the water and sinks to join the other remnants on the sandy bottom. It's shallow here, so we get the fun task of pulling that mess off the lake floor, too. I shake my head and let out a long sigh. We really shot ourselves in the foot with this one.

Spring break delivered us a bad case of boredom. Due to last night's shenanigans, problem solved. We now have the chore of cleaning up the mess we made.

By the sounds of the rowdy groups passing by in their fancy boats, it looks like spring break delivered better plans for the residents from this side of the lake while we dredge up the soggy debris.

Kyle lets out a low grunt. I look over and catch him ogling a group of bikini-clad teenage girls catcalling at him and the other boys as their boat passes by. I roll my eyes in my friend Leona's direction. Her mocha eyes return the gesture. She and the other two escapees volunteered to help us clean up the mess made by our stupidity. This is how we roll. We stick together.

"Close your mouth, Kyle," I mutter, leaning into his line of vision.

He mops the sweat from his brow with the back of his hand. "Ain't nothing wrong with looking." Some of the guys grunt their agreement, sounding like a bunch of pigs.

"Yeah, but it's tacky to drool, dork," Leona fires back.

Not all of the residents from Shimmer Lakes Trailer Park are of the poor white trash lineage. Leona is from the poor black background. She lives with her dad in a small trailer down the street from mine. Mr. Dan is a nice man, and we all consider him a hero because he was also a soldier like Dillon's dad. Mr. Dan went to war, too. And although it gave him back, it didn't return him the same. He suffers from post-traumatic stress disorder and has had a hard time fitting into society since returning. Some days he doesn't even make it out of bed, but he does the best he can for his daughter.

The other two helping us today are the King twins. They are identical in looks and nature. Maxim, who we call Max, is a few minutes older than his trouble-prone brother, Maverick. We call him Mave for short. Mave is all about getting into mischief, and to be honest, it's his fault this time, too.

Max plays the guitar and Mave rocks out on the drums in Dillon's band, Bleu Streak. Both have wavy brown hair that brushes well past their shoulders and matching brown eyes. We grew up together, so it's pretty easy for us to tell them apart. Max's nose is slightly wider at the tip than his brother's. And that's not saying much because their noses are just as thin as the rest of them. They both are tall, well, maybe they're average but everyone seems tall from where I stand. And they're way too bony, even though they eat like hogs. They always have something in hand, devouring it and whining simultaneously that they are starving. I personally think those two have a bad case of worms. We actually hide our favorite snacks when we see them coming, because the dudes will eat you out of house and home. No joke.

Max flips another blackened board into the wheelbarrow and groans. "This is all your fault, Mave. You have the worst luck mojo. Ever."

"Dude," is all Mave mutters, keeping to the task of pushing the full cart over to Mr. Dan's pickup truck and dumping it into the bed.

"He already feels bad enough, Max. Leave him alone!" I shove into his scrawny shoulder as I walk by him.

"Whatever, *Mommy*."

"If you jerks wouldn't act like *babies*, then I wouldn't have to mother you all the time."

"I'm gonna need a bath after this, Mommy. You gonna wash and rock me?" Dillon waggles his eyebrows, earning a warning punch to the arm from my brother.

"Not cool, bro." Kyle shakes his head and yanks up another decrepit board.

Dillon raises his soot-covered hands in surrender toward Kyle, but flashes his dimples and winks at me. *The big flirt.*

"Enough horsing around. I'm ready to be done staring at our dead boat," Leona interjects while tucking a blonde dreadlock under the brim of her sunhat.

We all take a quick pause to pay our last respects, before getting back to work.

The boys discovered the boat in the back of one of the old sheds on the property a few years ago while they were plundering around. It was Aunt Evie's dad's boat, so she gave us permission to do whatever we wanted with it. It wasn't fancy like the pleasure boats from across the lake, but we knew how to improvise.

After some junkyard digs and a little bartering with a few boat mechanics, we had ourselves a *closely* restored 1953 Chris-Craft Sportsman. After more digging around in the shed, we unearthed two sets of antique wooden water skis. That's when we knew we were in business.

Our setup may not have been as fancy as the rest, but it was just as functional. We taught ourselves the fine sport of waterskiing, spending most of the warm months on the lake as long as we could scrape up the fuel money.

Kyle grabs up the metal skeleton of one of the boat chairs and sighs. "Sure wish we had a rewind button." The entire group grumbles in agreement.

Last night we were hanging out on our dock like

we do most nights, wishing for some entertainment. I had no gas in my car and no money to remedy that problem, so we couldn't even go cruising around. We were outright bored. And that's when Mave rolled up on his bike, lugging two huge sacks of fireworks. His uncle had given them to him after a New Year's Eve event as payment for helping with a pyrotechnic show. He had been holding on to them for some reason. It's a wonder they hadn't already starred in some catastrophe around here before now.

"I've got an idea," is all Mave said as he headed to the boat with the sacks. We sat glued in our spots, not sure if we were up for a Mave idea. They normally ended poorly, so we should have known better from the start. He looked back over his bony shoulder and hollered, "Ain't y'all coming?"

So like the bunch of idiots we are, we followed behind him. After grabbing a canoe and connecting it to our boat with the ski rope, we headed out to the middle of the lake to put on a show. Dillon captained the boat with Mave by his side. The rest of us were pulled behind in the canoe. Once we reached the middle, the two boys set out to splitting the night sky with the flashy fireworks. That went well for all of two seconds.

Then the stupidity began. Kyle jumped over to help them out as they were loading an ignited firework. With the rocking of the boat, the fireworks launcher fell over and the next thing we knew, the entire boat was lit up like a giant fireball. The boys jumped to the canoe while Dillon worked on freeing the rope, but he couldn't get the knot untied, so we were helplessly tethered to the burning boat. Giving up, he took a giant leap off the side of the boat. In the process, his foot hit the throttle, causing the blazing boat to take off like shot.

A loud boom erupted during the runaway course and the gasoline can took flight in a flash of fire. Before we could decide to abandon the overloaded canoe, the boat plowed into a dock on the other side of the lake. The boat and a good portion of the dock went up in flames, and we were dumped into the lake. Luckily, none of us idiots were injured. *Well, not too bad.*

"I'd go for a fast-forward button right about now," Mave mumbles, his arms weighed down with soggy remains.

We drive off load after load until the sun is setting and shore is completely swept clean. Only a scattering of ash and the lingering scent of smoke remains as proof of last night's catastrophe. After returning Mr. Dan's truck, we set out to our side of the lake in hopes of ridding ourselves of the sweat and soot. The boys strike out in a sprint as they tear off their filthy shirts, and each one does some daredevil dive off the end of the dock. Leona and I are too tired for any type of flare, so we merely walk to the end and step off into the cool water as the night closes in around us.

I ease over to the ladder and try to free some of the soot from my skin. The water ripples around me, and I know it's Dillon before looking. For whatever reason, it's become our little spot over the years. It's normally where we end up when Dillon wants to talk about a new song or about a falling-out with Cora. Sometimes we just cling to the ladder and dream about a future far away from here.

"You alright?" he asks, reaching over and wiping my cheek. His thumb works over a spot several times before he drops his hand.

"Might as well be." I dip my head into the water to sleek my hair back and let out a groan. "Our poor boat. I'm gonna miss it."

"Me too. I'm really sorry, Jewels." He releases the ladder and treads the water in front of me, waiting for me to soothe him and tell him it's okay. Words that he needs to hear after the chewing out I'm sure he received from Cora. He gets no slack from her, so he seems to always be seeking it out from me and Aunt Evie. Of course, we both baby him. Someone has to, right?

"It was an accident. Don't worry about it." I reach over and push a lock of hair away from his eyes and offer him a smile. "We just gotta find a new hobby." I know that's not a lot of soothing, but that's all I got tonight.

Dillon's gaze goes from remorseful to intense. Wanting to get away from it, I push off the ladder and start to swim off, but his long arms stretch out and anchor me to him.

"I'll make it up to you one day, Jewels. I promise."

I nod my head in agreement to appease him,

23

knowing he's naïve enough to think he can pull it off. I try to wiggle free, but Dillon takes hold of me a bit rougher.

"I'm beat, Dimples. Let me go." I push against his chest but his arms remain locked around me.

"One day the band is going to hit it big. When we do, I promise to buy you a brand new boat. Better than any of those over there." Dillon hitches his chin toward the other side of the lake.

"Awesome. Now let me go." I wiggle around, hoping to slip from his grip.

"You don't believe me?" He pulls me a little closer, his tone challenging.

I look over at the crowd wrestling in the water, no cares in sight, and wish I could brush off my worries so easily. "You know how things are, so don't try making unrealistic promises."

"I'm gonna prove you wrong... And the day I do, you have to hand over the keys to your fine ride." He releases one hand and holds it out to seal the deal.

Every day we've lived has been a struggle. Not for a blame boat, but for necessities such as groceries. I want him to prove me wrong, so much so, I'd happily give him the keys to my Mustang.

My weasel of an uncle hightailed it with some floozy the year after Aunt Evie took us in. The foolish man was so blinded by lust that he left his 1976 Mustang II Cobra Hatchback. Aunt Evie generously signed the title over to me on my sweet sixteenth birthday. *Talk about a sweet gift.*

The exterior is shiny black with a mean silver

racing stripe that starts on the hood and sprints all the way to the back bumper. This baby is fast when it's standing still and is all mine. It's great as long as I have some money to put into the gas tank, which normally I don't, so my baby sits under its car cover most of the time.

"Okay, Dimples. It's a bet." I place my hand in his and enjoy the false security I find in his grip.

"We can seal it with a kiss for better measure." He nods in seriousness and puckers his lips.

After delivering a forceful splash of water to his grinning face, I take off toward the shore. "In your dreams, dork!" I holler over my shoulder and keep swimming as fast as my tired legs will carry me.

I leave the group on the shore and head down Sunshine Street. It's the street facing the lake, and I'm lucky enough to hold residence on it. I can sit on our small porch and look over the lake and pretend I'm at a retreat, if I'm in the mood to imagine. The view of the crystal-clear lake is gorgeous. If I have to be stuck in a trailer park, at least I'm blessed enough to be stuck in this beautiful one. All of the streets at Shimmer Lakes Trailer Park have too nice of names. They sound like they should be from a children's board game. Dillon lives on Peachy Path, just behind us, and the twins are a street over on Buttercup Circle. Too much sugar drips off those names for my likings. It's a *trailer park*. Hello! There's nothing sweet about it.

The campground section of the park is called Lulu Lane. This is the only name I like. It speaks to me for some reason. It calls to me now, so I make a long loop around the property to have some time alone. It's a modest place, only a handful of campsites and rows of rectangle trailers, but it is my safe haven.

By the time Kyle and I arrived at Shimmer Lakes, we were both malnourished and infested with head lice. Aunt Evie took to mending us up and showing us a simpler, yet better, way of life, which in the beginning included us both having to go close to bald in order to get rid of the lice. Dillon thought we were both boys for the first months of us being neighbors. My aunt kept reassuring us that it was only hair and that it would grow back, and eventually it did. I was only six at the time. Now I know that's mighty young to remember much, but some things you can't ever forget, no matter how badly you want to.

Thinking about that bald time, my fingers test my scalp, finding a headful of frizzy locks, the coarse texture declaring it's time for a shower. After one last glance at the lake, I head to our trailer and pull open the metal door. It lets out a groaning pop as I quickly yank it shut behind me before the cold air makes an escape. The moist air inside is pretty chilly from the window air conditioning unit. I walk over to it and find it set on blizzard, aka high. So I bump it down a notch. It's a must to have it on full-blast during the humid days, but the nights are more kind, so we can turn it down then. Aunt Evie must have been too tired to worry with it tonight. Her door is closed, so I know she is out for the count. I grab up some clean clothes along with my shower supplies and head back out to the bathhouse. We have a small bathroom, but the pipes make all kinds of racket and I hate to wake her.

I set out, on foot, down the coquina road. The only sounds are that of my feet crunching over the road and the gentle lapping of the water along the shore. The bathhouse is just two streets over on Happy Hill, so I'm there in a flash.

I ease into the abandoned bathhouse, and lock myself in my usual stall at the end. I set the water at nearly scalding in hopes of loosening my achy shoulders. As I'm washing the grime of the day and lake off, my thoughts stray to the changes about to take place.

Graduation is only a few weeks away. The next chapter in my life will begin soon. I'm excited to start a new chapter, yet I'm also not ready. I'm still battling with the whole *do I stay or do I go* decision. I'm pretty sure I have to stay. I can only afford community college and there are really no writing and journalism courses there. It's not my dream come true, but normally dreams don't come true in my neck of the woods.

With that despairing thought, I finish rinsing the conditioner out of my hair and shut the shower off.

Footsteps echo through the shower room, but I pay it no mind until a girl whispers out, *"Dillon."*

The stall opens and clangs shut right next to mine as his familiar chuckle mingles with her annoying giggle. The good angel and bad angel appear on my shoulder at this moment. I tell the good angel to hush up so the bad angel can help me cook up a plan. Being that he is one of my best friends, it *is* my responsibility to harass him in this moment.

"Dimples, is that you?" I holler to the next shower stall over and have to laugh when he grumbles in aggravation. He knows he is so busted and won't be enjoying his lady friend on this night.

"Don't call me that!" He groans just as a faint thud hits the stall's wall beside me. I can imagine it was his forehead hitting it in frustration.

"But you're just a boy!" I laugh some more with his little friend's laughter joining in. "Honey, don't let that manly physique fool you. He really is just a baby."

Dillon grumbles and groans some more. The girl keeps giggling.

I'm barely dried off before I start pulling on my clothes. "Good night, my sweet Dimples!" I yell before darting out of the bathhouse and straight over to Leona's trailer. I find her stretched out on the small couch watching the *Late Night* show, with her eyes halfway shut. She tries to stay up to watch the bands that perform on these shows. It's as close to MTV we can get, beings that none of us have cable.

"Get your happy butt up. We got business to take care of." I pull her off the couch and to her feet.

She seems to wake up and slides on her shoes. "Who's our victim tonight?"

"Dimples. He's entertaining a girl in the bathhouse, and I think we need to put out that fire," I say on a laugh as we walk briskly over to the small community laundromat where the ice machine is housed.

Leona helps me fill two buckets with ice and water before hauling them over to the bathhouse. We ease back in and tread lightly to stifle the echo of our steps. I hear Dillon whisper something, causing the girl to giggle. It's all I can do not to giggle myself. The idiot should have known not to linger in the very spot he got caught in. Leona and I leverage the buckets up against the wall and do a silent countdown before launching the ice water over the top of the stall. Squeals and yelps follow us as we quickly dash back out.

"That should cool the lovebirds down," Leona says once we reach her door.

"Good night," we both call out as I head home.

I quietly reenter the trailer and tiptoe to my small room without bothering to turn on a light. I plop on the small bed, ease open my window, and wait. Dillon serenades the trailer park most every night, whether he intends to or not. It's just chords and melodies he strings together at random, but they are always beautiful.

It doesn't take long before the strumming of his guitar starts drifting from his porch. There's a potent edge to the song, with aggravation rippling through the melody. A smile pulls at my lips from knowing what's behind it. No matter, it's still beautiful and eventually lulls me to sleep.

• ♫ • ♫ • ♫ •

Morning comes way too early. My small bed is pushed up against the wall by the window, so I only have one side of the bed to wake up on. Today it is definitely the wrong side. My shoulder slammed into the side of the canoe on impact with the dock during our stunt-gone-bad. Today it finally decides to hurt, as well as my back. I ease off the bed and walk over to the small mirror taped to the back of the door to inspect my shoulder. A dark bruise is painted on the back side.

I glare at it before opening the door and padding to the small kitchen area. Aunt Evie is sitting at the table, already dressed for the day in a white tank top and tie-dyed skirt. My great-aunt is a hippie in her own right, but she is a uniquely meek woman. Although she's not hard on me and Kyle, she does expect us to know the rights from the wrongs that she has instilled in us. I can't even fathom what horrible situation we would be in today, had she not taken us in.

She thumbs through a hymnal while sipping her coffee, so I grab a cup and join her.

"Whatcha doing?" I ask while trying to stretch out my sore back against the back of the chair.

"Looking for some songs for Dillon to play at church tomorrow."

"You think they're going to want a jailbird playing the offertory hymn in the morning?" I rise slowly to grab a few aspirins and a Pop Tart.

"Ain't nobody perfect. They won't hold a stupid

30

stunt against him. Speaking of which, I forgot to tell you that the Lakeshore Times called yesterday." She jots down a page number before eyeing me. Her watery blue eyes hold a measure of trepidation for some reason.

"Awesome. I'll swing by the front office and call them back before I head to the dock this morning." I make note to leave a few minutes early. *Oh, what it would be like to have a home phone.* "I wonder what writing assignment they have for me."

Just as Dillon has been born to create music, I feel the calling to write. My fingers get itchy sometimes, and I just have to sit down and pour out my heart on paper. I am lucky enough to get the opportunity to write for the local paper every now and then. I also publish the campground's monthly newsletter that I had talked Aunt Evie into letting me create my freshman year of high school. It's just a one page bulletin about the coming events and some other whatnot information.

"They don't have a writing assignment for you, Jillian. They want a statement about the mess y'all caused the other night."

"Ugh. No comment." I place my head on the table. Great. Just great. My jailbird status has probably cost me that ray of hope for working with the paper full-time one day.

"Young lady, you need to start making better choices. If you don't, one of these days you're gonna make a choice that's going to haunt you for the rest of your life."

I lift my head and blink back a sudden stinging of tears. Swallowing them down, I stand up and head to my room, but turn back to gently wrap my arms around her. "I'm really sorry for screwing up again, Aunt Evie."

"I know, honey." She pats my arm before I release her.

I beat on Kyle's door to rouse him while heading to my room. After a quick rummage through my clothes, I decide on a pair of cutoffs and a holey T-shirt. There won't be any sorrow over having to throw them away at the end of the day, like I had to with yesterday's ruined outfit. I plait my hair in a long side braid to keep it out of the way for the long day ahead and make my way back to the living area, relieved to find Kyle sitting at the table eating his own Pop Tart. Sometimes he can be a booger to get out of bed.

He flashes me a good-natured smile that lights up his green eyes. They are a few shades lighter than mine and always seem to hold a healthy dose of optimism. "Yo."

"Did you feed Dog?" I ask him.

"Yep. He wouldn't quit barking until I did," he mumbles while tearing into a second pack of Pop Tarts.

I smile at our goldfish with appreciation. Aunt Evie surprised Kyle and me last Christmas with the little fish. He's probably as easy and as cheap of a pet you can have, and we like Dog pretty well. He keeps us content in the pet department, but sometimes we long for a furry, frisky dog. Luckily, all we have to do is hop on our bikes and strike out to Shimmer Lakes Farms. The owner has a gorgeous yellow lab named Peaches, and neither one of them mind us paying her an hour or two of attention once in a while.

After Kyle finishes up breakfast, we meet the guys outside. It's already screaming hot, and I'm just too sore for the twenty minute bike ride, so the decision to drive my baby is pretty simple.

"Leona got called into work," Dillon says as he directs the guys to the backseat. He towers over them by a few inches, so he always gets shotgun.

We all pile in like a bunch of sardines. The familiar, irritating feeling of knees jabbing me in my back starts up immediately, so I don't even have to look to know Mave is directly behind my seat. I work at keeping my annoyance tamped down as I scoot the seat as far up as it will go, hoping he takes the hint. At least he's not backing out on helping us. *Stay positive, girl.*

Sliding the gearshift into first, I eye Dillon before pulling off. "Good morning, Dimples. Was your night chill?"

"You ain't funny, Jewels." He leans his head on the passenger window.

I lay the pedal to the metal and cut out of the parking lot in a jolt, making Dillon tumble around unexpectedly. He's a big boy, so it's pretty comical. The peanut gallery in the backseat laughs in agreement.

"Jewels!" he growls, finally looking over at me.

I ignore him and crank up the music, alternative rock screeches from the speakers, effectively waking us all up for the workday ahead.

This guy named Jack, who lives in the trailer park, is past-due on his rent to Aunt Evie. Lucky for us he is an out of work construction worker, so she agreed to let him work off his rent by helping us out today. He grabs a hammer and goes to work right along with us, so we manage the rebuild with minimal fuss.

As the day progresses, so does my frustration. The heat has put a mean whooping on me. Shimmer Lakes is nestled in the deep southern part of the state where the air is so thick and sticky during the hot months that mosquitos can get stuck in midair. No joke. *Well, okay, that was a joke.* But southern humidity is not a joke. My hair is completely soaked with sweat and my clothes are sticking to me with no pity. Between the throbbing blisters the hammer gifted my right hand and the ache clamping down on my sore left shoulder, I feel pretty weighed down by the time we gather up Jack's tools.

We pile back into my car by suppertime. Once we are all shoved back in, the begging and pleading begins for food. *I knew it was coming.*

"I'm starving." Mave moans, sounding in pain.

"Me too!" Max adds with the others mumbling in agreement.

Too tired to put up a fight, I make the mistake of asking, "Where to?"

A litany of *I don't know* and *not there* spill from

their aggravating lips.

"We had pizza last time. I want something different," Kyle whines. We eat out maybe once a month, so it's always a struggle to choose.

"I don't want subs," Mave pipes in, shooting down Max's mumbled idea.

"You boys act like a bunch of old ladies. Can't make your minds up, but turn around and bicker when someone makes a suggestion. I ain't got patience for this mess today."

I crank up the Pearl Jam CD to drown out their squabbling and head to my favorite hangout. Fat So Moe's Burger Joint has the best burgers around, hands down. We push through the front door and find the jolly owner at the counter.

"Yo, Moe!" Kyle hollers out.

Moe looks up from the counter, resembling Santa Claus but with a really long goatee and several silver hoops through his ears. "Yo, bro!"

Moe wears shorts and T-shirts year-round with combat boots. He is a cool character for sure and has starred in many of my fictional stories. He talks as though he should live on a surfboard in the ocean instead of running a burger joint in the backwoods of Georgia.

"You scrubs finish walking the plank for the rich and flameless?" A wide grin pulls his lips back, showing off that endearing gap between his two front teeth.

"You ain't funny." I give him a playful glare. "Can I have the pimento cheese burger with Cajun fries and a vanilla milkshake?"

"Sure thing, sweetheart. How 'bout you boys? Salad?" Moe holds up a head of lettuce in tease.

The boys give him a look that reiterates him not being funny before ordering two burgers apiece with fries and sodas. We go to pay with the last bit of money we could scrape up. I think we should have an entire dollar left for the tip.

Moe shoos the crumbled stack of money off. "This meal is on me. You kids got done dirty with the whole arrest show. I think you've earned a break for the day."

We try to push the money on him anyway. Aunt Evie wouldn't think too kindly about us accepting a free pity meal, but Moe says a few choice words on the fairness of this town and starts getting riled up. We think better of it, put our money back into our pockets, and thank him diligently.

The boys take up one booth, so I slide into the one behind them and prop my feet up on the opposite bench. The cool vinyl feels heavenly against my tired back.

I pick at my food for a while and listen to the rowdy heathens goofing off in the next booth. Each one has earned a slight sunburn in the last two days. At least we will look like we were on vacation when we return to school in a few days.

Pushing the red basket of food out of the way, I settle my elbows on the edge of the table and try to decide if it's worth calling them down. Moe keeps chuckling in good humor at them, so I keep my lips shut.

"You like fries a lot, don't ya, Kyle?" Max asks.

Kyle nods his head and shoves another handful of fries in, totally missing the joke. He has french fry confetti sprinkled in his hair and hasn't a clue that Mave is still adding to it. Dillon says something that cracks the whole table up, and now Max has soda shooting out of his nose. I know they are slightly younger than me, but I just wish I could let go like they do. Nothing seems to bother them, and it makes me jealous. I feel like I've had to grow up too fast due to the life dealt to me.

Dillon looks over and finds me glaring in their direction. We hold each other's gaze for a few beats before he heads over and plops down across from me. Without asking, he begins to devour my food.

My eyebrow hitches up as I drop my feet back to the floor. "Hello?"

"No need in wasting it," he answers around a mouthful of my burger, shrugging his shoulders. "What's the matter, Pretty Girl?"

I try to shrug back, but my sore shoulder is so stiff it won't let me. There's no containing the wince and this catches Dillon's attention. Before I know it, he's dropped the burger back into the basket and has slid in next to me. Brows pinched and mouth set in a hard line, he eases my shirt off my shoulder without asking permission. The angst of his sigh tickles the side of my neck as he leans in to give it a closer look.

"Good grief, dude! Stop groping my sister," Kyle complains, with the twins roaring in laughter.

"I'm next," Mave declares.

"Shut up, Maverick!" Kyle and I shout at the same time, both of us cutting him a sharp look.

Dillon shakes his head while brushing his fingers lightly over the deep bruise. "We hurt her shoulder the other night, Kyle."

I kind of like how he takes the blame for the injury. Carrying the blame all the time becomes quite daunting.

This gets the boys' attention, so they all shuffle over and inspect the injury like they would actually know what to do. It's almost laughable. Except, it's not. I'm in a lousy mood and don't feel like being fussed over.

"I'm fine. It'll be fine." I brush Dillon's hand off my shoulder and start scooting until he gets the hint and lets me out of the booth. "I'm tired. Let's go."

"Can't we stay for a little while, Jillian? Moe's got the pool table set on free play," Kyle calls out just as I reach the door.

I turn back around and find each one giving me their best puppy-dog eyes. One minute they are fawning over my injury, and the next they are acting like a bunch of selfish brats. This instantly shoves me further into my sour mood.

"Sure. Stay as long as you want," I mutter.

They turn tail and quickly head to the game room, already bickering over who gets to break. No one notices me walking out the front door.

Maybe it's time for a little lesson on being more considerate.

I climb into my car and roll up to the side entrance near the game room and lay on the horn before wheeling the car around. I look in the review mirror in time to see them all run out of the restaurant. Kyle has his arms in the air in frustration, while the twins look confused, but Dillon just stands there with his hands on his hips, grinning. I don't know why, but that makes me smile, too.

I offer them a tiny wave before pealing out of the parking lot.

•♫•♫•♫•

Sunday morning finds my crowd doing the late for church shuffle. By the time we arrive, the tiny sanctuary is packed and I have to refrain from groaning out loud. Kyle scooted in before me and swiped one of the last spots on the pew with the twins. The only remaining choices are to sit up front with Aunt Evie or sit directly behind them. It's never a wise choice to sit behind the King twins. For one, they are way taller than me and I can't see over their big heads. Secondly, they are such a distraction.

"Hey," I offer while sliding onto the back pew beside Leona and her dad—they were obviously late, too. One glance up and a whimper falls from my lips. I'm staring at the back of Mave's head today, which is even worse.

"Everything okay?" Leona whispers.

"Yeah. Some campers had a mishap Aunt Evie had to deal with." My poor aunt never gets a break.

I shake off the frustrating vibes and focus on the soothing melody coming from the piano as Dillon plays the offertory hymn. Leaning slightly to the left, I'm able to have a clear view of him. Seeing him seated behind the piano, stylishly dressed in a black button-down shirt with the sleeves rolled up to midway of his forearms and a pair of grey dress slacks, pride bubbles up my chest and lands a smile on my lips. Cora makes him dress properly for church, even on the Sundays he doesn't play the piano.

Leaning forward, I scan the twins. As always, they are in the normal jeans and T-shirts. At least Kyle wore a blue button-down shirt with his jeans. Surely, God doesn't care what we wear as long as we show up, but I do like to dress nice for my visits to his house on Sundays. Today it's a simple coral-colored sundress. I guess it's one of those unspoken things I've picked up from Aunt Evie over the years. She's a dress wearing kind of woman when it comes to church. She even leaves the tie-dye at home for the occasion.

I refocus on Dillon as he plays "Victory in Jesus" for the call to worship song. He plays with such seriousness and reverence—his head bent toward the keys with a stoic expression on his handsome face. Witnessing this is such a gift and I'm a little disappointed when he eases the song to a close, then gets up discreetly and slides onto his designated spot on the front pew beside Cora. *Would it be rude to shout encore?*

Preacher Mike Floyd takes his place behind the podium, and I lose him behind Mave's big head. "Good to be in the Lord's house this fine day," he says, and people amen their agreements.

He leads us in a quick prayer before instructing us to turn to Proverbs Chapter 7. He then dives right in and reads verses twenty-four and twenty-five. "The Lord's Word says, 'Hearken unto me now therefore, O ye *children*, and attend to the words of my mouth. Let not thine heart decline to her ways, go not astray in her paths.' This world wants to lead us down the wrong paths. Youth today have too many temptations. Too many opportunities to easily make the wrong choices."

Yep, they allowed the jailbirds into church this morning, but we are about to receive ourselves some learnings.

I slump even farther down in the pew and hold back the childish desire to stick my tongue at half of the congregation with their knowing glances trained in my direction. Good grief.

The preacher is all of five minutes into the sermon when Mave's head starts doing the bobbing around thing. The dude is going to have one sore neck. Mr. Dan leans up and nudges Mave on the shoulder to try to rouse him back awake. This works all of five more minutes, when the head bobbing picks back up with a soft snore to accompany the show. I can see over his head, now that it's bent over, but the view makes me a little nervous.

Preacher Floyd's dark eyes are zeroed in on the

snoozing boy as he continues his rant. "We all need to keep our focus on God before we find ourselves on a destructive path we can't find the exit for."

Without missing a word, the preacher eases over to the front pew and picks up an unopened box of tissues. He strikes a pitcher's pose and launches the box, bouncing it perfectly off the top of Mave's head. Mave lets out a loud snort and looks around disoriented. Kyle starts laughing.

"Shut up before you get a box of tissues to your head, too," I whisper while landing a quick slap to his shoulder. Preacher Floyd seems to be on a mission, and this won't be making it any better for us. Kyle transforms his laugher to a cough, so I sit back and leave him be.

"Mr. King—" Preacher Floyd begins.

"That's Maverick, sir," Max blurts, jabbing a finger toward to his twin.

I give the end of Max's hair a mean tug to hush him up. Pointing out who's who won't be helping the cause.

The preacher shifts his gaze over to Max before looking back to Mave. "Young man, I do believe God may have something important you need to hear today, so wake up and listen up." The congregation amens this as Preacher Floyd takes his position back behind the podium, hidden from my view for the remainder of the service. Mave seems wide-awake now. Every so often, he rubs the spot where the tissue box made contact with his head.

Preacher Floyd repeats those two verses, I think

specifically for Mave's benefit. "Hearken unto me now therefore, O ye *children*, and attend to the words of my mouth. Let not thine heart decline to her ways, go not astray in her paths," he reads loudly and with much emphasis. Then he adds Psalm 119:105. "Thy word is a lamp unto my feet, and a light unto my path."

The theme of this sermon is quite clear—we are obviously heading down the wrong path and need to get off it real soon, before we mess up even more. Between Preacher Floyd's fervent words from God, Cora's wicked sternness, and Aunt Evie's wise warnings for us to make better choices before the consequences catch up with us, I think they are hopeful at being able to turn off our stupid buttons.

Fingers crossed, they will succeed.

Much later, the congregation files out while Dillon plays the song, "The Old Path." He croons the lyrics in a somber tone, singing about staying on the right path with God and not straying from it. I'm not sure if this was a specific request or if Dillon thinks he's funny with the song choice.

After he concludes the song, I catch up with Aunt Evie outside and hear the rest of the crowd drifting behind us. They are whining about needing food—no surprise.

"I'm starving," Mave grumbles, right on my heels.

After he manages to step on the back of my sandal a second time, I quicken my pace to get away from his habit of annoying me to death.

"Well, my friend, I do believe if we stay on this here path set before us, we will be rewarded abundantly," Dillon says.

They are following Aunt Evie—the regular food source on Sundays. Today will be no different. The mac and cheese is keeping warm in the oven with the ham, and the deviled eggs are keeping cool in the fridge with the layered salad and coconut cream cake. My mouth waters just thinking about it.

"That sounds like the kind of path I can handle," Max says.

"Lead us, Aunt Evie, and let us not astray from your righteous cooking," Mave says solemnly, and the guys crack up.

I step ahead of Aunt Evie with not wanting to get in the way of the tongue lashing the boys are working on receiving.

"I will let not thine belly decline her food," Kyle declares, throwing in his two cents.

I glance over my shoulder and see this lady has finally reached her limit.

She stops abruptly and faces off with the smart-mouthed idiots. "Well, I'm glad that you young'uns ain't as stupid as I had suspected. You're smart enough to remember Bible verses well enough to misquote them, so maybe there's enough sense in you to be able to get it right."

My aunt doesn't get riled up too very often, and as I watch her place her hands on her thin hips, it's apparent the boys succeeded. *Fools.*

She hollers over to the preacher, and the boys

start to squirm. "Preacher Floyd, these here boys were just quoting those fine verses God had you share with us today. They'd like to share with you what they learned from the message."

They've gone and done it now.

I'm about to settle in my spot and see just what they come up with when Aunt Evie hooks my arm with hers.

"Jillian and I need to go finish up dinner. Do you mind taking them home when y'all done?"

A knowing smile eases onto the preacher's lips. "No ma'am. I don't mind at all. Come on, boys. Let's go sit inside and have a talk." He pats Mave's shoulder firmly and directs them to follow him. They all file back in the church with their heads hung low.

Needless to say, the boys don't make it back to the trailer for over an hour. When they do arrive, they eat in silence, and then do the dishes without being asked. They even thank Aunt Evie and don't swipe the leftovers to take home as they usually do.

THREE

Summer is like that really hot guy who teased you all spring before finally getting around to asking you out. He's too charming to resist and you have high expectations for the date, so you take the time to paint your nails and spend extra attention on hair and makeup. Even going as far as having a friend help you select the perfect outfit. But when the date finally arrives, you discover his charm was too flimsy to even make it to the dessert course. There was nothing behind that sunshine smile and flirty promise.

The summer after graduation is no different. It feels like my life is on the cusp of something awesome and exciting. I waited all summer for it to show up, but by mid-August it's become clear that feeling is nothing more than a delusion.

I should have known better.

Between managing the campground and cleaning condos, nothing about the summer has been charming. My main duties at the campground are keeping the bathhouse and mini-laundromat clean and trash pickup, for which I've done the last four summers, but this is my first year cleaning vacation rental condos on the other side of the lake.

So my days are spent cleaning and cleaning and cleaning some more... I clean up after the poor campers and then go clean up after the spoiled, rich vacationers. What a life.

Those people, who are so posh and spoiled, don't know how to pick up after themselves. They are pigs, quite frankly. I think they live by the motto: *it stays where it lands until the help cleans up.* They can afford to pay someone, aka me, to worry about such things. They are too lazy to even pack all of their junk. The only thing I'm required to turn in is money and jewelry. Everything else is considered a bonus, and I normally walk away with a trunkful of bonuses on a regular basis. I've acquired a nice supply of beach towels, sunglasses, suntan lotions, fancy perfumes, and plenty of unopened food. The boys love this, of course. It never fails that Max and Mave conveniently hang out at Aunt Evie's trailer on the days I clean. They are more than willing to help take care of the food supplies I lug home.

"I'm still hungry," Max whines, eyeing the empty tins of Spam and the crumpled saltine wrappers that are littering the dock.

"At least it was more substantial than the mayonnaise sandwiches we had last night," I remind him before taking the last swig of my RC cola. Times have been tough.

"Beggars can't be choosers," Leona adds.

"Y'all sit tight for a minute." I got an extra condo cleaning in today and struck gold in the food department, so I hustle back to the trailer and grab up the pints of fancy gelato hidden in the freezer.

Such a rare treat deserves a little flare with being presented, so I shrug on a trench coat and start stuffing the cartons and some plastic spoons into the pockets. As soon as my flip-flops slap against the dock, the crowd turns their heads and looks at me with confused expectancy.

"Drumroll please," I say, holding the front of the coat over my freezing hand. Mave taps against the decking and as soon as he stops, I whip out the small carton in a dramatic flourish. "Ta-da!"

The crowd acts like it's Christmas morning, eyes wide and smiles lighting their faces as I divvy the pints out. We peel off the lids and dig in.

"This ice cream is creamier than any I have ever had," Kyle says after a bite. "It tastes like fresh strawberries."

"Try this one." Leona swaps cartons with him. "Doesn't it taste like the peaches from that orchard nearby?"

"Hmmm," is the only answer my brother offers.

I dig into my carton of chocolate hazelnut. The rich, nutty flavor melts on my tongue. I spoon out a bite and offer it to Dillon as he gives me a spoonful of his vanilla. Everyone keeps up sharing in the various flavors until the cartons are scraped clean and I have a slight stomach ache.

"Thanks, Jewels. That was a killer treat." Max gives me a hug and waves at the boys to follow him. "Let's take care of the trash pickup for our Pretty Girl."

Dillon and Leona stay behind to help me clean up our picnic.

"I need to go get ready for my date," Leona says as she tosses the trash she collected.

"Date with who? Where to?" I ask, folding the trench coat for lack of anything else to do.

"A guy named Tony. He works at the shoe store

beside me at the mall. We're going dancing." She grins wide with excitement. "See ya!"

"I wish I had enough energy to do such things," I mutter while watching her skip away. I'm wiped out and dateless, as always.

"What such things?" Dillon asks from beside me.

"Like dating." I shrug and start to head home, but he stops me.

"I know a date you'd have enough energy for." Those dang dimples pop out as he holds up a finger. "I'll be right back."

Stretched out on the sandy shore under our favorite willow tree, there's no doubting Dillon nailed it. Looking up at the long, lacy willow branches dancing to the acoustic melody Dillon is creating with his guitar, it's pure heaven. As He plays softly, like a lullaby, my eyes droop until closing altogether until the chords abruptly hush. I glance over to find his head bent down and those midnight brows pinched together as he makes notations in his leather music journal. He eases his eyes over to the Bible sprawled open beside him for a second and then goes back to scribbling in the journal.

"What's with this obsession you have with the Bible?" I ask, sounding as drowsy as I feel.

Dillon pulls his attention away from the journal and focuses those nearly purple eyes on me. "The most beautiful lyrics ever written are in that book."

"Dimples, you make me swoon," I tease before yawning.

He snorts. "Don't make fun of me."

"I'm not. Seriously, I've fallen in love with songs you've created from Bible verses." He strings them together on a melody so sweet, you know beyond a shadow of a doubt he is fully worshiping God with them. They seem sacred and holy.

Dillon holds my gaze for a few beats, nods his head, and goes back to studying the Bible and making notes. Watching him search and compose music is such a divine experience. He is here physically, but he is in his own spiritually creative world. It's magical, and I know I am blessed to witness it.

I don't realize I'm holding my breathing until he begins playing the guitar again and I release a long exhale. He strums a few chords and softly croons lyrics to the notes.

Though the waters roar with trouble
Though the mountains may shake
There is a river that will flow with peace
So be still and always know
Be still and always praise
Be still and always love

Dillon plays a bit more, humming all the while with his eyes closed, face turned skyward as his shaggy black hair dances in the breeze. He seems wrapped in an enchanting spell when he creates music. It's a beautiful sight, and this is my most favorite way to spend an evening.

The music trails off as he opens his eyes and catches me staring. I've somehow become wrapped in the spell and I can't look away. He watches me just as intently and then begins strumming a new song. He sees my questioning expression over the unfamiliar song, and I'm awarded by a one-dimple appearance before his gaze goes serious again.

"What song is this?"

He shrugs. "It's not a song yet. Just a *promise* of a song."

I don't know what it's promising, but it is beautiful. I can see it becoming my favorite. It's slow and seductive and full of longing.

"I love it."

"I hoped you would," he says softly.

We stay in our own bubble with him serenading me with the promise of a song until the boys zoom by in the little colorful truck we use for trash pickup, whooping and hollering for Dillon to join them. He shrugs a shoulder at me again before gathering his stuff and jogging over to the truck. He hops in the back with Mave.

I shout out to Kyle, "Don't you dare break that truck!"

He grins and waves as he takes off in the direction of the old sheds. I guess they are going on a new treasure hunt.

The beat-up truck used to be a bright vulgar yellow in its nineteen seventies youth, but now it is a montage of colors. Max thought at one point he may one day become a *car artist,* and so he has practiced on the work truck over the years with leftover paint and an old paint gun he was able to acquire from his uncle's car garage. The hood is a metallic black with spatters of silver. It was pretty cool until the guys made it tacky by adding various wavy streaks of neon green, glittery orange, and metallic blue along the sides that look like a drunken psychedelic rainbow. The bed of the truck and the tailgate is a graffiti black music notes dancing over the red pearlescent paint underneath. It looks like a paint shop threw up all over the poor truck, but at least it's not that gross yellow anymore. Plus, it's a work in progress. You never know when Max will come home with another paint stash and more ideas.

After the truck disappears from view, I lay back and take in the stillness of the early night sneaking up on me. The nagging feeling that something awesome and exciting wants to happen lingers, making me antsy. I feel like I'm missing out on something spectacular, because I'm just not good enough to obtain it.

Eventually, I drag my tired, disappointed body to our small trailer to wash the condo cleaning off. After a long shower, I find Aunt Evie sitting at her normal spot at the small table with her devotional book. I grab the last pint of gelato from the hidden spot in the freezer and walk it over to the table with a spoon and present her with my small gift.

"Cherry. Your favorite."

Aunt Evie lights up when she sees it. "Awe. Thanks, sweetie. You scored big today." She opens the lid and offers me the first bite. She should enjoy the treat, yet here she is thinking of me before herself—as always.

"Enjoy it. It's all yours." I sit beside her and prop my chin in my hands.

"Are you sure?" she asked while working the spoon into the creamy treat.

"Absolutely." I watch as her eyes drift shut from the pleasure of the first bite. Being able to offer her this gift, albeit small, makes me smile. "The cabinets and fridge are stocked, too. If we can keep the twins away, we should be good for another week."

"Really? That's great, Jillian," Aunt Evie says with much relief. I suspected she didn't have grocery money, and she just confirmed it for me.

"We really need to put our foot down about the past-due renters." I start chewing my thumbnail, trying to restrain my comments.

"You let me worry about that, please," she says between bites. "People are having a hard time making their ends meet right now."

Living in the poverty that we do, you have to lean on one another. When one is doing better than the others, they don't squirrel it away for themselves. They spread it around as thinly as they can. Someone's electric bill or rent may get caught up anonymously or a box of groceries will show up mysteriously on your porch. In our low-income world, it's not about outdoing your neighbor as it is on the other side of the lake. Nope. It's about trying to keep your neighbor's head above water right along with your own. I've seen Aunt Evie do a lot of this for her neighbors.

"We're barely making it, Aunt Evie. If they don't pay, then how are we going to make *our* ends meet?" Being broke is no joke. The uncertainty and unrelenting nagging that plagues your thoughts, as to how to make things work, leaves you feeling totally hopeless.

"Things will get better." She tries to reassure me, but I can tell she doesn't believe her own words.

"No worries. I've saved enough to handle most of our bills for the month." I pat her on the arm before hurrying to my room to gather the money. I recount it, knowing it'll barely get us by, and bring it back to the kitchen. "Here ya go."

"Jillian..." Her voice trails off. She doesn't want to accept it, but times are tough and she has no choice but to do so.

"I like doing my part. It's the least I can do." I place a kiss on her cheek and give her a warm smile before heading to my room. The smile drops and is replaced with a grimace once my back is toward her.

I was hoping she would tell me that some people came through with their rent. Of course that didn't happen, so now I am left with no gas money until my next paycheck. Worst part is I rolled up on fumes earlier. The bike will have to be my mode of transportation for the next week, and I'm not looking forward to that at all. I get that these people are poor and struggling, because I'm in the same boat. But I don't sit around and do nothing. I grab up my bicycle and go to work.

It's late by the time I snuggle in the bed and lay

here listening to Dillon serenade the trailer park. He's playing his promise of a song, and the melody feels to be longing more so tonight. Maybe it's just me who's longing and feeling it in the song, but we seem to be on the same page a lot of the time.

There's always been a solid bond between the two of us from the very start. At around the age of ten, I remember an eight-year-old Dillon coming down with an awful bout of the stomach flu, so severe that the boy couldn't even keep water down. Cora was told to either show up for her work shifts or never come back. She had no choice but to leave her sick little boy in Aunt Evie's care. He was too weak to even speak those few days. Aunt Evie had Kyle stay with the twins in the hopes that he would be spared, but I refused to leave.

I wanted to help tend to Dillon, but Aunt Evie kept warning that I'd get myself sick, if I didn't stay away. The few times she would step outside to check the mail, I would hear him in the small living area, quietly weeping. He tried to be brave, but Dillon really wanted his momma. And who could blame him? When my aunt would sleep or wash those few days, I would sit on the floor by the couch and hold his hand while he slept. I just couldn't stand to be away from him, knowing how miserable he was.

Three days later, Aunt Evie asked if Dillon felt up to eating something, and he requested two pimento cheese sandwiches. At that point she declared him better. Unfortunately, by sundown I was puking my guts out, feeling close to death. Aunt Evie told me in so many words that was what I got for not staying away from Dillon. I was exiled to my room with a trashcan placed by the bed. Each night of my three-day virus, I would wake up to Dillon on his knees by the bed, holding my hand and begging God to heal me. We have always hurt when the other hurts and it started way back then.

I'm laying here now, near tears at the helpless situation we are in, when I notice the music has stopped. I peep out the window and find Dillon gone. The next thing I know, he is pushing through my door. He sits on the floor and leans his back against the bed, so I slide down to the floor and sit by him. It's a tight fit. His feet actually touch the opposite wall of the bed.

He says nothing. Just sits here in the dark. It's a bit cloudy out tonight, so I can barely make out his somber features in the muted moonlight.

"What's wrong, Dillon?"

"You just been on my mind tonight," he whispers as he looks over at me. "You alright?"

His hair slips in his eyes, so I reach over and brush the soft locks away instead of answering.

"You want to talk about it?" he asks.

"Not really," I whisper, tearing my gaze away from his to stare off into the dark.

He nudges the bag I gathered earlier with his foot, causing the plastic to crunch in the quiet. "What's this?"

"Just some junk I'm gonna try to sell to the thrift store tomorrow." I'm hoping it'll be enough for at least a half tank of gas.

He shakes his head in aggravation. "It ain't always gonna be this tough. Things will get better."

There he goes making promises again. How can he be so sure? Seems to me things just keep getting worse.

We sit here with our sides pressed together. Dillon slouches down some so he can rest his head back on my mattress and I lean my head on his arm. Things are better, just knowing he's here for me. Sometimes that's all I need.

"Let's make love," he whispers after a while.

I give his tempting suggestion some thought and decide it's a perfect idea. It always makes me feel better afterwards. He switches on the small lamp as I scoot over to the dresser and grab my notebook and pen. Dillon always refers to composing music as making love. It's sort of our inside joke. As we work on a song that entwines disappointment and dreams for nearly two hours, I feel the worry and anxiety slowly recede a little.

Hope fell down and drifted so far away
Until the dream came along and showed her
A better way

Nowhere to be found on the real, drowning
In the real, so much more than lost
Only then the dream appeared but at a great cost

When the melody fades on dusk of a

Misplaced day

Doubt and fears drift in and hope is called
So far away

We've crossed out more than not and have gone through over a dozen sheets of paper. I look over the lyrics and shake my head. Dillon Bleu is too young to be so wise. He pulled my worries right out of me in the way only he could—through lyrics. I start yawning, and Dillon takes this as his cue. He gives me a sideways hug, slides back out of my door, and returns home.

He sensed me needing him tonight. He showed up and did what he does best. He made me feel better and forget about my worries for a spell. Sometimes that's the best gift a girl can ask for, especially if you live in these parts.

I listen to him play a new melody from his porch, knowing it will eventually go with the song we just worked on creating.

Morning finds me reluctant with the bike ride. I unenthusiastically go through my morning routine, trying to talk myself into wanting to pedal to work. Unfortunately, it's not working, but I have no other choice. After I'm dressed in my cleaning lady uniform of worn-out jeans and tee, I grab my bag and grudgingly stalk out toward my bike. I'm surprised to find a bag draped on the handlebar. I peep inside and find some of Dillon's belongings—an old watch, a pocket knife, and a couple dress shirts that I'm pretty sure his mom would skin him over if she knew he got rid of them. I smile at the sweetness of this. That boy knows I need some quick cash and has willingly given up some of his things to help me out. As I said, we have always had each other's back. This thoughtful gift gives me just enough encouragement to climb on the bike and pedal my broke self to work.

FOUR

Fall has been creeping up on us for a while now, but the weather has fought it all the way to the bitter end. I was beginning to doubt fall was going to pull it off, to be honest. But October has arrived and finds me settling into college life. Classes are typical basics, but I am taking a creative writing course, which is the highlight of my life at the moment. If I'm not working, I'm in class. It is a rarity to do anything else.

Tonight is one of those rare moments, but I'm nearly too tired to take advantage of it. The community college is just across the road from the university, so I've made a few friends. I wouldn't say I'm close to any of them, but friendly enough to receive an occasional invite to a social gathering. The boys decided they were included and have already headed over. Whatever. They deserve some fun, too.

"Come on, slow poke." Leona checks her watch. "It's getting late."

We are both in my closet-sized bedroom as I hesitantly get dressed. I stand in front of my small mirror checking the back view of myself in a pair of almost too-tight jeans that I have finally decided on. I slide on a black lacy camisole and push into a chunky pair of scuffed black boots. Nothing special, but that's me.

"Leona Hill, you are the only chick I know who can pull off wearing maroon-colored bellbottom pants." I eye the colorful halter top she paired with it. On me it would look ridiculous, but with her mile-long legs and arms, she's totally rocking it.

"Quit stalling." She tosses me my cropped leather jacket.

"I'll go for a little while, but you'll have to find a ride home." I shrug into my jacket before flipping my head forward and finger combing my hair. I like sporting the natural, sort of unkempt, wavy-locks look. It works for me and is very low maintenance.

"Deal." Leona dances out the door, with me reluctantly following behind her.

The other side of the lake only takes minutes to get to by car. We pull up to music thumping in the night and a shore speckled with dancing drunken teenagers. Totally not my scene at all. I immediately scan the crowd for Kyle and am relieved to see a can of Coke in his hand. If he were underage drinking, I would kill him. He knows better, though.

Leona is pulled away almost immediately by some hot guy. This always happens. It's like the girl has a hidden beacon that navigates all the cute ones right to her. She seems happy about this, so I give her a quick wave before she disappears for the rest of the night.

Some time passes with me speaking to a few guys while the preppy girls in miniskirts and high heels glare at me. I glare right back at them and can't help but smirk when a few of them stumble from their stupid designer shoes bogging down in the sand. What sense do those outfits make for a beach party on a chilly night?

I have no desire to stay here in some social competition with the high and mighty, so it's an easy decision to cut out. They have already won, obviously. Don't they realize this?

It takes me a while to spot Kyle again. He's sitting on some truck's tailgate and is all about some Goth girl dressed head-to-toe in dreadful, bulky black that seems to be swallowing her whole. It's like she is hiding something in that shroud of darkness. Oh yes, I am already writing a story in my head with her as the lead character. With her chunky jewelry and interesting piercings, she's like some piece of abstract art that needs to be studied, so I get why my brother can't seem to look away from her. I just don't care for the intensity at which he is studying her.

"Wow. Talk about a world of dark and light meeting," I say just out of their earshot as I head over.

It's too funny, because Kyle is her total opposite. He's wearing a light teal, long-sleeve T-shirt with light washed jeans. His dark blond hair is perfectly styled. If you didn't know him, you'd think he was from this side of the lake. I did get the outfit from the rich thrift store over here. Kyle is all light and breezy and his female companion is all dark and brittle.

"I'm gone," I say as a way to get his attention.

"See ya." He doesn't even look up.

I'm not worrying about how his butt plans on getting home. Not my problem, as far as I'm concerned.

"Maybe Goth girl has a broom she can fly you home on later," I mumble.

"What was that?" Kyle asks, eyes still focused on her darkness.

She is shooting daggers at me with her glare. It's the same judgmental look I've been given all night, and it's rubbing me wrong that she actually thinks she has the right to be casting them at me as well. Doesn't she realize the guy hanging on her is from the same lineage as this piece of trash she is scowling at?

Say something to the witch or walk away?

Shaking my head, I decide it's not worth it and turn to leave, but Kyle snaps out of the spell she has cast on him and grabs my arm.

"Oh, hold up a minute."

"You clean my family's townhouse," Goth girl blurts.

The owners are always gone when I clean, but their security cameras keep an eye on me while they are away. I try to figure out which fancy house belongs to her family, but don't recall cleaning one with a witch's cauldron or any spell books.

"Yeah. And?" I infuse as much attitude in those two words as possible and shrug my shoulder.

The cleaning company offered me a few townhouses to maintain year-round. It's good money. I just don't like when someone feels the need to make me feel lower than I already feel because of it.

Kyle looks at me apologetically and walks away from her as though she were nothing more than a shadow he'd grown tired of standing near. I hear witchy woman suck her teeth, but don't look back to see if she's casting a hex on us. I'm just not in the mood.

"Would you give Dillon a lift home? You know how uptight Cora is about curfew." He makes a sour face while we ease closer to the bonfire.

I do know it. If the boy missed curfew with her finding out, he would be out of sight for *days*. Talk about another set of opposites. Aunt Evie quietly beckons respect by meekly offering respect in return. Cora's personality demands respect through threatening hissy fits. The feisty redhead is my least favorite person, and it's no secret she feels the very same way about me.

"So now my agenda includes delivering Dillon home before Cora goes all psycho-mom on the poor boy."

"Exactly."

"Fine. Just head home with the twins sooner rather than later, please."

Some girl calls out Kyle's name. She's a much brighter choice with a neon-pink sundress and nearly yellow-blonde hair.

"Sure," he distractedly mumbles while heading in her direction.

I find Dillon amongst a group of teenage girls who are drooling all over his man-child self. A leggy brunette looks to be just about to climb on top of him.

His tattered hat is pulled low over his deep-blue eyes, but I can still see that I have caught their attention. He meets my eyes as he tries pulling out of Miss Grabby's grasp. I give him a quick wave and am rewarded by a flash of those darn dimples. He cut his eyes in her direction before looking back at me and rolling them, starting up one of our silent conversations.

His nose wrinkles slightly. *This chick is too much.*

I smirk at him. *Yeah right, buddy. You know you love all that attention.*

He subtly shakes his head with his eyes taking on the façade of innocence. *No, I don't.*

Whatever. I shake my head at him and laugh. *You're eating it up, and we both know it.*

He glances heavenward and then in the direction where the vehicles are parked. *Save me.*

I shake my head. *Nah.*

We keep this up for a few more minutes until I decide to head over and try my best to embarrass him in front of the flock of girls.

"Hey, Jillian. Hold up a minute," Hudson Williamson calls out. He catches up with me just before I make it to Dillon.

"What's up?"

He brushes his fingers through his brown curls and gives me one of his easy smiles. "I thought we were meeting for coffee yesterday?"

"Oh, shoot. I forgot." I shrug while biting my lip. Although I outgrew my secret crush on him by the tenth grade, he still makes me nervous.

Hudson never spoke to me in high school, but has suddenly noticed my existence now that we bump into each other at the coffeehouse situated between the two campuses. I ignored him in the beginning, but he's starting to grow on me. He's turned out to actually be a nice guy, but I'm mindful at keeping my distance.

Hudson's dad is the bigwig real estate tycoon who owns everything this side of the lake. If Mr. Williamson could talk Aunt Evie into it, he would own my side of the lake as well. He would have the trailer park flattened and replaced by a bright and shiny new resort. Thank the good Lord, Aunt Evie is adamant about not letting him have his way.

"You can make it up to me by letting me treat you twice next week. I could use your help on a sales pitch I'm working on for my dad."

I'm half listening to him and Dillon at the same time. Hudson goes off on a tangent about joining his dad's real estate team, when I see Dillon glance at his thick leather watch. It's nearing his curfew and he knows it. I laugh to myself about this. *Dimples is getting nervous.*

"Ladies, I really hate to leave you." They all whine their disapproval. "But I have a private gig I gotta get to," Dillon says in his best rock star impersonation.

There's no holding back the snort over his blatant lie that they seem to believe so easily. They are hanging on his every word, for Pete's sake.

"Excuse me?" Hudson speaks.

I look back at him. "I'm sorry. My mind drifted..." My gaze wanders back to Dillon as he heads over. Maybe it's the bonfire reflecting over his face, but I swear there's an evil glint setting his eyes ablaze.

Dillon is several inches taller than Hudson and takes advantage of it by towering over the guy. He acknowledges Hudson with one of those male chin jerks, full of attitude, before turning his attention on me.

"Jewels, we need to be getting you home so you can reapply the ointment to..." He coughs and takes on a look of embarrassment. "It's time to reapply it to your *rash.*" As he drawls out the word *rash*, the big lug nods his head in a southerly direction and eyes my nether regions.

I could kill him on the spot.

Squinting my eyes at Dillon, I say to Hudson, "These baby boys...You can't take them anywhere." We both laugh, but Hudson takes a few steps away from me. Great. Now this dude thinks I have *personal* issues, thanks to Dillon Bleu. *There went my two free coffees.*

I stomp by Dillon's little fan club. "Come on, Dimples," I yell as we pass them. "Let's get you home so you can make curfew. Wouldn't want you to get a spanking." I laugh and watch a few girls trying to tamp down their giggles.

"Jewels, I done told you I ain't into that kinky stuff," he says and lands a vigorous slap on my backside. Before I can knock him out, he runs off toward my car and jumps in—knowing I would leave him if I had the opportunity. Before cranking the car, I punch him in the arm with all my might. This only makes him laugh.

"You punch like a girl, Jewels. Use your whole arm and don't tuck in your thumb."

Dillon balls his fist and shows me where to place my thumb. He proceeds in instructing me on how to properly punch for the next several minutes, and allows me to deliver several more punches to his arm. My hand is sore by the time I give up and drive off, but it doesn't seem like I made a dent in him.

A comfortable silence accompanies us on the short trip home until Dillon suddenly grabs my arm. "Stop at the church, Jewels."

I glance over and find the glow of the dashboard lights catching on his painful expression. I recognize immediately what it's about. Sometimes it's like all of his creativity worries him silly until he can express it. I get it, because sometimes my fingers will ache relentlessly until I can get somewhere alone and pour my thoughts out on paper. I know what he wants to do, but tonight I'm just too tired. My day was spent cleaning up after the *filthy* rich society, and all I can think about is stretching out in my tiny bed.

I ease my eyes back to the road and shake my head.

"You have to. I have a private gig to perform tonight." He nudges my shoulder, but I still shake my head. "I'm not kidding, Pretty Girl."

"I'm still not over the last time we broke into the

church. Your momma nearly beat the mess out of us, and Aunt Evie actually let her," I say, glaring at the road.

When I was not even eight and the boys barely old enough to ride their bikes without training wheels, we decided to pedal our adventurous selves out to the small clapboard church to hang out. We crawled through a back window and spent the day pretending it was our castle. I was queen for the day, up until they finally found us, and Cora took to spanking each one of us with the first thing her hand got ahold of, which was none other than a Bible devotional book. *Talk about being beat by the word!*

"Please." He peeks from underneath the edge of his tattered hat with those alluring eyes, rimmed with thick black lashes, pleading with me to give in. They actually have power over me. Humph. Dillon just won, and he knows. He flashes those dimples when he detects me relenting.

"Why not? It's your butt if you miss curfew and not mine." I wheel in and park at the back.

The church has a spare key hidden under a flowerpot at the back door. Dillon is privy to this so he can practice the piano anytime he wants since he plays for the church every third Sunday. I'm not sure the church knows he normally brings the twins to practice, too. Dillon has helped both the boys hone their music skills. He gave it his best shot with Kyle, but my poor brother is in the same boat as me. We are tone deaf.

Dillon fishes the key out and unlocks the door

before we push through and head to the small sanctuary. The familiar scent of lemony furniture polish lingers in the air and invites us on in. It's always such a reverent feeling to be here when this place of worship is silent and dark. I've never been freaked out as some may be, though. I have always felt welcomed—busy day or silent night. This cozy little church, with short rows of pews sitting on a worn wood floor, can hold about one hundred people. Only hold a podium can fit on the tiny altar instead of a full size pulpit. Instruments scatter along the wall behind it.

I take a seat on one of the front pews and settle in as Dillon sets himself behind the piano. The guy instantly looks at home. His fingers stroke the keys slowly and quietly at first as though they are thinking. He then takes off in his own rendition of Billy Joel's "Mr. Piano Man," dramatically singing about singing a song and feeling alright.

The quiet space instantly becomes alive and tangible with Dillon's vivacious energy pouring out of the instrument and mingling with his deep, silky voice. I feel the goose bumps rise along my arms as my body reacts to the chemistry he emits through his music. He plays the piano by ear, which blows my mind. Really! How can someone do such a thing?

Dillon ends this part of the concert and stands. He does a silly curtsey by the piano bench before seeking his next instrument selection. I laugh in spite of myself as I watch on.

Next on this private gig is a well-worn banjo.

Dillon fastens the strap over his broad shoulder before plucking twangy notes on the instrument. He glances up at me with a grin before launching into "The Ballad of Jed Clampett," the theme song to the *Beverly Hillbillies,* making me giggle. He seems aware that this show is on a timeclock, so he quickly grabs up a violin and slashes the strings with the bow before deciding against it with a slight shake of his head and a wrinkled nose. The small drum kit catches his attention as he slides his hat on backwards. He's quick to pick up the sticks and get down to business.

The place comes alive again with the rapid drum solo from the song "Wipe Out." Boy is that one long and fast drum solo. I'm almost certain the boy didn't miss one beat in it either. That wild drum performance made me tired just watching it, but seems to energize him even more. The color is high on his cheeks and a fine sheen of sweat has his face glistening.

"Woo-hoo!" I shout as he stands and bows dramatically before placing the sticks back on the floor beside the humble set of drums that he just made sound like a million bucks.

Dillon pauses long enough to undo the pearl snap buttons on his cuffs of his plaid shirt and roll up the sleeves, but not long enough to catch his breath. I still see the energy bouncing around his deep-blue eyes and know this performance isn't quite over yet.

My friend has saved the best for last, hands down. He straps on the old black electric guitar and turns the amp on low. Testing the chords, he adjusts the strings before turning around to face me. He strums the first few chords, and I know immediately he is playing one of my favorites, "Alive" by Pearl Jam. Dillon croons the lyrics in a velvety rasp, and I'm now swooning like those girls from the party.

His voice is just as brilliant as Eddie Vedder's. I say that reverently because I'm in love with Eddie Vedder, and Dillon knows it. He gives me this small, exclusive gift tonight, and I am reminded of how dear he has become to me over the years. He's my best friend, even though I am a little bit older than him. I know our friendship is not common, but as I've stated before, our circumstance has bound us together. We have always had a deep connection.

When the song eases to a close, I quietly ask, "Just one more. Please."

Dillon says nothing, just takes off into another one of my favorites by Pearl Jam, "Black." I let the melody and lyrics overtake me, appreciating the moody intensity that alternative rock bands create in their melodies and lyrics. It feels more real to me than the cheesy pop songs my generation seems to crave. Not me. I live in a harsh, real world, so this music genre has always felt more relevant. Pearl Jam, Creed, and Soundgarden are some of my favorites.

I close my eyes and listen to Dillon croon out lyrics filled with a somber mood. It makes me think about disappointments and regrets and desires and confusion, how some are rewarded with a beautiful life and not understanding why others do not.

As the song fades, I open my eyes and find his

staring back at me. A sly shudder creeps along my body and makes me feel uneasy. I know one day, and I feel like it's going to be sooner rather than later, Dillon Bleu will walk out of my life and on to a better one. He's too talented not to. This little moment between us is bittersweet for me and causes tears to prick at my eyes.

He seems to pick up on it, and his serious demeanor slides into a lighter one as his lips quirk up on one side.

"I wasn't that bad, Jewels. Don't get all weepy about it." He rolls his eyes as he puts the guitar away. I grab a hymnal and hurl it at his head, but he catches it in midair and grins at me. "No need in getting physical. You already beat me up one time tonight. Now how's about you chauffeuring me home?"

I let him get away with making a joke out of what could have been a serious moment and follow him out. As we make it outside, I take a deep breath of the crisp night air, hoping it will chase off the uneasiness that has taken hold of me. Dillon replaces the key under the flowerpot after he locks up and glances at his watch again. Curfew is getting dangerously close for him now, but he seems hesitant. I lean against the side of the church and tilt my head up to check out the clear night sky. The moon is full and the stars are in abundance. I love these peaceful nights.

I'm in no rush due to not having a curfew, so I'm being a bit mean to Dillon by making him ask to go home. He's not crazy about having to point out his dependence on me. He has a driver's license, but Cora has refused to let him drive much yet. I know the main reason is she can't afford a vehicle for him.

"You ready?" he asks in a casual tone, yet he seems to be stalling, too.

I glance over to him. He has his hands shoved in his jean pockets and is looking toward the Mustang. I shrug my shoulders and turn my gaze back up to the sky. "Hmm... I think I'm not quite ready to head home just yet." I know he has to get home. Truly I do, but this is too fun. He's starting to get fidgety. Cora is home waiting on him tonight. He can't just sneak in as he does when she's working.

My eyes drift shut but blink right back open when I feel the unexpected warmth of his arms circle around me. He yanks me against his chest and secures his mouth to mine in an instant. Stunned, I stand here in his arms as his lips move fervently over mine, trying to wrap my mind around the fact that my best friend is kissing me.

My mind demands me to push him away, to put an end to whatever he just carelessly started, but the pounding of my heart drowns out the voice of reason as my lips wake up and join in the kiss. This is going to cost me, but I'm willing to pay the consequences later. Or that's what I'm telling myself in this moment. It feels too exciting and incredible to stop, and I find myself trying to pulling him closer.

The anxious tempo of the kiss eventually settles into more of a sweet melody. Dillon holds me gently, with his hands threaded through my hair. Sinking into his caress, my hands rest on his chest and I can feel his heart hammering against my palms. Even with the height difference, we seem to be the perfect fit.

Dillon begins this unexpected kiss passionately, but ends it slowly on a whisper—just as he would perform one of his songs. He doesn't release me, but eases back enough to meet my eyes. It's as if he is awaiting my reaction, but I'm too stunned to voice these wild feelings. I stare back at him with my eyes wide in surprise.

He just pushed us over an invisible line and there's no going back.

"Dillon..." I finally whisper, my eyebrows knitting together in confusion.

He shakes his head, silently asking me to not say anything. So I don't, but slowly shake my head to return his sentiments. No words are needed. Those silent gestures conveying everything words could— *yes, we kissed, and no, we probably shouldn't have...*

I begin to squirm, wanting out of his grasp and away from the awkwardness, but he holds me in place and gives me a devilish grin.

"That's for trying to make me miss curfew." He actually has the audacity to lean in for another kiss after delivering that boneheaded remark, effectively ruining the moment.

I flinch away from those sinful lips and grab his arm to check the time on his watch. "You have ten good minutes and about a mile. If you take off in a sprint, you can make your curfew, Dimples." I push him off and take several steps back before pointing to the road.

"Wha..." It doesn't take long for him to catch on. Clarity dawns on his face as he releases a loud groan before taking off in a run down across the parking lot and on to the highway.

"You stole that kiss, you jerk!" I holler behind him.

He keeps running but yells back, "You can take it back anytime you want!"

I shake my head and watch him run with all his might before he disappears into the darkness. I don't feel bad about making him run home. I checked to make sure he was wearing his sneakers and not his boots first. I would have taken him home if he had on his boots... *Maybe.*

Slightly perturbed and a lot confused, I prop myself up on the hood and try to make some sense out of what just happened. I don't know how to react. My thoughts are muddled with all sorts of emotions—giddy, anxious, hopeful, a little ashamed, happy, sad...

The biggest part I'm struggling to grasp is the fact that my first real kiss was with Dillon Bleu and it was *fantastic*. I've kissed a few guys, mostly awkward pecks at the end of a date. I've never been with anyone I wanted to actually make out with before. But what just happened was beyond a kiss, it was an experience of absolute wonderfulness.

Laughter bubbles out of me as I lie back on the hood. *I just made out with my best friend.*

I wait long enough to know Dillon has made it

home before heading in that direction. The lights are off in his trailer as I park beside mine. I go inside quietly and ease into my dark room and swap my clothes for a ratty shirt and pair of night pants before crawling into bed. I'm lying here still playing what happened, over and over. My lips are still a bit tingly. I run my fingers along them and smile in spite of it all.

Too much adrenaline has me too keyed up to sleep, so I pull out my short stories journal and try to get lost in the fictional world.

The pen hits the paper and creates a story about a dark witch who accidently turns her black magic against herself during a spell-gone-bad. She is transformed into nothing more than a gloomy shadow and mournfully drifts through life, waiting for someone to notice her...

Not feeling it, I put a pause on the story and flip several pages to begin another one that feels more inspiring. This story is about best friends running away together on a sea adventure. They stow away on a ship and set out to explore the world. Of course, the girl falls madly in love with her best friend, and he in return. They spend the rest of their days on a deserted island, living off coconuts and love. This story seems to write itself, and I fill page after page with their adventures.

When my eyes begin to cross, I wrap my arms around the journal like a security blanket and slowly drift to the land of nod.

Before I drift too far, a pinging sound starts up

against my window. I try to ignore it, but someone is being pretty persistent tonight. It's not an unusual occurrence. The whole crowd has done this exact gesture several dozen times apiece. Someone always needs to talk.

There are also those manhunt nights. I've been practically dragged out of my window to participate in these late-night games. Shimmer Lakes Farm has the grandest corn patch around, and my crowd never misses the opportunity to take advantage of it during the season, striking out after midnight and playing tag in the pitch-black. There's just something so mystical about the night air rustling through the tall cornstalks while wandering around in the midst of them.

We've only had a few mishaps over the years. Kyle plowed into a parked tractor one night while trying to outrun Dillon and ended up needing seven stitches over his right eye. This was a few years past the church break-in incident, so Cora took to tearing each of us up with a tree switch for that one. The other incident was minor, in comparison. We took to playing a manhunt tournament in the middle of growing season, and the twins just couldn't resist the temptation of the abundant sweet corn. Those boys ate their weight in raw corn and then commenced to spending the next two days not being able to leave the bathroom. Their mom banished them to the bathrooms at the bathhouse. So for those few days you could find them sitting in the shade outside the building, normally with one either heading into the bathroom or coming out. Those boys were miserable.

I'm about to ignore the persistent visitor completely until my tired mind snaps into focus. *It could be Dillon.* I sit up and ease open the window, but he has disappeared already. I'm disappointed until I spot him on his front steps with his guitar in his lap. We watch each other for a few beats before he starts strumming the melody to his promise of a song.

He plays it through several times as I watch on, his eyes never leaving mine. I'm beginning to wonder if this song is conveying a promise between just Dillon and me. Maybe it's been a promise for a while and I'm only beginning to see its possibility tonight. I watch him until my eyes get too heavy to remain open. He nods his head in a gesture that says for me to lie down. I offer him a shy wave before snuggling into the bed while listening to the guitar create the beautiful song. I fight sleep as long as I can, knowing the spell will be broken tomorrow, and things will never be the same again.

FIVE

A few weeks have passed by since the kiss, but it's seems like my friendship with Dillon is stuck back in that night. We've decided to pretend it didn't happen. Or Dillon has decided and I've had no choice but to go along with it. Okay, I guess, but now there's this awkwardness between us. The kiss was obviously a mistake. I just want my best friend back and things the way they were.

Today is Dillon's birthday. The guys are planning a celebration of sorts and are making me help out. That would be fine, except Max is trying to hook Dillon up with his cousin, Clare or Clara, or something like that. Nothing against her, but I'd rather not have to witness it. Since the kiss, Dillon has avoided me as well as other girls. It's like I broke him of it somehow. I guess I'm that lousy of a kisser.

The morning after the kiss, everyone met up to help Aunt Evie scrub the small campground cabins down for the seasonal closing. That way, except for dusting and fresh linens, they would be ready for spring. It really irked me when Dillon avoided me like the plague that day, always working on another cabin away from the one I worked on. I had begun to worry that he really thought I had some sort of rash as he had declared at the party. But I thought it was best to let it go and not bug him about his odd behavior.

I know Dillon. He will come around eventually.

"So the new guys are coming to the party?" I ask Kyle while driving around the campsites for trash pickup.

"Yeah. They killed it last week at the concert." Kyle hops out before I can come to a complete stop to grab a few bags.

Thinking about the concert makes my stomach twinge, so I sit tight and let my brother grab this load.

Dillon and the twins were asked to perform with these two other guys at a free concert in the park. Trace Leigh and Logan Carter just split with a band they had played with for a few years. This concert was sort of a trial to see if the guys mesh, so I went to support them, but Dillon refused to ride with me. He actually asked his mom to drop him off and pick him up. That was a dead giveaway. What teenage guy wants his mom escorting him around? Especially in front of these new dudes.

The weirdest part is that even though he has gone to weird measures to avoid me during the day, Dillon has not missed a night of serenading me with his promise of a song. Why do I know he is playing specifically to me? I tested it to be sure. I've been waiting all kinds of late hours before I ease my window open. Never has the song begun until then. A few nights I've dozed off while waiting out a time to open my window, and he has waked me by the pelting of pebbles on my window until I open it and listen. I don't get what's going on, and it's so blame frustrating. I'm getting ticked off just thinking about it. Maybe it's some little crush and he doesn't know how to deal with it. I guess only time will figure it out.

"Get the lead out, Jillian," Kyle says, forcing me out of my head. "You drag your heels any slower and we gonna miss the party." He slings another bag in the small truck's bed before hopping back in the cramped cab.

I slip the truck into first gear and ease up to the next batch of trash bags. "What's the big rush? All we're doing is meeting at the game room and giving him a stupid out-of-date deli cake."

Kyle cuts his impatient eyes at me. "It's Dillon's flipping birthday. We gonna celebrate it the best we can." He shakes his head and lets out a harsh huff. "You've both been acting totally weird lately, like an old married couple who's bickering. You need to knock it off."

"What?" I slam the brakes and pull up the emergency brake handle. Before I can climb out for the last of the trash, Kyle grabs my arm.

"You heard me. I don't know what happened between the two of you, but you gotta get over it. We're all he has, Jewels. Cora has to work a double at the diner today, so we are *all* he has."

My brother is right, of course. Dillon has nobody but us, so it's time I get over whatever it was that happened and remember what's important.

We finish dumping the trash in the dumpster and head home quickly to wash. By the time I emerge from the shower, I've resolved to show Dillon a great birthday. I fish out a few twenties I had stashed for emergencies and send Kyle and Mave off on the task of grabbing up pizzas to go along with the cake.

While they're gone, I search through my clothes to find something nice. It's a chilly night in this early November, but we are holding the party in the game room at the campground. It's closed for the season, so it's all ours. It looks like a slightly bigger version of the cedar cabins and is a big draw to campers, although it's in severe need of upgrading. Since we won't be outside in the cold, I decide to show Dillon and his date how nice I can look. I settle for a black leather miniskirt Leona gave me a while back, due to it being a bit big on her tiny frame. I'm about a size thicker than her, so it fits me like a glove. I rummage around until I find my deep-purple top with long sleeves. The neck is super wide, so it hangs off one shoulder, punk-rock style, the way I like it. I finish the look with ankle boots and several studded belts. After applying minimal makeup and fluff my long wavy hair, I call it done.

I head to the door, but pause. I need to give Dillon a gift. Not just any gift, but something as special and unique as he is. I head back to my stash of condo freebies and rummage around the colognes and shirts and guy shades, but nothing seems to fit the bill. I'm close to giving up when my eyes land on my journal. It holds a few new songs I've written since the kiss, but have been too big of a coward to share them with him. Maybe this will be a good way to mend our little split. He is always begging me for more songs. I grab a pair of scissors and neatly free the songs from the binding, roll them up in a tube, and tie it off with a leather cord that has a cross on it. It's one of my favorite bracelets, so I think it makes for the proper bow.

I gather up some of my favorite CD's and some courage before heading to the game room.

With the music booming through the speakers in a fast tempo that matches the racing of my heart, I watch as Dillon walks in grinning, exposing those dimples under his stubble. He's wearing an Oasis Rock Tour T-shirt with faded black jeans, and his leather jacket and boots. His hair is in perfect disarray, the blue streak a bit more vibrant than the last time I saw him.

"Looks like someone has been to the beauty shop," Leona comments.

"Yep," I mutter my agreement, taking in the total package of Dillon Bleu. Between the hair and outfit, the guy already looks like a rock legend, and I'm quite sure he will be one day. I'd bet on it.

He meets my gaze before his eyes travel down the length of me and back up. A heated look passes between us, but before his hot gaze secures to mine, it trips back to unease. Instead of speaking to me, he sidesteps and heads over to the guys.

Great. The birthday hasn't lessened the

awkwardness in the least.

Kyle hands him a soda and they all tear into the pizza. With my appetite completely gone, I keep my distance by hopping up on top of the bar beside Leona and sip on a soda while trying not to sulk. I'm ready to be over our weirdness, but I guess he is not.

Max strolls through the door a little bit later, with a tall bleached blonde in tow, and walks over to give Dillon a manly slap on the shoulder, at which Dillon actually winces. Something doesn't seem just right with his upper back, but he moves on so quickly that the boys don't catch on. I smirk though, because I did. There's not much this guy can get past me, and I'm pretty sure it is the same the other way around as well.

"What in the world has Max dragged along with him?" Leona asks beside me, her long legs dangling to the beat of the music while she picks the pepperonis off her slice of pizza.

"I think she's Dillon's birthday gift." This causes Leona to laugh and I join in. This is so Max, to bring a girl as Dillon's gift. I swipe a discarded pepperoni and shrug while trying unsuccessfully to look away. I keep trying to avert my gaze, but find myself right back to staring at him and his company.

An hour later, the place is lively with a couple dozen teenagers dancing around or playing pool. This is the only part of the year we are allowed to hang out here, so everyone seems to be taking full advantage of this opportunity.

"So you play the keyboard?" I ask my dance

partner and one of the newest members of Bleu Streak.

"Yeah. I've sung lead some, but it's not really my thing." Trace gives me a lopsided grin with his bright eyes bouncing with energy.

Trace is a Kurt Cobain lookalike, minus the worn-out features. He has the lightest blue eyes and shoulder-length pale blond hair that seems to float around his face, it's so light. This dude is animated and such a free spirit that I can't help but enjoy his company. I'm not much for making new friends, so this pleasantly surprises me. He's from a nearby suburb, so he's sort of in between our side and the other side of the lake, socially speaking.

I glance away from Trace and catch Dillon watching us. I wait for him to look away from being caught, but he keeps those intense eyes pinned to me without shame.

"New Year's is going to be epic. Logan has all the hookups when it comes to stellar gigs." Trace rambles on about all of their big plans.

My eyes wander back over Trace's shoulder to the table where Dillon is playing cards with some guys. Blondie has been glued to Dillon since she arrived. He's only danced a few songs with her, choosing to hang out with the guys instead.

Dillon's mouth is in a hard line with his eyes narrowed, not looking too pleased. *Well, the feeling is mutual.* I try to pay him no mind, but it's like we have always been two magnets drawn to the other.

His message tonight, through the staring and

stern set of his handsome face, is telling me to walk away from Trace. And my message back, through a few sharp glares and slight headshakes, is that he has no room to tell me what to do.

"Trace, I need a Spades partner," Dillon yells a little too harshly. He seems to catch himself and pushes his grimace into a forced smile. "Come help me out, dude."

Trace offers me an apologetic smile before heading to the table, ending the dance and fun I was having.

The guys eventually grow tired of Spades after a half dozen games, so Dillon opens his few gifts. Kyle gives him a bottle of cologne he swiped from my condo freebies. I'm cool with it since it happens to be Dillon's favorite brand. Leona gives him a new guitar pick with *Bleu Streak* etched on it.

Dillon's dimples are on full display, thoroughly delighted by the two gifts. The twins are the poorest of the crowd. No one ever expects a gift from them, hence Max bringing a girl.

My gift is too personal, so I decide to wait until later. If he doesn't straighten up, I may not give it to him, period.

"I'm starving," Mave yells while I catch Max swiping a finger-full of icing off the edge of the cake.

"We better go ahead and cut it before the dang thing disappears," Kyle grumbles, giving the twins a pointed look for which they ignore while licking icing off their fingers.

My brother yanks the cake away from them and

when he turns to walk it over to Dillon, I notice the entire piped edge of frosting from one side of the rectangle confection is completely gone.

We eat the old cake that turns out to be surprisingly moist. I guess the date really doesn't have to dictate the freshness every time. We sing "Happy Birthday" at exactly one minute before midnight and continue to sing one minute past. It's a weird thing we started years ago, before we even hit the teenage years. We celebrate each other's birthday to the very last minute of the day. We want to remind our friend how important he is to us, since most of this world seems to not care.

As the song ends, Blondie tries to give Dillon a birthday kiss, but he turns his head and receives it on his cheek. She grabs hold of his right shoulder to leverage another kiss, but he winces under her arm and tries shrugging her off. He finally manages to untwine himself from her. This time she takes offense and walks away. *Poor girl.* Rejection from this guy is a pretty tough pill to swallow.

Dillon rotates his arm around a bit when he thinks no one is watching. *What's going on with you, Dimples?*

The party will probably wear on for a few more hours, so I slip out the side door and head home. Once I'm in my small room, I look down at my outfit one more time before peeling it off and swapping into my usual oversized T-shirt and hole-riddled sweatpants. *I dressed up for nothing.*

I stretch out on my bed and try to decide if I'm

89

going to wait up or just go on to sleep. I seriously doubt he will be serenading me tonight. My eyes slam shut, hoping to block out my disappointed feelings and find sleep soon.

Something rouses me abruptly, but I'm not really sure what that *something* was. I lay still and wait for it again, eyes searching the dark. I almost come unglued when a leg swings through my window.

"*Shh*… It's just me, Jewels," Dillon lands on top of me, nearly knocking the wind out of me.

"You scared me to death," I whisper-yell, trying to push him off.

Dillon doesn't budge, just lies on top of me, so close our noses touch and our breaths mingle. He stares like he's searching for something. Waiting for him to find whatever that may be, I push a few strands out of his eyes, but they flop back down tickle my face. We stay this way for a while, neither one of us wanting to move. Having him close, after the recent rift, feels good.

"Someone crawling through your window is nothing new." Dillon comments, still not moving.

"I suppose you're right," I mumble, taking in the smell of mint gum on his breath.

I've had more than one visitor fall into my room at one point or the other, needing something. I guess it's because I'm the oldest is why everyone comes to me.

When Leona was twelve, she crawled through my window and openly wept. She had started her period that night and couldn't bring herself to confide in her dad. I remember putting my arm around her shoulder and whispering, "We got this." I went to Aunt Evie's bedroom and filled her in on what was up with Leona. She nodded her head and said, "We got this."

My aunt drove over to Walmart and stocked Leona up on all of the necessary supplies. She even grabbed a huge box of chocolates that we *women* sat up late devouring. She then went over to Leona's and explained to Mr. Dan what was going on. So once a month, until she was old enough to take care of things herself, Leona would fall into my room, and with a dramatic eye roll, saying it was that time again.

Max showed up in my room one night with women trouble. He was having a hard time getting any girls to take him seriously. It was his own blame fault. I told Max if he would knock it off with all of the goofing around and the wild pranks, then maybe someone would be able to take him seriously. I also informed him that most girls did not like to be referred to as being *hot thangs* and *babes*. I schooled him till dawn the next day about what he was doing wrong. He took my advice and straightened up for a while, but by the end of the following week he was back to his old goofy ways. Some are just not teachable.

Of course, Mave has showed up on a regular basis over the years to just hide from whatever trouble the idiot got himself into at that moment. If it's out there to get into, Maverick King finds it. If he doesn't find trouble, it somehow finds him. The dude is a haphazard.

Dillon has been the exception to the rule, always using the front door and barging his way into my room when he needs me, without knocking. Well, up until now, I suppose.

"Take a walk with me?" He shifts most of his weight off to the side, motioning for me to get up.

"No. It's too cold," I mumble and stay put, wishing I was bold enough to pull him back on top of me.

"Then put on a coat. Please..." He begins scooching over until I have no choice but to stand up or fall to the floor.

I move over to the closet and begin rummaging around for a thick jacket with a hood. It's not freezing by any means, just nippy. I slide his gift into the inner pocket of the coat while pushing my feet into a pair of Ked's knockoffs.

"Alright, Dimples, let's go." I motion to the door, but he's already wiggling himself back through my small window. I'm amazed he's able to get his long body in and out so easily. Reluctantly, I follow. He finishes pulling me through and sets me on the ground outside.

Once I'm steady on my feet, Dillon releases me, but gathers my hand in his without hesitation. We head over to the dock. The moon isn't so full tonight, but the night sky is crystal-clear, so it's easy to see the way. We stand at the end of the dock for a while, but eventually have a seat on the planked top and gaze out over the water. I love the soft, tinkering lullaby of the lake water.

I look over at Dillon and find him lost in thought, so I nudge his knee with my own. He looks over with an apprehensive smile that is barely there.

"Happy birthday." I pull the songs from my pocket and hand them over.

He eyes the tube of papers while a slow grin pulls at his lips. "This what I think it is?"

"Yep. They're all new, too."

He slides the leather bracelet off and tries handing it back to me, but I shake my head no. "It's a guy bracelet. It's part of your gift." I take it out of his hand and tie it around his wrist.

"Thanks, Jewels. This is my favorite gift." He raises the papers with reverence.

I lean back and eye his right shoulder. "Speaking of gifts…You got new ink today, didn't you?"

Dillon gives me a sidelong glance. "Just how did you know about that?"

"Come on, Dillon. I've known you a lot of my life. There's not much you can get past me. For one thing, you wouldn't take your jacket off all night, and you've been babying that right side of your upper back." I ever so slightly place my fingers in the spot and feel the soft give of a gauzy dressing.

He glances at me sideways again before looking out over the water. "I don't think I'm ready to show it to you just yet."

"Why not?"

"It's pretty personal."

"Okay."

He looks back to me, skeptically. "Okay? That's

it?"

"Yes. It's your body, and I know a tattoo to you is a personal expression. I won't nag you about it."

Dillon stares at me warmly and seems to appreciate my response. A shiver skirts along my chilled body, so he pulls me closer and wraps his arm around me. I automatically lean my head on his left shoulder.

"So tell me why you woke me up and dragged me outside in the wee hours of this morning." I breathe in the subtle hints of his cologne. It's a woodsy smell that reminds me of our walks through the small wooded area behind the trailer park. I nuzzle closer to the side of his warm neck without thinking twice about it and take in another long breath.

He remains quiet, but his arm tightens around me. Tucked into his side, this little place feels like home. Like it's exactly where I belong.

"I'm waiting," I say after a few minutes of silence.

His body grows rigid. "I want to..."

I raise my head to look at him. I reach up and brush a few locks of hair away from his forehead and search his handsome face. "Dillon?"

"I want to apologize for stealing that kiss." This apology is only a whisper.

"Why did you kiss me?" I whisper back.

"I couldn't wait any longer," he says in a husky voice, while holding my gaze.

Before I lose my nerve, I climb into his lap and rest the tip of my cold nose to his warm one. "I want that kiss back now," I quietly demand before leaning the rest of the way to reclaiming my kiss.

A sigh of relief slips from his mouth as he takes over the kiss. It's a delicate unrushed caress. It feels right and I savor it. His lips are so warm and surprisingly soft. I wait for him to end the kiss, but eventually realize he has no more desire than I do for it to stop. I pull back and stare at him as we both become breathless.

"My Jewels," Dillon murmurs as he places my hand over his heart. It beats strong and vigorously. "I was scared I totally screwed things up with you." He rests his forehead to mine.

"Never. You will always be my best friend." I scoot as close as I can to him and brush a kiss along his ear before whispering, "My Dimples."

He chuckles lightly and rewards me with a glimpse of those babies. "Yes, I'm your Dimples," he says, finally relenting to my name for him.

We stay out on the dock until the dawn of the new day appears on a haze of greys and peaches. We shuffle back to our trailers, with him boosting me back through my window and stealing one more kiss before heading to his own bed.

I snuggle deeply under my quilt and relive the sweet moment I just shared with Dillon. It was definitely an unexpected turn. It gives me hope that exciting and awesome experiences are obtainable after all.

• ♫ • ♫ • ♫ •

It's Thanksgiving weekend and this place is a ghost town. Aunt Evie let Kyle go with the twins an hour away to their grandparents' home for the weekend. The twins were pretty psyched about the endless amount of food at their disposal. Kyle is growing like a weed, so he was all for going with them. Leona works at the mall—enough said. With the sales events, I won't see her until at least Monday. My pocketbook definitely won't allow me to go see her. That's just too much temptation.

So it's just me and Dillon, lazing in the swing on the beach. He helped me out with trash duties earlier, and now we are free for the remainder of the day.

"Go on a treasure hunt with me," Dillon says, easing the swing to a stop.

As soon as he says the words *treasure hunt,* I automatically rise and we both head to the sheds.

This is something we've done since we were old enough to wander off together. The whole lot of us has come down to these sheds and walked away with a bounty of treasure over the years. Well... It's treasure to us anyway. This is where we discovered our boat after all.

We scoot into the bigger shed and memories assault me, sending a smile to my face. Aunt Evie's family didn't believe in throwing anything away, which has been a big plus in helping us combat our boredom over the years. Never have I slipped into one of these buildings without discovering something new.

Another treasure unearthed in this place was a dirt bike. It took the boys over four months of searching around for all of the scattered parts before they could get it up and running.

And it only took Mave less than four days to completely destroy it.

The guys set up some shady ramps, which I absolutely didn't trust, along the edge of the woods. They all managed okay as long as they kept their speed reasonable. Leave it to Mave to push it way past the limit. The daredevil and that bike took an unexpected nosedive into the lake after crashing through a few trees. The bike was completely ruined, and Mave earned a broken arm. I can still see him trudging up out of that water holding his arm. He looked more confused than hurt.

"Dude, something don't feel so right with my arm," he said as he tried to hold the misshapen appendage up. He had to play the drums one-armed for six weeks. In all actuality, it probably helped to improve his skills. His left-handed drumming improved dramatically during that period.

Speaking of drums, this is where we found Mave's first drum set, buried underneath some gross smelling burlap sacks. The set was nearly dry-rotted, but he didn't care. That boy wore holes into the tops of the drums from playing them so much. A week after we had to finally trash the set, Aunt Evie surprised him with a used set she bought at a local pawn shop.

"Playing the drums seems to be the only thing

that keeps Maverick out of trouble," she said the day they were delivered. Mave planted a sweet kiss on her cheek, as he always did as a thank-you, and then went to pounding on that set until they also fell apart.

Leona found trunks of vintage clothes last year and spent the remainder of the school year rocking out all sorts of mod outfits. The only item I swiped from one of the trunks is this faded army jacket I'm wearing today with some old jeans and a Beatles T-shirt. I scored the Beatles shirt from the thrift shop across the way where Leona and I plunder through the racks at least once a week. Living in such close vicinity of the rich does have its perks. Those people wear something one time and deem it unworthy, and then send it packing on down to the secondhand stores.

I look over at Dillon and see that he is wearing another name brand hoodie I found for him. Dillon has always been an exception to my white-trash rule. He has never looked like he fit in with us. He always looks impeccable, even in jeans and T-shirts. I guess with Cora not really having white-trash roots, Dillon doesn't either.

My clothes are clean, don't get me wrong. I just feel lacking.

Dillon catches me looking over a shelf at him He gives me a peek of those dimples before something in a box catches his eyes. I turn back to my thoughts as I stroll down the aisle. There are three distinct rows in this shed, and it makes for easy plundering.

"Hey, you remember our garden?" Dillon waves

a small garden trowel in the air.

"How could I forget?" I laugh at the memory.

Preteens, Max and Kyle came barreling out one of the sheds with armfuls of gardening supplies and cracked plastic kiddy pools one spring day. They had spent the week before helping Ms. Raveena with tending to her rose bushes. Ms. Raveena is a northerner from Buffalo who retired in the South. Her long, black hair has an attractive streak of grey in the front, and the boys call her Grey Streak behind her back. It's all in good fun, because the crowd adores her. She even lets the twins go through her cabinets and fridge like they own the place. She and I share the same theory on those two.

This little old lady's pocketbook is deep enough to live on the other side of the lake, but she says she prefers the simple life over here instead. She hauled in a brand-new trailer and set out to making herself at home amongst us poor folks. I like to visit her cozy little place. Unlike most of the trailers around here, her floors don't sag and no mildew smell is evident. She has the prettiest little yard. It resembles a mini flower showcase.

Ms. Raveena inspired the two boys to want their own garden, and they had talked her out of enough topsoil to fill the half dozen or so pools.

"The stench of that fertilizer will live in my olfactory nightmares forever," I say, causing Dillon to wrinkle his nose.

Mr. Wayne lives a street over from the little lady and is an avid gardener as well. He pretends to be a grouch, but I know better. He smiles a lot when he thinks no one's watching. But I'm always watching. Always looking for a story or glimpse of something to inspire my words. I like to create different worlds for people other than the ones they live. Mr. Wayne has starred as a ruthless secret agent, unearthing a hidden supply of nuclear weapons buried in the bottom of the lake. He has also starred as a fun-loving drug smuggler, stockpiling his stash throughout his garden and only cultivates in the middle of the night.

Don't ask me where this junk comes from. I guess it's my way of taking a break from reality. I could take you around the entire trailer park and tell a tale I've created for each resident. Okay, guess I got off the subject a bit...

Mr. Wayne privately competes with Ms. Raveena to see who can grow the best flowers. I secretly like the little lady's the best. She has lots of vibrant colors throughout her yard. The feeling you get from walking around the small, lush space is fun and whimsy. Mr. Wayne leans toward a more subdued color palette. Don't get me wrong. It's a really slamming yard, too. It's more tranquil.

So anyway, the boys promised to Kool Seal Mr. Wayne's roof in exchange for some of his top-secret fertilizer. The rest of us strolled up to the rear of the sheds to see Kyle and Max's progress the day they received their allotment of fertilizer. They were scooping handfuls of the black mixture into the beds and mixing it throughout the soil as Mr. Wayne had instructed.

Just let me tell you, the stench coming off those two boys and the garden beds was the funkiest kind of stink I have ever smelled. We couldn't stop gagging, so we hauled tail. Later they joined us by the lakeshore, but they reeked from the fertilizer so bad, I demanded they take a dip in the lake. They reemerged still stinking to the high heavens, so we took them over to the maintenance shed and doused them down with diluted bleach before hosing it off.

Come to find out the top-secret fertilizer was a combination of cow manure and fish guts that had been decomposing for a while.

I nearly gag just thinking about it. That was one heck of a stink.

The boys became the butt of many a joke that summer. Kyle earned the nickname fish-face, and Max was called heifer after that incident.

After Mother Nature carried off the stench from the makeshift garden beds, the boys were antsy to plant. The problem was they had nothing to plant, so we struck out on our bikes and pedaled over to the Shimmer Lakes Farm and begged the owner for some spare seeds.

"You kids are welcome to walk the freshly planted rows and take any stray seed on top of the ground." He looked at Max and Mave sternly and said, "But if I see any dirt caked up to their knuckles from digging, you'll have to return all the seeds you find."

Their shoulders drooped a bit from the warning, but they reluctantly agreed. It was the only shot we had to get seeds, so everyone kept reminding the twins of that as we hunted. We looked at it as another treasure hunt and searched the rows all afternoon until we had a good-sized collection of various seeds. We sorted the seeds, planting the ones that looked similar together and impatiently waited to see what the mystery garden would produce.

Six weeks later we were blessed with a bounty of vegetables – cucumbers, squash, green beans, okra, and plenty more. The tomatoes were so juicy and plump, we would eat them like apples right off the vines. Kyle was over the moon when the first signs of watermelons began to form off one plant. That was his favorite. It was more vegetables than we knew what to do with, so the boys left small bags of produce on everyone's porches throughout that summer.

I guess that top-secret fertilizer was worth its weight in stench. It was the only year we had a garden. The following summer the boys hit the teen years and thought they were too old and too cool for such.

It's still one of my favorite treasure hunt memories, though.

I'm rummaging through a bin filled with an assortment of trinkets when Dillon eases behind me and wraps his arms around my waist. "Find any treasure yet?" I lean into him and snuggle into his warm embrace.

He places a kiss on top of my head. "Yep." He hugs me a bit tighter. "She's right here in my arms."

I turn to face him and can't help but smile. What girl wouldn't want to be called someone's treasure, right? His dimples are on full display, and I lightly touch my fingertips to them. "I think I've found my treasure, too," I whisper before leaning forward and placing delicate kisses over each dimple. "My Dimples."

"And always my Jewel," he murmurs before kissing me sweetly.

• ♫ • ♫ • ♫ •

Dillon and I spend every waking moment together during this momentous fall. That's nothing new. We've done that for years. But now it's more of just him and me without the rest of the crowd. We find excuses to be alone, and no one seems to be paying us any attention. So we're either hiding out under our willow tree with him composing endless amounts of music or plundering around the sheds. It's like our eyes have just opened to this possibility for the first time in such a way that we can't get enough of each other.

Dillon still serenades the trailer park each night, but it's later now. He always crawls through my window, and we sit on the floor by the bed and whisper about what future we want together. I know we are too young to have such conversations. But when you live the way we live, your future dreams are all you have. Getting wrapped up planning our future has become our nightly routine.

Our dreams have not wavered over the years. Dillon says his quest is to become a rock star and my wish is to someday write a book. Sadly, I know deep down my wish won't be coming true. My ties are too tethered to this place, and Kyle is my responsibility more than anything. I want Kyle to have a chance at a better life, so my life may have to be placed on the backburner to make sure he gets a shot at it.

I sit on the worn couch in the game room with Leona by my side as we watch the guys rehearse for their big New Year's Eve gig, both our heads bobbing to the beat Mave is provoking from the drum kit. Logan plays a mean bass and is joining in as the others follow. I like how they meld their sounds, weaving each instrument's sound to the others to create such killer songs.

Dillon leans close to the mic and starts crooning out the lyrics to a cover song, long shaggy hair falling down his face. It's easy to envision female fans swooning for him and male fans fanaticizing about being him one day soon. It's a future he's just on the brink of entering. I feel it in my bones.

He looks up and gives me a sly wink, catching me swooning myself.

We've always had a way of silently communicating with one another, but now our wordless conversations carry a different and more intimate message than before. I can be watching the band practice, and all Dillon has to do is give me a certain look and I know what he's thinking about. His silent messages whisper about love, hope, and excitement.

It's a promise of great things to come, and I'm beginning to hope that dreams are attainable.

SIX

I should have known better. I should have known that no matter how hard I fell in love with him, Dillon Bleu was an exciting and awesome human who was *unattainable*. Sure we pulled it off for a while, but...

"Five. Four. Three. Two. One..."

"Happy New Years!" The crowd cheers, but I don't join in. There's a huge lump lodged in my throat, and no matter how hard I swallow, it won't go away.

Dillon and the rest of Bleu Streak light up the stage at the Lakeside Music Hall for another round of songs as couples finish up their celebratory kisses. Dillon serenades this crowd with a song I wrote for him. It speaks of first loves and attainable hopes and dreams. Unexpected tears slide down my face. All I want to do is go home, but he made me promise I'd stay until the end, so I keep to hiding in the corner and demand myself not to fall completely apart just yet.

My time with Dillon Bleu has run out. The clock had been ticking down rapidly and I've chosen to ignore it like a fool. I knew it was coming, but had no idea how fast it would happen.

Dillon is making his dreams into plans, plans that take flight after this very gig. He's leaving me as I knew he would, but naively hoped it wouldn't be so quickly. Trace got up with some guy out in California and got Bleu Streak in on an opening act contest. The winner will get to tour with some pretty cool rock bands for the next year. I know deep down whom that band will be, and I also know that once they pull out in a little while, they won't be coming back. Who could blame them, really?

I wipe away the tears, but more trickle out to replace them. Dillon has just begun playing the melody of his promise of a song. He's looking directly at me as he smoothly croons the lyrics into the microphone. It's the first time I've heard them and now I'm crying so hard I can barely see him.

My Jewel, my life
You're my night and you're my day
You'll always be with me
Even though that's still too far away
You don't see you the way I do
Such a treasure
Such a jewel
I want you now and I want you always
Just a little while, my love
Just a little while
Give me just a little while…

He continues to sing some more, but I make for the door. This hurts too much. He's just a boy, making promises to me in those lyrics. And there's no way he can keep them. I make it to my car and slump over the steering wheel.

Moments later, Kyle is yanking the passenger car door open and slumping in the seat beside me. He slams the door shut and faces me with confused anger. He stares me down, waiting for something, but I don't say anything.

"You want to tell me what in the heck that's all about?" He waves back toward the building.

Dillon and I have kept our new relationship just between us. I didn't want Kyle upset over it, but I guess the cat's out of the bag now. Dillon singing that song was definitely a bold way of announcing it. I'm guessing he thought he was safe on stage, away from my brother.

"I'm going to kill him!" Kyle slams his fist on the dashboard.

"Just calm down. What's your problem?" I rub my temples and try to ease the headache I've earned from crying.

"He's like a brother to us, Jillian." Kyle stares out the window and takes several deep breaths. When he speaks again, his voice is low and I have to strain to hear him. "You knew he would be leaving."

This declaration causes the tears to pick back up again. Kyle reaches over the console and wraps his arm around me.

"This is why I want to kill him," he says, but there's no fire to the words this time. Just pity.

It's two in the morning when I see Dillon finally

gliding through the Music Hall doors. Kyle hasn't left me since I fell apart, so he sees him too, and before I know to react, my brother is out of the car and tackling Dillon in the parking lot. I jump out screaming at him to stop, but it doesn't help. Trace and Mave are there in a flash, pulling Kyle off of Dillon.

"Stop it now, Kyle! You're gonna get your butt arrested!" I'm about to push between them, but Logan pulls me back.

"Watch yourself, little lady. Let the guys handle this," Logan says coolly, ticking me off even more. Logan Carter looks like a hot younger version of Lenny Kravitz and speaks just as smoothly as him, too. He emits a cool vibe. He drapes his arm around my shoulder as he casually watches these two guys go at each other as though it's the most ordinary thing. Nothing seems to bother this dude.

We stand there and watch as they all wrestle around some more. Kyle growls out all kinds of not-nice words as he lets out his frustration, but Dillon only allows a few grunts to slip from his lips.

It takes several long minutes before Trace and Mave can manage to break it up. Both boys are pulled to their feet, with Trace standing in front of Dillon and Mave holding Kyle back. Both are rumpled and breathing heavy. Dillon has a small split on his bottom lip that is trickling blood, but I see no other damage. Kyle has no visible signs of the fight. I'm pretty sure Dillon didn't even swing at him.

"How could you, man?" Kyle asks. "You're like

my brother, dude!" He lets out a few more explicit words as his face twists in pain.

Dillon pushes Mave out the way and grabs Kyle up in a fierce hug, shocking the whole lot of us. I wait for Kyle to fight him off, but my brother actually starts crying and hugs him back.

I realize in this moment that maybe this is more about Kyle's disappointment in Dillon leaving him than what's going on between Dillon and me. Those two have been attached at the hip since preschool, right along with the twins. He is losing a chunk of his family in one fell swoop, just as I am. This thought beckons more tears to fall. We've practically lived together all of our lives.

The rest of the band seems to understand the privacy of the moment, so they head over to Trace's van and begin loading up the equipment.

"I love her, Kyle," Dillon whispers as he still embraces him. "I love you too. You are my family."

"Then why do this?" My poor brother sounds so broken.

"I've got to, man." Dillon steps back and beckons me to him. "I've got to give this a fair shot. Music is all I know. I just feel like it's now or never. I have to go." He wraps his arm around me. "I'll be back. I promise."

"Don't make promises, dude." Kyle pulls away and walks over to open the passenger door and climbs in the backseat. We follow suit, and I drive us home in a thick silence. Really, what else is there to say? Dillon deserves this shot. Being from our trailer-park background, there's not many of those that come along. I want him to follow his dreams. I don't want to hold him back, but that doesn't mean this doesn't hurt. It feels like someone has ripped my heart out. My stomach aches and my throat stings with the pain of knowing he is leaving me.

I park and we all head in. Kyle goes straight to his room and Dillon follows me to mine. We only have about an hour before the band plans on pulling out, and all I want to do in that time is have him hold me.

Dillon lies on his side. I cuddle up next to him and run my hand up the back of his shirt. My fingers glide over the subtle outlines of his tattoo as I try to memorize the feel of it.

"Can I see it again?" I ask. He sits up without hesitation and tosses his shirt on the floor.

He was in my room, just like tonight, last week. On Christmas night, no less. Aunt Evie had cooked us a delicious feast, and after Cora and the twins left, Dillon stayed to hang out with me. It was a slim Christmas, with everyone declaring the meal and each other's company to be gift enough. We put our small artificial tree up and draped it with silver tinsel and brightly-colored twinkling light, but no gifts were placed underneath. This wasn't the first Christmas we had with no gifts, but those ones always sting a bit. I hate not being able to give my loved ones tokens of my affection to show them how much they mean to me.

Dillon and I hid in my room. With him holding me, the disappointment slipped away and was

111

replaced with contentment. I told myself, as we cuddled together on my small bed, Dillon was all I needed.

We were kissing and holding each other when he unexpectedly pulled his shirt off. This surprised me at first, and I began muttering nervously that I wasn't ready to move any further, but he shook his head and turned around to reveal his new tattoo to me. I sat up in shock when I took in the elegant lettering just above his right shoulder blade. *My Jewel* was etched along his skin in sleek, black ink and was surrounded by intricate line designs swirling around emeralds. He's always said my eyes look like emerald jewels, hence my nickname. I couldn't believe he would actually brand my name on him permanently. That is a pretty strong commitment, and I hope he won't live to regret that decision. It was the best gift I had ever received on Christmas. Or so it was until he spoke.

"It's another promise, Jewels," he had whispered as he peeped over his shoulder to gauge my reaction. "You're mine, and I will be back." And this was the point where he broke the news to me about his departure, leaving me stunned. I couldn't muster another word to him that night. I just nodded my head or shook it as he explained the once-in-a-lifetime opportunity that just happened to be all the long way in California. The guys couldn't possibly get any farther away. Or that's what I naively thought, until he explained the potential of the tour going international. That was the point where I knew, beyond knowing, that I had lost him, whether he was willing to admit it or not. Dillon had asked me to say something, but all I could do was shake my head in a daze of disbelief and disappointment.

We have just begun a new chapter in our young story together. A story I was so excited to see develop into what I had genuinely believed would be our happily-ever-after. And it was ending way before a good love story should. So yeah, I'm awfully disappointed.

I've had only a week to prepare for this moment and I'm still not ready. I guide my lips slowly over each letter and try to memorize the feel of his skin and the smell of him. I repeat this gesture over each letter until Dillon becomes restless. He seems to not be able to restrain himself any longer, so he turns and tugs me into his lap and kisses me, and then kisses me some more. I can taste the metallic tang of his blood from the cut on my tongue as our lips crash together, but I don't care. It won't stop me from having these last kisses.

Who knows how long it will be before I receive anymore, if ever again. I'm not a dumb girl. I know life can push you into a lot of changing. Things change. People change. And feelings can change. Everything can be so fickle.

"I'm so proud of you." I murmur the words across his lips, not wanting to break the connection. "You got this," I reiterate, promising myself no more tears until he is gone.

I don't want him to leave here burdened by grief,

but free. Free to take flight and live his dreams. I hold onto his heated skin for dear life, not wanting to break this fragile bond.

He holds me until Max and Mave show up at my window and demand he comes out. "Dude, the sun will be coming up soon. We gotta bounce on outta here." I hear the excitement in Max's voice. Those boys get a chance at a better life, too. I'm trying really hard to be happy for them all and not be jealous. It's not an easy feat.

"Five more minutes. Now get outta here or it's gonna be ten," Dillon says.

"*Dude*." Mave taps his watch before they disappear.

"I wish you could come with me," he says again as he pulls me in for another kiss. He grasps the back of my neck and tugs me even closer.

We already had this conversation about a million times in the last week. Kyle needs to finish the last two years of high school, and I need to stay here and make sure that happens. I have a commitment here to help Aunt Evie, too. The years are catching up to my great-aunt. After all she has done for me and my brother, I can't just disappear in the night like the boys can. I have responsibilities that I cannot just walk away from.

"I'll call you soon," Dillon says as he retrieves his shirt from the floor and pulls it back on.

My insides seize up, but I hold it together.

Before he can climb out the window, there is a knock on my door. I nearly fall out when I pull it open and find Aunt Evie standing on the other side. *Busted.*

"That boy ain't leaving until he gives me a goodbye hug, too," she says, shocking us both.

Kyle walks in and stands behind her. His eyes red-rimmed and the frown on his face wobbling. Dillon gives Aunt Evie a hug, and then one to Kyle before returning to me for another one. We say nothing until he turns to climb out the window.

"You know you have been welcome to use the blame front door all this time, young man," Aunt Evie says with a smile, causing us all to release a nervous chuckle.

"Was I the only one who didn't know about this?" Kyle asks, incredulous.

"Looks that way." I offer him a shrug and follow Dillon out the door toward and the awaiting van.

It's idling in anticipation with only us and the dark morning sky to see them off. Dillon climbs in the passenger seat, and then leans out of the open window for one final farewell kiss.

"I will keep my promises, Pretty Girl," he says, pulling away from me.

I reluctantly let him go and back away from the van. The van creeps down the coquina road, the noise of the tires crunching against it covers the sob that slips from my lips. After the taillights round the corner, I sit in our small yard and fall to pieces. Eventually, I will have to figure out how to gather all of the fragments and get on with my life, knowing the pieces will never properly fit back together.

SEVEN

This has been the loneliest time of my life. The trailer park doesn't seem right at all with Dillon and the twins gone. They have always been a steady part of my life; now they are gone and I just can't cope with it. It's been *months* and everyone tells me it will get better, but it hasn't so far. I'm young and heartbroken, but it's more than me pining away over some guy. A big chunk of my family has left me. Kyle and I hang out more often than not, but the treasure hunts and midnight mischief just aren't the same. We are obviously behaving much better these days. My brother has snagged himself a girlfriend too, so you know what that means for me and my loneliness.

Sure, I talk to the guys, but it's really sporadic and always hurried. Dillon sent me a cell phone a few months ago, so that's made it a little easier to keep up with each other. He sounds so excited and determined when I talk to him, which is normally really late at night. It sounds like the band is struggling to make a name for themselves. Of course, they won the opening act spot on the All Rock Tour, as I knew they would. But they are considered freshmen and are having to prove themselves to the music industry. It's taking a lot of hard work and dedication, so I try to always sound upbeat and supportive when Dillon does get the chance to call, but it's not easy when every cell of my being aches from missing him.

The phone calls always go the same. Dillon gives me the scoop on what concert venue they will be going to next, on who they are meeting with to try to get an agent and all that business stuff, and what rock legend he has gotten to meet. I do what best friends are supposed to do. I cheer him on and continue encouraging him to keep pushing forward. But as soon as we say goodbye and I put the phone down, I crumble. I'm such an emotional wreck. I miss him in such a raw wild way, and I need to figure out how to get over it, for my sanity's sake.

"Whatcha doing, sweetheart?" Aunt Evie asks, pulling me out of my depressing thoughts.

I'm stretched out on the end of the dock, scribbling these miserable feelings in my journal as I try to find some comfort from the familiar lake as it laps gently under the dock.

"Wasting time." I sit up and close the journal.

She eases down beside me, with all kinds of joints popping in protest, and slips her sandals off. She pulls her long bohemian skirt up a bit so she can dangle her feet off the side of the dock and into the cool water. Even though summer is about to take off for another season, the lakeshore is pretty quiet this early evening. There's a light breeze that has brushed the humidity off, thankfully. I roll the legs of my jeans up and scoot closer to the edge to dunk my feet in.

"Sure has been 'bout too quiet around here without them boys causing any ruckus," Aunt Evie says with a chuckle. She knows what's got me down and wastes no time delving into it. "It's been tough on you." She runs her fingers through my long waves in a motherly manner as she watches me with sympathetic eyes. She may have the title aunt, but I've viewed her as my mother ever since that day she welcomed me and Kyle home.

I just shrug my shoulder. Really. What can I say? It's true.

"Good things come to those who wait," she says lightheartedly, but I find myself sniffling in an instant. She wraps her arm around me and lets me quietly sob for a spell.

Good grief. I'm such a cry baby anymore.

"I miss him so much," I whisper, batting away the escaped tears.

"That boy is your other half and you are his. And nothing is going to change that. Let him live this stage of his life. Stay strong, sweetheart. He'll be back before you know it."

Why on earth would he want to come back?

"I have no doubt that Dillon Bleu will be back, Jillian. Don't give up on him and don't give up on yourself in the meantime. Focus on school and keeping Kyle straight for now." She nudges me with her foot to get my attention, but she already has it with her mindreading skills.

I look over and nod my head. "I'll try."

119

Kyle zooms up in the little truck and beeps the silly-sounding horn to get my attention.

"It's trash time again," he hollers after cranking the window down.

I give Aunt Evie a weak smile and head off to take care of my duties. I slide into the passenger side and face toward the window. My brother leans forward, attempting to make me look at him, but my focus stays glued to the window. He's obviously noticed my swollen eyes.

"I really want to hurt him," Kyle whispers before popping the truck into gear and spinning the tires on the coquina gravel.

EIGHT

A year goes by...

They say distance makes the heart grow fonder.

Nope.

Made mine grow bitter.

The hurt has gradually morphed into anger over the last year. The phone calls becoming less frequent have only helped the bitterness to grow faster. My enthusiasm has wavered, so when Dillon does manage to get a call in, I'm short with him and ask no questions.

Last month we hit an all-time low. I was in the midst of studying for my final in business ethics—not my favorite subject by a long shot. This is when Dillon decided to finally call me after weeks of silence, so my frustration levels were already stomping on my last nerve.

"Hey, Pretty Girl," Dillon said, already sounding a bit weary.

I probably should have said something when I hit the talk button, instead of greeting him with silence I'd grown accustom to.

"Hi," I mumbled, the thrill of the sporadic calls

long gone.

"Guess where I got to perform last night?" I could hear him trying to tamp down his excitement, but he was failing.

Now, I know I should have closed the textbook eagerly and given my boyfriend my undivided attention. I should have begged him for every single detail. But I didn't so much as inquire nicely. To be honest, I was tired.

And if I'm going to be completely honest, I was jealous. Still am.

Dillon is living out an amazing dream and there I sat in my closet of a bedroom in my tin can of a house, studying for an exam at the community college.

Angry and jealous.

So, instead of being polite and supportive, I kept studying and mumbled a terse, "Where?"

Dillon didn't answer right away, but when he did, he revealed his own ugly issue. "You sound distracted. You got company?" This is his little turn this year. He's started with this notion of me growing tired of waiting on him and thinks I'm going to move on with someone else.

Well... Since we are being honest, some days I think about it. I'm almost twenty and live like a hermit. It's lonely, and I'm starting to doubt Dillon is ever coming back for me. There are all kinds of wild notions running through my head as to what he may be up to all the way out there in California. He *is* the lead singer of an up-and-coming rock band. I may not be a highly educated woman, but I've got enough sense to recognize the reality of that situation.

So, back to the conversation.

"Yes, Dillon. I have company. I'm on a hot date with this hunky textbook." I was all-out mad at this point and let loose a sarcastic-laced rant. "I know insignificant things such as my exam at school tomorrow don't matter to you. But I really need to study so I can pass and not have to be a freaking cleaning lady the rest of my pathetic life!" Chest heaving, I flicked the pen across my small room and threw down the thick business textbook. It sounded like a ton of bricks landing and even caused the trailer to shake slightly. "So do tell me where you got to perform at last night."

Dillon went quiet again and when he answered, I heard all the hurt I had inflicted on him. Mission regretfully accomplished.

"I think it's best I just let you go," he said barely above a whisper before hanging up.

I've not heard from him since, and I can't bring myself to call back. I can't even begin to describe how much I miss Dillon and hate him at the same time. More correctly, I hate that a choice he's made is keeping us apart.

A voice keeps whispering that maybe it's time to let him go, but that's an unbearable request. Our bond was set a long time ago by the harsh trials life had divvied out to us, tangling our souls in a way that we'll never be completely free from each other. Even if he never comes back…

I both love and hate that bond. Love that we have such a divine connection. Hate knowing I'll never be able to set Dillon Bleu free.

NINE

Months gone by…

Another month passes and then another, with me hearing nothing. Not one word from Dillon. I have heard all about the fun and adventures of the life and times of Bleu Streak via Max and the gang. They call or text every so often to tell me about some crazy, cool something-or-other that they got to do. They also call regularly to ask for new songs. I'm just not in the sharing mood as of late, so I keep brushing them off. These calls come weekly, yet I still hear nothing from Dillon.

So I guess that's it. It's over. If I'm not boiling mad, I'm hiding out somewhere bawling my eyes out. This is not a life. It's definitely not the romantic notions Dillon and I had dreamt up in that month before he left. We were so naïve.

I get that he doesn't have the money or the time to come see me anytime he wants. It's not like a music career can thrive from the backwoods of southern Georgia. He's where he *needs* to be. And sadly, I'm where I *have* to be…

TEN

And yet another month…

"I miss you."

"You sure about that?" I ask curtly. Dillon finally calls. I'm relieved yet downright aggravated.

"Come on, Pretty Girl. Be nice to me." He pauses but when I remain quiet, he continues. "You know I'm in love with you, and I know you love me, too."

Such words coming from a seventeen-year-old, I think to myself. Well, he's closing in on eighteen, but still. It's mighty young to understand the notion of love.

"You say you love me so much, then why haven't you called in over three months?" I ask, tears floating down my face. *I feel so pathetic.*

"I thought it was best to give you some space to finish up your semester. I didn't want our dumb bickering screwing up your grades."

Cradling the phone with my shoulder, I park the golf cart on the cold, deserted beach and slump down on the seat. Taking a deep breath, I wipe my eyes and search the lake for some courage to ask the question I'm not sure I want answered. "What's going on between us?"

"*Life* is what's going on, Jewels," he declares, but the answer doesn't make me feel any better. "I'm working so hard. Really. I just don't want to ruin what we have. Baby, this is a test... a trial we can get through. I promise we can. Just be patient. Please."

"Okay," I agree weakly.

We sit in more silence for a few beats. It's tempting to beg him to come see me, but I can't ask him something he can't deliver right now. I know that wouldn't be fair.

"The band is heading to Virginia Beach next week for a one-night show before going to New York."

"That's cool, Dillon." It's the first time they've been anywhere close to the east coast. My stomach twinges at him being that close and not getting to see him.

"I just wish there was time for a quick trip to Georgia."

My nose stings and more tears show up with my disappointment. "Me too."

"You want to see me, Pretty Girl?" Dillon asks, lowering his voice.

"More than anything." A sob hiccups out before I can stop it. I'm a hot mess.

"Well, the plane tickets and concert passes should be delivered tomorrow for you and Kyle."

I sit up straighter. "What?"

"Please say you'll come see me. I'm dying to see you. *Please*." His sweet begging sends a grin to my face.

"I'll be there, Dimples!"

128

"I've missed you calling me that," Dillon says in a serious tone.

"I miss *you*," I say, like that's not already obvious. All I've done the entire phone conversation is cry like a baby.

"I love you, Jewels."

"I love you, Dimples."

• ♫ • ♫ • ♫ •

Excited doesn't even come close to describing Kyle and me. We've been working super hard to get things lined up for our weekend trip. A friend of ours has agreed to take care of the garbage duties and bathhouse cleaning while we are gone, in exchange for getting to camp out in the park. Sounds fair enough to me, and Aunt Evie okayed it, so all's good.

One thing about relationship angst is that I've had lots of inspiration for new songs. I've written half a dozen stellar songs in the past two years. There's been a lot more than that, but I've weeded through them for only the best. They're neatly wrapped in a shirt box to present to Dillon for his eighteenth birthday. Two are moody ballads and four are more upbeat rock songs. I can't wait to give them to him.

With our bags packed and loaded in the Mustang, we're ready to head out to the airport. We swing by the campground office to say goodbye to Aunt Evie, but she's nowhere to be found.

I walk back to the front counter to where Ms. Nell is jotting something down on the sign-in sheet.

"Thanks again for helping Aunt Evie out while I'm gone."

She glances over the top of her glasses and smiles. "You're welcome, dear."

"Do you happen to know where she's at?" I glance at the clock behind the counter, excitement building to get on with this adventure.

"She went over to help Ms. King move her niece in. The poor girl just needs somewhere to stay for a few months. Since the boys are gone, Ms. King agreed to let her stay here."

"Okay. We'll just head over there. Thanks again." I wave to her and head to the door as the phone begins to ring.

"Oh, no. They're on the way now," I hear Ms. Nell say, so I turn back around. "Evie fell off the porch. Hurry!"

We take off in a run before she hangs up the phone. Sure enough, when we get there poor Aunt Evie is laid out in the yard, moaning while she holds her upper thigh.

Before I can wrap my mind around what's happened, Kyle and I are speeding behind the ambulance on our way to the hospital. The emergency room isn't busy, so they take Aunt Evie straight to x-ray. We find out within an hour that she has broken her hip in two spots and needs emergency surgery. Everything happens so fast—me signing off on the operation, followed by them wheeling her away from us on a stretcher.

In a state of shock, my brother and I shuffle

numbly to the waiting room. Within minutes, I snap out of my fog and pull my phone out and call a cab for Kyle.

"No, Jillian. I'm staying." He shakes his head and thrusts his fingers through his shaggy blond curls.

"Yes, you're going. There's still time to make the flight." I stand up and push him out the door so we can grab his luggage from the Mustang.

"Dillon is going to be crushed. You should be the one to go." Kyle looks miserable. I'm right miserable myself about our predicament, but there's no other way around it.

"Dillon will get over it. You know it needs to be me to stay and take care of her." Kyle continues shaking his head, so I throw a palm up in the air. "Enough now. You're going, and that's it."

I have to practically shove Kyle in the cab once it arrives. As the cab pulls off, my brother looks out the back glass at me, brokenhearted. Making him go is the right thing to do. He'll appreciate it one day, or maybe he already does.

After cab disappears into traffic, I head up to the hospital room they assigned to Aunt Evie and wait for her to come out of surgery. I call Dillon and fill him in on what happened.

"That's awful," he grumbles into the phone. "How is she?"

"She's still in surgery. They said she may need to stay here for about a week," I tell him while staring blankly at the beige wall. "I'm sorry I couldn't go."

"I understand, Jewels. She needs you there."

"Let me know when Kyle arrives, please."

"I will, and keep us posted on Aunt Evie. I love you."

"Love you." I hang up the phone, clamp my eyes shut before the tears can run free, hunker down in the chair, and prepare myself for another period of waiting.

They deliver a groggy Aunt Evie to her room later this afternoon. She's barely able to keep her eyes open. It pains me to see her look so frail and surprisingly old. This is a look I've never seen her wear, and I don't like it one bit. It just doesn't suit her at all. It's a reality check that I'm not sure I'm ready to handle.

"Your trip..." She moans.

"No worries. You know I wouldn't leave you. Kyle has gone ahead. I had to practically beat him out the door, though." I laugh, trying to lighten the mood.

"You're so loyal... So dedicated to me." She slurs her words as she speaks. She's making me exhausted just by looking at her. Her eyes slowly shut, but moments later she cracks them open and continues with her line of thought. "I've never had that in my life." She smiles weakly.

The thought of her husband abandoning her sends a pinch to the middle of my chest. Poor Aunt Evie never deserved to be treated that way. Especially since she's always the one to be there, loyal and dedicated for everyone else. They don't make 'em as good as Aunt Evie anymore.

"I won't ever leave you." I hold the hand not

bound in IV tubes and tape, and give her a genuine smile.

She returns it with a weak one. "That's what I'm afraid of, sweetheart." She dozes off before I can reply. I don't even know what to say to that, anyway.

"I love you," I whisper and place a kiss on her forehead. This woman deserves to be loved more than she has. This thought saddens me. I ease back into the guest chair and watch her sleep.

I can only hope to become at least half the incredible woman she is one day.

Two days pass quickly with nurses coming and going at all hours. They get Aunt Evie up as much as possible. She's a good sport about it, but the pain remains etched in her delicate features. She goes quite pale until they can deliver another round of pain meds, but she never mutters any whines or complaints. She's a tough cookie.

I come and go between the hospital and the trailer park. Ms. Nell has been a godsend with keeping things on track with the camping rentals. Weekends are always busy, even in the cooler months. I've stayed way too busy to dwell on missing the concert. Kyle sent me some pictures he snapped during it and some at a backstage party.

While I wait at the airport for Kyle's flight to arrive, I scroll through the pictures again. The newest one came in around four this morning, about the time the guys were supposed to be hitting the road. It's of the band, unruly hair and smug grins, standing in a line in the hotel room—showing off their bare chests with a word scribbled on their skin.

WE MISS OUR JEWEL

Dillon stands at the end of the line with his own message marked on his chest.

LOVE YOU

The plan was to arrive one night early so that when the band arrived the next day, we would have the entire day together. Then after the concert, they would hang out at the hotel until they had to pull out the next morning. It was a rushed trip, but it was one I was willing to take. I'm just glad Kyle got to go. He's been moping around here like a sad little puppy that's lost all of his buddies.

The announcement of Kyle's flight pulls me away from ogling Dillon. Pocketing my phone, I stand and head over to the terminal exit.

When he emerges from the crowd in the terminal, I don't believe my eyes. I burst out in a fit of laughter. "What happened to your eyebrows? They're gone!"

Kyle rolls his eyes. "A parting gift from the one and only Max King." He gives me a quick hug before we walk over to claim his one bag of luggage, but there's no holding back my snickering. "Stop staring at me," he says playfully.

It's been a while since he was a part of an infamous Bleu Streak prank. But I'm no fool. My brother is quite pleased with this.

"So, how was it?" I ask once we are heading to my car.

"Awesome! The guys are getting better, if you can believe that's even possible. They've got quite a following already." He tosses his bag in the trunk and then grabs me up in a bear hug. "The guys said to give you this for the new songs. Dillon said to give you a big ole kiss, but I declined. Told him I can get Hudson to take care of the kissing for me." Kyle's lips slant into a smirk as he pushes back his sleeve, revealing a nasty bruise. "A parting gift from Dillon."

I laugh. "Ouch. I guess you earned that one." *Man, I wish I had been in the midst of their chaos this weekend.*

"I've got a whole sack full of Bleu Streak T-shirts and hoodies and some other junk. Dillon wants you wearing them daily," Kyle says, as we load up in the car and maneuver out of the airport parking lot. "He said they're having to spend a load of money to make money, but sounded hopeful about the band getting signed by a record label soon. Dudes are too good not to get signed."

"Yeah?" I glance at him before turning onto the highway.

"Yeah. They're just the opening act, but how the fans were screaming and all kinds of rowdy you'd have thought they were the headline of the show."

I wanted to ask a million questions but tamp it down and let Kyle ramble on and on about some girl he met backstage until we arrive at the hospital to check on Aunt Evie.

"The doctor says we can take her home in another day or two, but she will have to have physical therapy," I inform him as we trek down the hall.

"We'll handle it," Kyle offers as we push through

the door of our aunt's room and are immediately greeted by a bounty of floral bouquets.

"It smells like Ms. Raveena's garden in here," I comment while taking it all in.

They are exquisite and have all been delivered in the last hour. I inspect the cards on the bouquets as Kyle catches up with Aunt Evie. She's already teasing him about his face sans eyebrows. Each card is inscribed with some silly joke and is signed by none other than Dillon and the band. I smile at the sweetness of this and swipe the entire collection of cards before settling on the edge of her bed. I then set in on a comedic act for the next hour or so, and we end up laughing until tears trek down our cheeks.

Later on, as I drive home, my smile falters. Life sure is challenging. Focus is key. Frowning, I don't give into to the selfish moment begging for release. Instead, I set my focus on where it needs to be.

Focus on the business of the trailer park.

Focus on getting Aunt Evie better and things lined up for her to go home hopefully soon.

Focus on the fact that my brother got such an awesome gift this weekend.

As long as I don't focus any attention on myself, it's easier to overlook my own heartache.

ELEVEN

Three years is a long time. *Over* three years is a VERY long time.

The thing about time, even though life may feel stuck on pause, is that it just keeps on getting it. My life may feel like it's stuck on a perpetual pause, but a lot has happened. I graduated from community college with an associate's degree in business. It does nothing for my passion for writing, but it has come in handy with managing Shimmer Lakes Trailer Park and Campground these days. My dream? I think not. But it's a small sacrifice to pay, if Aunt Evie doesn't have to work so hard and Kyle gets to attend a well-known college in South Carolina.

As I listen to the rain tinkling against the tin roof of my porch, pride blooms into a smile on my face. With my thoughts hovering on my brother, I prop my chair against the wall on two legs and balance the modest plate of lunch on my lap. He is getting a real chance at life, too, and is claiming it like a boss. The guys leaving sort of forced Kyle's hand in having to grow up a bit. Without the distraction of the twins, my brother's grades did a complete one-eighty. We were all pleasantly surprised to find Kyle to be a whiz in computer programming. That's what he is majoring in, and the sky's the limit for him now.

The new millennium has rushed in on us and new trends have encouraged changes to be made. For some odd reason, rich folks have taken up the hobby of camping. Not the type we here are used to, with tents and sleeping bags. No. I'm talking high-dollar fancy camping with campers nicer than any trailer this park has ever housed.

The other side of the lake has no spare land to accommodate this new trend. They've squished every extra inch of their side with commercial properties with lots of glitz and glam. Luckily we had land to spare. It took the help of Hudson to persuade Aunt Evie to agree to remodel half of the campground into an RV park. We even put in a pool. The renovations paid for themselves the first year, and this year is just money in our pockets. That's a very new and very nice feeling, just let me tell you.

Hudson has surprisingly become a pretty close friend. His dad would probably kill him if he knew Hudson was over on this side of the lake more often than not, giving me and Aunt Evie pointers. He's a great guy, but I see him as only as a friend. He often likes to remind me that he sees more potential for us than just friendship, but I always remind him that I don't. He doesn't push it, so it's never become an uncomfortable barrier between us.

Leona has also left me. She now lives on the other side of the lake with her lawyer husband in one of the fancy townhouses that I actually used to clean. She snagged her a slightly older man. Grant is in his mid-thirties and spoils her rotten. He even paid for her to attend an exclusive interior decorating institute. She graduates this spring and has already signed the lease on a building to open her interior design company. I'm happy for her, but I'm just so blame lonely.

Glancing around the screened-in front porch of my small cabin, I have to admit my life ain't so bad. Aunt Evie gave me this cabin after graduation so I can have my own space. I love it. It may only be a one-room space, but the fact that there are no wheels attached to it gives me comfort of it being permanent. The open room keeps company with a kitchenette, small sitting area, and my queen-sized bed. It feels luxurious after spending most of my life sleeping on a tinier-than-twin bed. It has a small yet sufficient bathroom and is decorated with secondhand finds, but it's all mine.

The small deck on the back that overlooks the lake is my favorite spot, but it's not covered, so I'm confined to the front porch today. That's okay, because it's a nice space as well.

Spring showers have shown up mercilessly and won't leave Shimmer Lakes alone. Taking a bite of my pimento cheese sandwich, I war with the decision to call the pool guy and set up another cleaning tomorrow. Surely, it'll be filled with leaves and other debris after this storm passes. I just had him out here two days ago and not one ounce of me wants deal with him again so soon. The guy is nice and all, but he asks me out every time he does the pool. To confess to him that I am in love with the rising rock star Dillon Bleu is quite laughable, so I always politely decline with no further explanation, and then go hide out in my office until he leaves.

Taking another bite, I resolve to just clean the pool myself. The rumbling of a big diesel motor sounds through the downpour, so I look over a few blocks down the road and nearly choke. I slam the chair back on all four legs, grab for my glass, and take several gulps of tea to help dislodge the chunk of food.

After three long years of random calls and letters, I can hardly believe it. My eyes instantly tear up as I watch an ultra-sleek black and silver tour bus, with Bleu Streak painted along the side in vibrant blue, pull up to Cora's. The bus towers over her tiny trailer and looks completely out of place.

I steal a glance at my worn-out jeans with rips at the knees and my faded Pearl Jam T-shirt, feeling completely inadequate. *No way will I fit into Dillon's shiny new world.* The rushing hiss of the airbrakes has my focus back on the tour bus. The side door slides open before several guys pile out and mad-dash it into Cora's little home. One is a good bit taller than the rest. My skin pricks with awareness and my heart stutters several beats as I watch him. He has a hoodie pulled low over his head and glances around from underneath it before ducking inside.

Stunned, all I can do is sit still and gape at the sleek bus. I'm both elated and disappointed that he would just pop up in the middle of a rainstorm after all this time, unannounced. During the last phone conversation with him a few weeks back, Dillon said they were in the final negotiations of their record deal. Undoubtedly, Bleu Streak has finally pulled it off.

Appetite lost, I grab up my glass and plate and shuffle inside. My skin itches in anticipation, and it's all I can do to not take off in a sprint over to Cora's. But something whispers for me to sit tight and wait… some more.

I'm sick of waiting.

After several anxious paces around the small room, I tip-toe over to the front window like a weirdo and peek out from behind the curtains to make sure I wasn't seeing things.

Nope. The giant bus is still there.

A frustrated sigh pushes past my lips when I notice it's blocking the entire narrow street. Bored campers are driving around on their fancy little golf carts. Each time one nears the bus, they have to drive through Mr. Wayne's yard to get by it. It's a wonder the old man hasn't already called to complain about the muddy mess they're making on his property.

It's my responsibility to handle this, so I pull out my phone and call the front office. "Hey Jen. Can you find me an available RV site?" Jen handles the RV park bookings during the tourist season. She is a vibrant young blonde who seems to always have an abundance of energy and never sits still.

"Sure. Just give me a sec." I listen to her fingers

clicking over the computer keyboard. "Hmm...Let's see. I have site fourteen and site twenty-two available."

"Twenty-two. It's more private. Book it under my name, please. Then I need you to go over to Cora's trailer and ask her guests to move their bus over to that site. Okay?"

"No problem," Jen says before hanging up.

Standing behind the curtain, I continue to spy on the bus, but it just sits idling. A few minutes later Jen pulls up to Cora's on a golf cart. She looks at the tour bus then in my direction. There's no way she can see me, but I can guess the message she just relayed to me. She darts inside. Within minutes, some dude exits the small trailer, climbs into the bus, and follows Jen over to the far side of the RV park. It's out of my sight, and more importantly, it's out of sight of others. This place will become a circus as soon as word gets out that Bleu Streak is here.

Jen zooms up on the golf cart and bounds inside without knocking. "OMG!"

Jen is friendly enough, but she is new to these parts and doesn't know any of our history. She could pass as my younger sister, with the exception of her being tall with hazel eyes. She's got a lot more energy than I do, too. Right now her entire body is vibrating with excitement or maybe caffeine... *Probably both.*

"Please call the security company and let them know we need to book a guard for the front gate ASAP." I try to ignore her questioning gaze. We use security guards during holiday weekends to keep out straying visitors who are trying to freeload at the pool or beach.

I guess a holiday just pulled up in a shiny new tour bus.

"OMG! *Dillon Bleu* just asked where he can find you! Said he went by Aunt Evie's but nobody was there. *Dillon Bleu* is looking for you!" She starts jumping up and down like a spastic fangirl.

I get it, truly I do. Bleu Streak is starting to blow up in a big way. TV appearances. Concerts. It's happening big time for those guys. They are all over the radio, too. I even have an advanced copy of their debut CD that won't be out until late summer. I won't tell her that, though.

"Please calm down and take care of the security guard before things get too crazy," I say again, but she's not budging, so I relent. "Okay, he's my best friend, if you must know. Now go. Take care of business."

She's grinning big time. "He said to tell you to stay put." She points her finger at me sternly and seems so proud to get to tell me this little message. She bounces back out the door and is gone in a flash. Jen is only a year younger than me, but boy, does she make me feel old.

Swiftly, a flash of panic rushes over me. I yank the band out of my hair and run to the bathroom to drag a brush through the knotty mess. I glance in the mirror at my makeup-less face and moan at my plainness.

"It's just Dillon," I say to myself, but the

butterflies dancing in my stomach don't believe me. Giving up on the notion of calming myself, I fumble to get the cap off the mouthwash before taking a swig of it to swish the pimento cheese out of my teeth. I scamper to the armoire that serves as my closet, but before I can pull it open a knock hits the front door.

Great. Just great.

I pad over barefooted and ease the door open to reveal the larger-than-life Dillon Bleu. We stand here, silently staring at each other with my gaze having to go farther up than last time. He's taller. *How's that possible?* His features seem more defined, but I can't get a good look at him. His eyes are shrouded by the hoodie, making him seem more mysterious than I know he really is.

Dillon takes one step forward and with one rapid swoop, he grabs me up and laces my legs around his waist. With his lips planted firmly on mine, he walks in and kicks the door shut.

The dam that's held my feelings in check for the last three years shatters and sends my body into a mad frenzy of relief and desire. My arms and legs tighten to near pain, but I still can't get close enough to him. There's just as much urgency in his touch with his fingers forcefully grasping my backside.

Without a word spoken, Dillon backs me up against the door and continues to consume me with his mouth. I thought, after all of this time, that whatever feelings he had for me would have evaporated. It seems as though they have only grown stronger.

The need to see him better overtakes me. I pull the hoodie off his head and gasp. "What did you do to your hair?" I ask, stunned, breaking our silence.

His lips trail a hot path of kisses along my neck, barely pausing to reply, "After all of this time, Jewels... you want to talk about my hair?"

He goes right back to nibbling on my neck, so I study this new hairstyle—it's a mohawk, of all things. His gorgeous hair has been completely shaved off on the sides, and his remaining black silky hair is sporting dark blue tips. The tattoo behind his ear is completely exposed now. He's sexy as all get-out. If there ever was a guy who could pull a mohawk off, it would certainly be Dillon Bleu.

I run my hands through it, beckoning a guttural sound from the back of his throat.

"It's surprisingly soft. I thought it would be full of gooey hair product." I thread my fingers through it again, testing the feel of it.

Dillon lifts his head and I nearly get lost in the depths of his dark-blue eyes. "Stop playing in my hair, Pretty Girl, and kiss me like you mean it." His words are released on a growl as he leans forward and reclaims my lips.

My throat thickens with emotion as the thought hits me—Dillon left this place a determined boy and has returned an accomplished man.

My tears splash over both our faces, as I let go of a fear I have held for the last several years. I never thought he would come back, and yet, here he is in my arms.

Dillon kept his promise after all.

He releases my lips and kisses away the tears on my cheeks. "I'm here." He reassures me as though he could read my thoughts. "I promised, remember?"

With my voice held captive by these overwhelming emotions, all I can do is nod. I wrap my arms firmly around his neck and bury my face into the inviting crook of his neck that has always felt like home and continue to cry. Dillon kicks his boots off, carries me to my bed, and settles me against the pillows. He leans back and yanks off the damp hoodie before climbing beside me. I snuggle back into the crook of his neck as his arms wrap around me. We stay this way, clinging to each other and our overdue reunion, while listening to the melody of the rain mingle with my sobs until I cry it all out and we both doze off.

• ♫ • ♫ • ♫ •

I awaken with a start to a darkened cabin. *Alone.* My hand reaches out and seeks Dillon's warmth, but he's gone. A sob builds so deep within me that my body begins to tremble before the cry releases from my lips.

It was only a dream…

My sobs grow louder with my disappointment. I want to scream. To rip this hurt from my chest.

The bed dips. "*Shh…* I'm right here. *Shh…*" In the darkness, Dillon pulls my thrashing body onto his lap and begins rocking me back and forth.

"Where were you?" I manage to say around a sob. "I thought you left me again." I can't believe how badly I just totally spazzed out.

"I was right here, Jewels." The warmth of his hand rubbing my back soothes me until he follows that with a chuckle.

"I find nothing funny." I screech, pinching him on the arm.

"I stole me a pimento cheese sandwich. I was starving," he confesses.

Now I feel completely stupid. "You're eating in the dark?" I lean over and turn a lamp on. Sure enough, he's holding a half-eaten sandwich. We both laugh now.

"Can't a man eat some supper, woman?" I notice the teasing tone of his voice and then see a plate on the edge of the bed holding two more sandwiches. I eye them and then him. "They don't make pimento cheese like this out west," he says sheepishly and shrugs his shoulder.

Still needing the reassurance that Dillon is really here, I ease around to sit behind him and wrap my legs around his waist. He's down to his boxer shorts.

"What are you doing almost naked?" I ask, holding tight to his taut stomach while he takes another bite of his sandwich.

"They were soaked through," he answers around a mouthful of food.

With nothing obscuring my view, I take in his broad shoulders, appreciating what lugging all that sound equipment has done to his body. I notice he has enhanced the tattoo a bit on his toned upper back. It's a bit bigger and more defined now. You can tell it was done at the hands of a wickedly skillful artist. I lean forward and place kisses over it, causing him to moan so deeply it vibrates through his body and against my lips. A long tattoo running down the back of his left arm catches my attention. The scrolled writing is tucked neatly along his triceps and is none other than a phrase from his favorite Bible verse, Ephesians 5:19.

Sing and make a melody in your heart to the Lord.

My fingers glide over it, wanting to take him all in. To memorize the newness of my old Dillon.

Dillon rubs my knee. "Why don't you take these pants off and get more comfortable?"

"Both of us without pants on would probably be a bit dangerous," I whisper, continuing to kiss and explore him. I've missed every inch of him, and there are definitely more inches to love now.

"No doubt about it," he says before taking the last of bite of his sandwich.

I glance at the clock and am shocked. It's two in the morning. We totally missed supper, and I realize I'm in need of a shower, too. "I need to wash."

Dillon looks over his shoulder and cuts me a devilish grin. "Okay, let's go shower." He stands up and places his plate in the sink.

"Me, first. *Alone.*" I climb out of the bed. My eyes dart to the bathroom door, then to him, and then to the front door.

Dillon picks up on my apprehension, so he stretches back over my bed, taking up the entire space. "I'll be right here. I'm not going anywhere," he murmurs, watching me with hooded eyes.

Maybe not tonight. I shake off that nagging truth and go grab a quick shower. Hurrying through it, I slip into a pair of night pants and a tank top. When I reemerge, Dillon is sound asleep. It still doesn't feel real that he's actually here. I'm scared to blink, knowing he won't be here long, so I pad over to the edge of the bed and watch him.

"Stop staring at me and get back in this bed," he mutters, voice thick with sleep.

When I don't move, his long arm reaches out and yanks me on the bed. He snuggles against me with one leg hooked over mine and an arm secured around my waist, like he's worrying I'll be the one to disappear.

We sleep for a few hours, until my stomach wakes us both with its gurgling. When the awful racket refuses to shut up, Dillon fishes out his fancy phone and punches in some long message before snuggling back down.

"Why didn't you tell me?" I whisper as I lay on his chest, listening to the soothing rhythm of his heart.

"I wanted to surprise you," he mumbles, sounding close to dozing back off.

"Why are you here?"

He lets out a long sigh and tightens his grip around my waist. "I got business here to take care of before the tour begins."

I think he's about to go back to sleep, so I nudge him in the side.

"I bought mom a house in California. I need to get her moved out there this week." His words sink in.

Naively, I thought he would make this place his home base. It hurts more than I want it to that he's not.

A little while later, there's a knock on the door. Dillon climbs out of bed and steps outside for a few minutes before returning with a suitcase, his guitar, and some grocery bags. After setting everything down in the kitchen, he steps back out. This time he brings in a tray with two coffees and a white bakery bag. He hands me a coffee and the bag before climbing back in beside me.

"How'd this get here?" I ask him while peeking in the bag. My mouth waters when I fish out a Bavarian cream donut. I take a big bite and moan at the sweet goodness. This isn't grocery store grub. This is the real deal and it melts in my mouth.

"My assistant grabbed it up for us."

"Your *assistant*?" I ask before taking a sip of the gourmet coffee.

"Yep. His name is Ben, and he takes care of all my stuff for me." He shrugs his shoulder before digging into the donuts.

I laugh. "You are so spoiled."

"Tell me about it." He sniffs himself, brushing off my joke with one of his own. "I need a shower." He swipes another donut, gives me a sugary kiss, and heads to the bathroom.

I enjoy another donut and finish up my coffee before I pad over to the small kitchen to check out what is in the bags. They are filled with all of our favorites. Or more so Dillon's than mine. I guess there were a few other items he's been missing. I dig out a jar of Dukes mayo, thick sliced bologna, spicy pork rinds, a tub of pimento cheese, double-stuffed moon pies, RC colas, and a couple loaves of bread. Putting the groceries away, I can't help but giggle while trying to I imagine some California guy named Ben, picking out all this southern junk for Dillon.

I've just got done making the bed when Dillon reemerges with only a towel around his narrow waist. He so lean and masculine, it takes my breath. He grabs up his suitcase and walks back into the bathroom, as I stare at him until the door closes. He's back out moments later, with his mohawk freshly spiked and wearing only a pair of distressed jeans, with his broad, nicely-defined chest on full display.

I perch on the end of the bed, watching him move around in my small space and wishing there was some way to keep him here all to myself. I'm still hoping I'm not dreaming. I discreetly pinch my arm and feel the sharp sting, so maybe I am awake.

That sleek phone starts going off, so he pauses to check it. His fingers fly over the screen like a pro before placing it on the nightstand. Even how he works that dang phone is sexy.

Dillon looks over at me and smiles knowingly.

Before I can decide to be embarrassed about being caught ogling him, he eases over and kisses me like it's our first time.

"Play me a song, Mr. Guitar Man," I whisper against his lips.

Without hesitation, Dillon pulls the case on the bed and fishes out his electric-blue guitar. He begins strumming the melody of "My Jewel," his promise of a song, and hums a few beats before he begins adding the lyrics. This song is the band's debut solo and is rapidly climbing the charts right now. I realize immediately he has changed the lyrics.

My Jewel
My life
I want you now
I want you always
Be mine now
Be my tomorrow
I'm not whole without you
Marry me now and let's start our tomorrow

He stops playing and places his guitar back in the case and returns with a ring box in his hands. He sings softly, *I need you completely*, as he opens the dainty box, showing me an elegant emerald and diamond ring.

Always be my Jewel
Today and forever

He picks up my left hand, kissing it before placing the ring on my finger. All the while, he continues humming his promise of a song to me. A song that has bonded us together all these years. He stops humming and waits.

"Yes," I whisper, causing him to pull me up in his lap and kiss me with abandon.

I pull away from him after a spell and run my hands along the bare sides of his head. "Only if you grow your hair back," I say sternly, making him laugh.

"Blame this hair on Max." Dillon smirks as he runs his hand through it. "I woke up one night last week with the punk buzzing the side of my head with his clippers, with all the jerks rooting him on. It was either go bald or the mohawk." He shrugs his shoulder as to say, *what can I do*? "Max doesn't know it yet, but he'll be starting the tour with neon-green hair," he says, confidently.

"You guys are ridiculous." We both laugh.

"Enough about that. This is our moment. I'll grow my hair back out if that's what my fiancée wants." He nuzzles into my neck and croons, "My Jewel," before he begins singing our song to me again, in delicate whispers in my ear.

We hibernate in the bed for the remainder of the day. Dillon seems totally wiped out. He said they've been working around the clock to get ready for the upcoming tour. So I spend most of the day either watching him sleep or watching him do some business on his phone. It rings several times, but he refuses to answer any of them. He keeps sending texts, letting the person know what they need answered. I love that he's not sharing this time with anyone but me.

The sun is setting now as he types something else into his phone. I'm stretched out beside him, admiring my gorgeous ring. It's not too flashy but definitely makes a statement. A nice-sized square emerald surrounded by sparkly diamonds and set in a platinum gold band, it fits perfectly. I absolutely love that it's not a traditional diamond solitaire. Of course, my man would come up with something unique to us.

Once he's done, he says, "Everything is set," before turning toward me. His vibrant purplish-blue eyes are sparkling and his dimples are on full display. I love him so much it makes me feel weepy. I thought maybe it was just the whole teenage first love feelings we had, but now he's back and those feelings have never left me. I know beyond a shadow of a doubt that Dillon Bleu is my soul mate. My fingertips skim over those dimples that have been such a sweet spot in my life. All of the good memories of my young life include this man, and I can only dream there will be so many more.

He turns his head and kisses the palm of my hand before scooping me in his arms. "I need you completely, Jewels. Will you be with me *completely*?" His voice is strained with his emotions.

I whisper a yes against his lips, making him crush me in his embrace. He lays me back down, hovering over me. "I'm serious, Jillian," he says, not using my nickname, emphasizing the seriousness of the situation.

My stomach twinges and my heart begins fluttering in a tizzy when he reaches over and pulls something else out of his guitar case, placing the meaning of *completely* on the bed beside us. Total understanding hits me while eyeing it. Nervous as I am in this moment, there's no way I can refuse this man anything. If this is what he really wants, then I absolutely want it, too.

"Yes," I whisper again.

TWELVE

Morning light filters in our small cabin, as we hold each other tight. It's our last private day being cocooned away together, and I'm reluctant to let it go. I want this man all to myself and to never share him again. Last night was amazing, and I want to revel in it for as long as I can.

I'm kissing along Dillon's neck, when there's a knock on the door. He kisses me once more before climbing out of the bed and wrapping a blanket around his waist. He cracks the door slightly, exchanging a few hushed words before pulling another coffee tray and white bag in with him. He closes the door and heads back over. This delivery system of his is pretty handy.

"We've got to get the lead out soon, Pretty Girl." He hands over a coffee.

"I've got to square a few things away and go beg Aunt Evie to let me go."

He offers me a muffin and quickly devours one himself. "No worries. She had to have known it was coming. Plus, you're a grown woman." Dillon winks as he starts rummaging in his suitcase. "A mighty *fine* woman."

I ignore his flirting, suddenly too wrapped up in the reality that my life is about change. "She's going to kill me." My attention travels to the front door, knowing as soon as we exit later today, my ordinary world will be transformed to something extraordinary. *This is happening too soon and too fast...*

Dillon drops the outfit he just fished out of his bag and crawls back on the bed with me. He kisses me until I forget my worries. Leaving me breathless, he disappears to the bathroom. The sound of the shower turning on and then the alluring melody of him singing fills the entire cabin.

I'm not ready to face this new life yet. Yes, I'm scared. What will Aunt Evie do without me? Sure, we've got a great staff now, but I don't want her stressing over it. On the nightstand, Dillon's phone dings to alert another incoming message. His phone never quietens, I'm learning quickly. I reach over to check it. *Dude—Mom loaded up—bus ready to roll out.*

I finally get up and start packing a bag, but an edgy hesitance has my movements sluggish. Dillon assured me that we can make a trip back in a few weeks to gather the rest of my stuff, so I'm just packing clothes and toiletries for the first leg of the tour. He promised to buy me whatever I may need along the way. I'm holding him to that one, because I really don't have much in the way of clothes except the jeans and T-shirts. Nothing that would be suited for his shiny new lifestyle.

I'm tossing shirts in the suitcase when Dillon eases behind me and laces his arms around my waist.

"I love you," he whispers in my ear, sending goose bumps to dance down my neck.

He smells beyond incredible, fresh cedar after a rainstorm, so I turn around and take a deep inhale of his neck. "Mmm...I love you, too."

"You got to get that fine butt of yours in gear, babe." He pats me on the part in question before releasing me. He grabs a beanie out of his suitcase and pulls it over his unruly hairdo. When he looks back at me, his eyes seem to be glowing with excitement. He is so breathtaking in a mere grey thermal shirt and dark jeans. He could wear a brown burlap sack and still be mouthwatering.

I finally find my voice after staring. "I know. You got a text saying it's time to pull out. I can't believe you've been here for three days and I've not seen the twins yet."

"I ordered them to leave us alone. The group hasn't changed much. The twins are still too bony and too much trouble. You've got plenty of time to catch up," he says as he zips up his own suitcase. "I'm going to load my stuff and be back for yours in a little while." After giving me one more kiss, and not a chaste one by a long shot, he heads out the door. "You've made me the happiest man in this world, Jewels," he says before closing the door.

A smile is plastered on my swollen lips as I look out the window and watch him saunter away. A few minutes later, I have the suitcase and a travel bag packed and placed on the porch, waiting to be picked up. I've just made my way back in when there's a knock on the door. Thinking it's probably Ben here to grab my stuff, I hurry back over to greet him. I'm a bit shocked to see Cora instead. The look on her face makes me instantly worried. It's not a look of happiness. She's finally freed of this place, but seems upset instead.

"Is it time to go?" I ask, not knowing what else to say.

She just stands there, chewing on whatever she's about to spit out, and now my stomach is beginning to hurt with dread.

"Just say it, Cora." I believe in ripping Band-Aids off in one quick snatch and not drawing out the inevitable.

"You need to stay here," she says, her features hard yet remorseful. "He's just getting his start. Now's not the time to introduce a girlfriend."

I hold up my hand and show her the engagement ring. "I'm more than that and you know it."

She eyes it and then shakes her head. "Dillon needs a good chance. He deserves better..." She pauses. "He deserves better than this place."

"I know this." He absolutely does. This is the only thing she and I have ever seen eye to eye on. Dillon Bleu deserves the world and more. I eye her cautiously as she stands at the door, not entering. Good. She doesn't plan on staying long.

"Do you love him, Jillian? I mean, *really* love him?" she asks. She's talking down to me like I'm a child. She's always done this, but now it's really rubbing me wrong.

"More than anything," I reply as the first few tears of anger and hurt slide down my face. *I should have known better.*

"Then let him go."

Bile rises in my throat as my stomach recoils at her demand. "But…"

Cora looks me dead in the eyes without any hesitation. "He deserves better than this." She motions around the trailer park.

Suddenly, I get it, hearing the true meaning hidden in her words. She's really saying that Dillon deserves better than *me*. She's never thought I was good enough for her son, but to hear her finally vocalize it stings all the way to the bone.

She knows I get it too, so she pushes on, driving the knife deeper. "If you go, you will only be holding him back. He's not even twenty yet. Really, the boy can't see past his lust for you long enough to see how he is endangering his career. It would have only taken them half the time to make it, if he weren't so busy worrying about you over the last few years."

Dazed, my head timidly shakes. "I don't see how that can be true. He's not visited once in all this time and I've not bothered him."

Only sporadic phone calls and letters have been the extent of our relationship. Yet here she stands, blaming me.

Always blaming me.

Clearing my throat, I try to defend myself. "I won't hold him back."

"Yes, you will, even if you don't mean to. Let him

go and be free from this place." Cora narrows her eyes when my head starts to shake in protest. "We all know you were secretly with my son when he was underage."

I almost laugh at this. She's trying to make it sound like a sixteen and eighteen-year-old couple is something inappropriate.

"We're both legal adults now," I snap, hating her for trying to make what Dillon and I have into something wrong.

"The papers won't see it that way. They will see an adult woman taking advantage of an underage boy. You know how the papers would love to twist that around until you are painted as a pedophile."

Her words make me sick. My hand cradles my stomach. "You wouldn't do that."

"I will do whatever it takes for Dillon to be rid of the trash in his life. He deserves better. This is not the life for him." The hate and determination in her eyes is palpable, leaving no doubt she would follow through with her threat.

I've heard all I want to hear so I slam the door in her horrible face. Her truthful words are ripping me apart. I know I'm not good enough, but for some reason I thought his love for me and my love for him could be enough. Dillon seems to think so. Maybe we are both still too young and too stupid to be making the decisions we thought we were ready to make. I just… I shake my head and the empty room.

I cannot be his regret, or his ruin.

I scribble on a piece of paper, *Last night was a*

mistake. You need to move on, and leave it on the counter. Tears are plopping thickly on the note as I place the ring on top of it. I grab my bags, load up the Mustang, and peel out of the maintenance exit before anyone can stop me. I can't be here when he shows back up.

I can't tell Dillon Bleu goodbye...

PART TWO
SECOND CHANCES

A Little Bit Older and Some Wiser…

THIRTEEN

Cora was right, and I hated her a long time for it. Hated her vehemently in the beginning for doing what she did. And hated her even more when I realized she was right. She forced my hand, completely crushing me, but she was only thinking about the best interest for her son. I totally get that now.

Of course, she was absolutely right. Hated her for it, all the same, but I would have ended up being the ruin of Dillon Bleu and his dreams. Aunt Evie warned me all those years ago that one day I was going to end up making a choice that would lead to consequences that would follow me the rest of my life. Boy, was she not kidding.

"You show up here one more time and I'm gonna go all redneck on your behind. The answer is no and will always be NO!" I holler at the jerk. "Some things ain't for sale. You need to get that through your thick head."

"I like when you get all feisty on me. It's sexy." Hudson laughs as he tries to grab hold of my hand, but I slap his away.

He thinks he's cute, showing up here at my office

today and refusing to leave. I get out of my chair and walk around him. He's propped up on the edge of my desk like he owns the place, and I have to restrain myself from shoving him off. *He wouldn't see it coming, and he would land on his butt before he knew what hit him.*

"You're pushing it, Hudson. Really pushing it." I stand by him and point toward the door, for which he totally ignores.

"You need a real man to take care of you, sweetheart." He has me all riled up today and is loving every minute of it.

"Will is all I need," I say, my chin jutting out in defiance.

The playfulness instantly seeps away and a somber look paints across Hudson's features. "One of these days Will is going to grow tired of this place and leave it for greener pastures. Then you'll be stuck here, all alone, *again*. You know it's inevitable, Jillian." He places a business card on my desk as he does every time. He taps it while looking at me sadly. "If you reconsider either one of my offers, give me a call." Once Hudson is at the door, he turns to look at me once again. He is nearing thirty but still carries that sweet boyish look. Age is only evident in his knowing eyes. "Hopefully, it won't be too late," he says before closing the door behind him.

I take the card and toss it into the trash. Hudson is a great friend and he knows the economy is not in the trailer park's favor, but giving in and selling it to him will never be an option. This place is the only life I have ever known. I can't bear the thought of it being leveled for a water park and fancy resort. Aunt Evie gave me enough cushion financially to keep this place afloat, but it has become overwhelming on how to turn things around. Half the residents stay here rent free due to falling on tough times. Their pleas to give them more time is wearing thin, but I just keep letting them slide anyway and try to find ways to make up for the income deficit. I'm just now realizing how much weight had been on Aunt Evie's shoulders, with having so many families depending on her to help them out. I sit here with the same crushing weight bearing down on my shoulders that she carried like a herculean. I'm close to collapsing.

Hudson also hounds me to no end to go on a date with him. And that is a big, fat NO. He knows I'm completely sold out to Will and totally in love with my guy. I don't understand why Hudson doesn't think Will is enough. Well, he absolutely is. Will has only been in my life for less than five years now, so we are still learning each other, but I can't imagine my life without him.

Will showed up when everything was in ruins and helped me pull it back together. Will doesn't care what my social status is in this world. He just wants me happy and to make me happy. Not to mention he is absolutely gorgeous with big blue eyes and dark hair. Now that's my kind of guy. I smile at the idea of me having a certain type.

I wander back to my chair and try to get over Hudson ruffling my feathers today. I've had a tough go of it over the last several years and he knows it.

Jen barges in without knocking, as she always does, sipping on her addiction—coffee.

"What's your flavor of choice today?" I ask while powering up my laptop.

"Caramel mocha," she answers, taking a seat on the other side of my desk. "What's on the agenda now, since you ran off my eye candy?"

"Hudson walked over to the dock to mope. Why don't you go cheer him up?" I suggest, and this sends her out the door in a flash. I *hope* that's where he went. It's what he normally does before taking off. That man seems obsessed with this place, nearly salivating during his visits.

Shimmer Lakes is a gorgeous piece of real estate, I get it. This side of the lake is still lush with an abundance of undeveloped land and wooded area. Aunt Evie gave every acre of this massive place to me. Selling it would make me an instant millionaire, but I would feel worthless for doing it. I know the old trailers are an eyesore, but those tin cans are people's homes.

Once I hear the office door close, I pull up the search engine on my computer and type in the two words needed to get me what I want. Within minutes the latest footage of Bleu Streak is displayed on the screen. Okay, so I admit I cyberstalk Dillon. I can't help myself. I pull up his concert footage on YouTube weekly and also watch all of his interviews...

It's been fairly easy to keep up with the band through media sites and Google. The twins are finally easy to tell apart. Mave has acquired two full sleeves of tattoos. His artwork looks like all sorts of interesting stories etched along his skin, and I would love to have a conversation with him about them. Max only has one elaborate piece of sheet music dancing along his one arm. Fans go wild for the twin rock stars. The dudes have a pretty impressive following on social media, as do Trace and Logan. Dillon doesn't dabble in any of it. There is a Dillon Bleu fan club page on Facebook, but I seriously doubt he knows it even exists. I know all about it. I'm a member of course, and check in on the page at least once a day.

There's no doubt in my mind or heart that I did the right thing by letting Dillon go, but that doesn't mean I don't love and miss him all the same. That day I drove off with Cora's words slicing my heart in two and hid out at Leona's for two weeks, making sure he was forced to leave me and embark on his tour. When I returned, my note was gone and Dillon left his own note with my ring sitting on top of it. The note reminded me that I was his and that he promised to always be mine. Not able to stomach looking at the ring and note, I stowed them away and fell into a dark funk.

The weeks that followed, I was absolutely miserable and literally stayed sick to my stomach from it. There's just no getting over Dillon Bleu. He's more than my first love. He was my dearest friend and the missing him is there clamping down on me every day. If I sit still and close my eyes, I can picture those dimples perfectly, and my memory can recall the alluring woodsy smell of his skin.

Pushing Dillon out of my life was detrimental, but I had no idea how much more badly it could become until I walked into Aunt Evie's office and found her lying on the floor, unconscious. My life finished crumbling in a flash. She had suffered a massive stroke, only five months after Dillon's last exit. I was able to get her to the hospital, but the damage was irreversible. That determined lady held on until Kyle was able to drive the six hours from school. We both sat by her bed and watched her peacefully slip away within an hour of Kyle arriving. Never one to cause a fuss, that lovely woman left us quietly.

When a highfalutin passes away on the other side of the lake, there is always lots media coverage and public mourners quick to declare how great that person was to the world. Nothing like that happened when this great woman died. Those ignorant people have no clue a saint left the earth that sad day. I know my dear aunt didn't get the praise and recognition she deserved during this life on earth, but I'm certain Jesus met her at the gates of heaven and personally escorted her home in a grand celebration fit for a queen. And I know the crown He presented her was more luxurious and majestic than any the royalty of England has ever laid eyes on. I know He rewarded her for saving Kyle and me because that was no easy challenge. That brave woman never complained one time about having to put up with us either. She always made us feel like her own.

I had to grow up fast in those dark days. Never did I think I would be planning a funeral all on my own at the age of twenty-two, or taking over a business and other responsibilities on top of that. Aunt Evie left it all to me, so there was no other choice. I was terrified.

Cora made it to the funeral and kept her eyes glued to me the entire service. Every time I looked up, she was watching me. After everyone left, she and I exchanged hurtful words that we will never be able to take back. And most days I wouldn't ever care to take them back.

I gave her what she wanted—her son a fair shot at his dreams without me getting in the way. I told her she had no right to come back to smear it in my face with her designer dress and salon quality hair, while I stood in that graveyard in a thrift store dress a size too big. She seemed to be able to wash the trash off in a pretty short time.

"You just remember to stay away. Just because Evie is gone, doesn't mean you get to go making a mess for Dillon now." That was the last thing she said to me the very day I laid the dearest woman in my life to rest. I was just glad Aunt Evie wasn't there to hear it. I was ashamed for being so belittled like that. It was easy to write Cora off completely after that day.

I gave into the temptation one time since her threats that day. It was nearly two years after Aunt Evie's death, when I couldn't stand it any longer. Well into my cyberstalking, I watched Dillon transform in those first two years. He ended up keeping the

171

mohawk for quite a long time. I guess that was his rebellion against me for rejecting him. True to his word, Max began that tour with short, spiky green hair. I often wondered how Dillon pulled that stunt off, imagining him shining those dimples as he shared with me the details of it. I pure ached to hear something as silly and simple as that moment I had missed between them.

At the end of that first year, the band wrapped up their first North American tour and went back to the studio to work on their sophomore album. When they reemerged several months later, Dillon's hair had grown back out with just a small streak of blue in the front. He looked edgy in a sexy, brooding way. The fans went crazy for his new look as well as the new album. That record was filled with heartache, and the lyrics combined with the moody melody made it an instant success. It went platinum within a month of its release.

I pulled an interview up late one night just so I could hear Dillon's voice. It was one from the band's promotional junkets for the new album. Dillon was asked in the interview how did such an outstanding album come to be. He said, "A broken heart is the best muse one can find."

The young female interviewer went inappropriate with that statement in two seconds flat. "Oh baby, I could help that heart heal right up."

Dillon gifted her with a one dimple show. "Thanks, but I'm not finished learning from this broken heart just yet." He left it at that and made the girl swoon even more and had me bawling.

A copy of the CD was delivered to me before the sales began. I cried for weeks after receiving it. Dillon's message was weaved into each song with the lyric speaking about broken promises and pointless goodbyes. I hurt him—message received, loud and clear. *If he only knew I was doing it for his own good.*

The need to soothe him became unbearable, so I loaded up in the Mustang and drove a few hours away to Atlanta to catch a concert. I stood near the middle of the crowd and was mesmerized just as much as any fan in the arena that night. Dillon's presence on that stage was indescribable. The man owned it. Absolutely owned it. He was stunning with his black hair styled in an edgy shag, wearing a snug-fitting deep-blue Henley with the sleeves pushed up to expose the ink on his well-defined forearms. I couldn't make out what the designs were, but one looked like a cross and the other arm had intricate wording. Nicely-fitted dark jeans and boots completed his outfit, making him look dangerous and tempting. His electric-blue guitar was strapped around his broad shoulders, and he was working the chords like he was born to do nothing but. The female fans were swooning. I couldn't blame them one bit. He looked larger than life and like every American girl's rock dream.

I stood in awe as the entire venue rocked out to songs artfully interlaced with Bible verses. I seriously doubt they knew, but I guess that doesn't matter. If there's one thing I've learned over the years from

Dillon Bleu, it's that music weaves into the listener's soul and really never departs. I totally get that and I bet you do, too. Have you ever heard the first few chords of a song play on the radio and know immediately what it is, even though you've not heard it in years? It's as though your memory automatically brings it forward from a secret spot, and you can sing every word as you did years ago. Dillon has captivated an incredibly sized rock nation, and these fans will always hold God's words in their hearts long after Dillon departs from the stage. The guy is a genius. This is his intentions and he masterfully pulls it off.

The songs pulled me in throughout the concert, and I just wanted to become part of it. And I felt that way too, with the vivacious music dancing out of the sound system and vibrating all through me. I was just as captured in the trance of the music as the rest of the fans, with my eyes closed, when I was brought out of it abruptly as the first chords of a song I had not heard in a while began rising from Dillon's guitar. My memory recalled it instantly, and my eyes snapped up to find Dillon staring directly at me as he began singing Pearl Jam's "Elderly Woman behind the Counter in a Small Town." I naively thought I was hidden from his view, but he had found me. My heart pounded and the need to flee or stay warred within me. Dillon sang about trying to remember an acquaintance from the past after a long separation. The longing in his voice had sent a despairing throb straight to my soul. I felt hopeless in the middle of that concert arena.

Dillon signaled to someone from the side of the stage during the guitar break and whispered something to them, before going back to singing. The next thing I knew, a stagehand was by my side, handing me a backstage pass and trying to escort me in that direction.

"Um. No thanks. I just want to watch from here." I tried to yell out to him over the music.

I looked back at Dillon. His head was bent to the microphone with his eyes still on me. He nodded his head in a beckoning manner, but I chose to ignore it. He sang about time fading away and then returning. Saying it had been too long. I thought over those lyrics, thinking how they were being played out in reality—a small-town boy stood before me as a big-time man. He had changed by not changing at all. He was different, but still felt so familiar.

Dillon had me captured in his gaze as he sang these meaningful lyrics. He was telling me he missed me and my heart was crying out that I missed him, too. As soon as I was in the same vicinity of him, it was like I could breathe again. Why could something that makes me feel so whole be deemed wrong?

Why couldn't I just simply love this man freely and keep him without the universe trying to steal him away from me?

The stagehand tapped me on my shoulder. "But ma'am, you've been requested to accompany me backstage."

I nodded my head in agreement, trying to

appease him. "I'll head that way in a bit. Right now I just want to enjoy the show."

The big dude leaned down. "Can I at least escort you to the front row?"

"No thanks," I yelled over the music again.

He stood by me the rest of the concert, for what I don't know. Dillon proceeded to play through a Jillian's favorite hits list it seemed the rest of the concert. The very last one he played was just a solo acoustic performance of "My Jewel." He slightly changed the lyrics as he crooned and strummed his guitar quietly. I may have been the only one to notice.

> *My Jewel, my life*
> *You're my night and you're my day*
> *You've always been with me*
> *Even though that's still too far away*
> *You don't see us the way I do*
> *Such a treasure*
> *Such a jewel*
> *I want you now and I want you always*
> *Just a little while, my love*
> *Just a little while*
> *I'll give you just a little while...*

I nearly came undone in the middle of that packed arena until reality pushed its way back to me abruptly, making my heart sink. Our lives were too different now. Dillon didn't deserve for me to interfere in his life. I would only make a mess of it. Before the stagehand could stop me, I bolted through the crowd and headed for the exit.

As I reached the door, Dillon called out in a husky voice full of determination, "I'm a patient man, Jewels."

And I guess either he is, or he's finally moved on, because it's been over five years since things ended that dreadful morning.

I've made a lot of bad choices in my young life and I'm not proud of it. I've asked God to forgive me, time and time again. I know His words say that I need only ask once for it to be granted, and our preacher backs that up in nearly every sermon. I know it's me. I need to forgive myself, but the feeling of unworthiness has become my constant. I just don't seem worthy enough. It all goes right back to my poor white-trash roots constantly taunting me. *You're not good enough…You're nothing…*

Sometimes I get really down on myself and wish the past to be altered, but then the certainty hits that if it were, then things could have turned out so differently. Dillon wouldn't be the rock star he was meant to be, and I'm pretty sure Kyle wouldn't be a bigwig computer programmer in Washington D.C. today. So I've not lived my dream of a writer, but I've been blessed to see my loved ones' dreams come true. Maybe, just maybe, one day I can get back to pursuing my own dreams, but for now I'm content just living this simple life with Will. I made a terrible mess in my youth with Dillon. I've vowed to make a better life with Will. Our life together is simple and good, without all of the emotional drama I've already endured.

I push my attention back to the present and click on the concert video. I just watched this one last night, but want to relive it again and try to decipher it some more. I've been finding some pretty unique footage lately of the band.

Last month I clicked on the London concert and was pretty surprised when the lights came up and Dillon was behind the drums, rocking out while singing into a microphone headset. The crowd went wild as he went to town on those drums while singing. The man laid ownership to any instrument placed before him. He wore a tattered hat backwards and looked so youthful.

He ended that concert brilliantly with a breathtaking a cappella rendition of "Rise" by Eddie Vedder. As he climbed from behind the drums, Dillon discarded the head microphone before pulling his hat back on the correct way. He had masked his eyes completely underneath the rim of the hat, to my disappointment. I've always been able to read him better if I can see his eyes. Standing before the microphone stand, he placed his hands on top of it. Leaning in, Dillon parted his lips and the words floated out of him in a velvety melody. His deep voice echoed throughout the silent venue. It was majestic and sent chills ricocheting all over me. The song spoke about moving forward and learning from mistakes, instead of dwelling on them. He was singing about reassurance and hope for the future. The rawness in his voice was filled with so much emotion, it caused my eyes to sting with tears. He was singing a message to someone who desperately needed to hear it. I just didn't figure out who that was until last night.

I'm still not certain why the message was needed, but now I'm eating up to know. A few weeks back before the London show, at the Amsterdam concert, Dillon, Logan, and Max sat perched on top of stools with the stage lights low. The performance was intimate and subdued. They played an exclusively acoustic concert, serenading the surprised crowd. The entertainment news was all over it, saying how the guys' change-ups were unique and refreshing.

To me, something was off and last night I finally put my finger on it. This latest video was footage of last week's Ontario performance. This was the last stop on the international tour. All the guys were running around the stage, playing all kinds of instruments. At one point the stage held two grand pianos. One was a dazzling blue and the other a gleaming black. Dillon claimed the blue with Trace at the black, and the two set out in an impromptu battle of the piano, causing the audience to go wild. They could have given Elton John a run for his money with how they poured their magical talent out all over those keys. Later the boys busted out banjos, a mandolin, and an accordion and went to town Mumford and Sons style. Dillon declared the audience his favorite and had the stagehands give out an overabundance of tour T-shirts. He then announced that their next tickets would be half off. Of course the fans went crazy at this point. By the last bow, Dillon was washed down in sweat and looked completely spent on more than one level. A few close-ups gave away weariness in his eyes that no one seemed to pick up on. I caught it though. He seemed to be apologizing unnecessarily to the crowd, even though they roared the entire concert with ample approval.

I watched the footage over and that's when I spotted the missing factor. Mave was absent in nearly all the last concerts. I am always so busy watching Dillon that I rarely pay the other guys any attention. This curious observation piqued my interest, so I went farther back to other footage. Some concerts a few months ago, Mave would play half the show before disappearing. He looked gaunt and pale. Then Dillon would finish the show with a solo acoustic performance or play the drums himself. Something's up with Mave, but I have no way of finding out, so all I know to do for him is pray.

"You watching those guys again?" Will asks as he strolls up to my desk, causing me to jump at being caught.

I flip the laptop screen shut. "You know I love their music. Can't a girl crush on a band?" I ask, and he shrugs his shoulders. "Well, don't be jealous. You're my main man. Are you ready for our date?" I brush the hair off his forehead and give him a kiss.

He nods and pulls me to the door. We head out for a quick bite to eat before hitting the movie theater. I always let Will pick the movie. It's a win-win. He watches whatever he wants and I can be left alone with my thoughts and not have to be social. I feel guilty. This is supposed to be Will-and-me time, yet I sit here and cannot stop thinking about Dillon. The missing him and worrying about him is growing stronger, and I need to figure out how to tamp it down.

FOURTEEN

A week later finds me in the front office with Jen. We are propped up at the check-in counter discussing the weekend itinerary. She is sipping on her third coffee of the day and I am wondering how she doesn't get the shakes from all the caffeine she consumes. She's a pretty perky person most of the time. If she starts with the shakes, I'll just have to cut her off.

I slide my gaze out over the trailer park. From here you can see the pool, the main beach with the big dock, most of the cabins, and the trailer section. The only thing out of sight is the RV Park, which is just past a thinly wooded area. It's sunny out, and the pool and lake are glistening in an inviting manner. I'm thinking about seeing if Will wants to picnic on the beach later in the day, when Jen speaks.

"I like Hudson's idea of a dock carnival. All we need are a few food vendors and an entertainment group. It would be cool to shoot fireworks across the lake."

I cringe with this suggestion. *If she only knew about the fireworks history around this place.*

"The cost would be minimal and you can open the gates for day-pass guests," she continues, nodding her head encouragingly. Eyes bright with hope.

Here's the thing about Hudson. He's really a great guy, and I still consider him a friend. He doesn't hold it against me when I get all riled up and go off on him. I think he secretly enjoys pushing my buttons. The thing is this guy always has great suggestions, too. The carnival idea is great and I'm all for it, if I can figure out how to rein Miss Excited Pants in some.

"You're not thinking about the trailer park residents, Jen," I point out, focusing back on shuffling through old itineraries for some ideas.

"Yes, I am," she says between sips of her latte. "They need some excitement. This place has been right boring lately. We need to pizzazz things up a bit." She's still nodding her head enthusiastically.

"I'm not crazy about *pizazz*." I turn to the computer and do a Google search for some other ideas.

She lets out a huff. "I know this. You're so boring."

I huff back at her. "No. I'm safe. There's a difference."

"Boring," she reiterates, shaking her head. "This place needs some shaking up and you need some yourself." She reaches over and gives me a playful shake.

"No. I have Will and I need nothing shook up."

Jen's obviously about to go off on one of her over-caffeinated rants, so I hold my hand up to stop her. A loud, forceful rumble catches both our attention, eyes darting to the front gate as an electric-blue Harley appears. A hulk of a man zooms past the office and is now heading straight over to my little cabin.

"Oh, dear Jesus. Please. No. No. *No*," I begin to frantically pray while watching him ease off the beast of a bike and saunter right into my cabin without hesitation.

"Hot dang!" Jen shouts and slaps the counter in excitement. "Looks like *pizazz* just rolled on up in the form of *Dillon Bleu!*" We continue to watch, and she lends commentary as she is nearly bouncing up and down. "He just walked right up in your place like he owns the joint. That's so bold. So sexy. Man, he's smokin' hot!" She slaps the counter and squeals again. "Hot dang!"

"Ugh. Really, Jen?" I place my clammy hand on my fevered forehead and try to breathe.

She eyes me with a smidgen of concern. "You okay? You're all flushed." Before I can answer, she starts giggling. "This man has you all hot and bothered."

"Shut up." I glare at her and she grins at me. We both look back and find him stalking across the lot in our direction, clearly on a mission.

He's wearing dark jeans and shirt with a leather coat—tall, dark, and dangerous all the way. I'm in so much trouble. He rubs a hand through his hair from what looks like frustration. He is way too extraordinary to be sauntering around in a mere trailer park.

I hop off the stool and do a mad-dash to my

office. "Tell him I'm out of town and it's best he just leaves," I whisper-yell before closing the office door and locking it behind me. I lean against it and listen as my heart hammers away.

Moments later, I hear the door open and his velvety voice fills the silence. "Hello," he says. And I can just imagine Jen swooning like a lovesick teenager.

"Hi," Jen says in a too-high-pitched voice. She giggles nervously. Oh boy. She's star struck.

"Tell Jillian she has company." Confidence flows from his deep tone.

"Umm... She's out of town. A road trip... To go visit her brother. Sorry." Jen is sputtering and stuttering all over her words. She's such a lousy liar.

Of course, Dillon is going to call her out on it. I hold my breath and listen through the door.

"Sweetheart, that woman's baby is parked by her cabin. Now go tell her to get her fine butt out here."

"Umm..." She pauses. "No. Wait. You can't go in there!"

Heavy steps echo down the hall before the doorknob comes to life, making me yelp. "Jewels, I know you're in there. Either open up or I'm going to break the door down." The door continues to jiggle. "I'm not playing games with you, Pretty Girl." There's a stern edge to his words.

He's not going away, so I reluctantly open the door and look up into his stormy blue eyes. The breath I was painfully holding stumbles through trembling lips and tears follow suit. He walks in and grabs me in a fierce hug and lifts me right off the ground, enveloping me in such familiar warmth it makes me shiver.

"Hot dang!" Jen's shouts, her squeals muffled from being wrapped in his embrace. "That's so hot!"

It's the last thing I hear Jen say because Dillon kicks the door shut in her face.

It happens all at once and way too fast—kissing and grabbing at clothes and I know I'm in trouble. Dillon is claiming my lips like a starved man. His jacket hits the floor and then he begins working my shirt over my head before I come to my senses. *What is wrong with me?*

"Stop," I say sternly, trying to snap him out of his lustful fog. I try to wiggle free, but he pulls me back to him. "No, Dillon. We can't do this."

"Right," he says caveman style. "Cabin." He grabs my hand and heads to the door, but I yank free from him. He looks back at me with his dark brows furrowed in confusion.

"We can't do this." I push him for good measure, anger breaking through my lust. "Just because I'm poor doesn't mean I'm cheap!" My hand twitches with actually wanting to slap him. *What is wrong with me?*

This seems to snap him back to reality. Dillon scrubs his hands over his face and takes a few deep breaths. "I didn't mean to insult you. Sorry. I just can't help it, Jewels. I missed you." He looks remorseful and is still trying to catch his breath.

"I'm sure you've got plenty of groupies waiting

to take care of you. Now I thinks it's best you leave." I point toward the door, trying to set my mouth in a sneer. I'm struggling to hold on to this mean-girl attitude. It's slipping fast.

"The only woman I've ever wanted has wasted too much of our time, trying to push me away. I'm done with the waiting, Jewels. I've given you five years. My patience has run out!" He eliminates the space between us in two swift steps, aggression and determination radiating off him.

Before I can form a protest or even blink, he lunges for me and tosses my body over his shoulder like a sack of potatoes. Jen has the audacity to cheer him on as he storms out of the office.

Dillon doesn't slow until he enters my cabin. He sits on the small couch and places me in his lap. It's not the bed, and that's a good sign. Hopefully, I made my boundaries clear. I can't afford to make any more mistakes, but he is just too *tempting*.

We say nothing for a very long time, trying to catch our breath while gathering our thoughts. As the confused haze of what just happened clears, it hits me all of a sudden—*Will*. Will could come up at any minute and catch us together. Nausea slams into me, bolting me from his lap. I hurry to the bathroom and lock myself in.

"Jewels?" Dillon mutters my name in a questioned warning.

Ignoring him, I fish my cell phone out of my pocket and frantically dial Leona's number. As soon as I hear her pick up, I whisper, "Dillon is here...

Will!"

"I can handle that," she says and I hang up. I'm not sure how she plans on doing that, but I know she will, so I let out a sigh of some relief.

After splashing some water on my overheated face, I steel myself and ease back out into the room. Sitting on my couch with his elbows resting on his knees, the man is larger than life. He is just as beautiful of a man as he ever has been. His black hair just touches his shoulders, and all I want to do is run my hands through it. It's the first time I've ever seen him without his signature blue streak. I walk closer to stand in front of him and continue to look him over. That jawline is even more defined, and his face is so chiseled with masculinity. I can only imagine how many walls this man's poster has been hung on. He's drop-dead gorgeous and way too enticing.

A faint scar on his chin catches my attention. It wasn't there five years ago. I glide my thumb over it with question. He doesn't answer right away so I tap it gently and wait.

"A mob jumped me in Sacramento after a concert and beat me within an inch of my life," he says somberly. I punch him in the arm at his poor joke.

His lips creep slowly into a crooked grin. "You still hit like a girl." He grabs hold of my arm and cradles my palm to his chin. The raised texture of the scar presses against my skin. "Max and Trace booby-trapped my dressing room door before a concert in Sacramento. A bucket was supposed to swing out and dump water all over me. The idiots forgot to take my

GOODBYES & SECOND CHANCES

height into consideration and the dang thing crashed into my chin. Trace had to open the show while they hauled in a doctor to sew up my chin. Singing through fresh stitches made for one long and painful night."

"I think them boys are a hazard to your wellbeing," I say, taking in his weary expression. I graze my fingertips along his furrowed forehead. He looks so drained. Something, or should I say, someone, has taken quite a toll on him. I ask the question I've wanted answered for weeks now. "What's wrong with Maverick?"

He pulls me into his lap and buries his face in my neck while releasing a long uneven sigh. "You don't know how badly I've needed you. Just sitting here with you..." His words fade out. He clears his throat and whispers hoarsely, "Jewels, you feel like home to me. I've been so homesick for you."

My eyes prick with tears at his statement, but I rein them in so I can focus on soothing him. I give in and run my hands through his silky locks as he continues to rest against my neck, breathing me in.

"Is he okay?" I ask once his breaths settle down.

"I had to check him into rehab this week," he says after another long sigh.

"What?" I pull his head up gently so he has to meet my eyes.

"He got mixed up with a bad bunch, and the next thing I know he's too high to perform most of the last leg of the tour." Dillon shakes his head in disbelief at his own words. "I thought we got past all that crap unscathed, but Mave… Well, you know Mave. It's like trouble finds him. The dude has always been too curious for his own good."

"Is he going to be okay?"

He shrugs his shoulders. "He promised me he'd get better, if I promised not to replace him in the band."

"I guess that explains all of your odd concerts lately," I say without a thought.

Dillon scrutinizes me with an eyebrow raised. "Just how do you know about that? I've not seen you in the crowd since that one night, and trust me, security is always on the lookout for you." This thought sends a trill through me for some reason—him still looking for me all of these years.

"I keep up with you on the Internet," I confess, heat creeping along my cheeks. My fingers continue to comb through Dillon's hair. I like how it seems to be relaxing him. Some of the stress around his eyes appears to be easing away. Guilt hits me hard over him having to go through this mess with Mave without me.

"Pretty Girl, you could have been having the real thing all of these years. You want to tell me what's going on? Why'd you push me away?" he asks quietly.

"I didn't want to get in your *way*. You were just getting started. Really. I would have just gotten in the way."

Dillon leans his forehead against mine with his eyes still holding me captive. "How could you have gotten in my way if you were by my side, where you belong?"

Good grief. He just doesn't give up.

We have a stare-down for a spell until Dillon begins yawning. Between the dark circles under his eyes and the fits of yawning, it's evident the extra work of filling in for Mave and then the emotional stress of having to put his friend in rehab has taken its toll on him. He needs to catch up on some rest and soon.

I untangle myself from him and stand. "Where are you staying?"

His hooded eyes sweep around the small cabin as he rests his head on the back of the couch. "I thought here would work." He takes in the small toy basket Aunt Evie used to keep in her trailer that sits by the couch, nudging it with his boot. "You took over Aunt Evie's duties of helping the young mommas out, I see." With this I begin to cry. Dillon eases off the couch and wraps me tightly back in his arms. "I'm sorry about Aunt Evie, and I'm sorrier I couldn't get here to you." He places a kiss on the side of my head.

"You couldn't help it," I mumble through my tears, knowing he couldn't, not with everything just taking off for him. My rejection helped to keep him away, too.

He walks us over to the bed and cradles me until I've mourned for all that has been lost. Once my tears subside, Dillon spoons me to him and begins to snore softly.

• ♪ • ♪ • ♪ •

Later this late afternoon, I quietly scoot out of the bed. I've been watching Dillon sleep for hours now. It's all a déjà vu moment. We have already lived this and seem to be doing it again. But life is different this time. And speaking of which, I head over to the office to call Leona.

Charging past Jen, I hold my hand up and cut her a stern look. This is enough to keep her quiet.

"What are y'all up to?" I ask as soon as Leona answers her phone.

"Just grabbing an early supper. How about you?"

"Trying not to have a heart attack," I say, pressing my palm against my chest. "I need some time. Can you tell Will I've come down with a nasty bug, and he has to stay away from me for a few days? I hate lying to him, but I just don't know what else to do at the moment."

"You want to talk to him?"

"No. I can't. Not right now."

"Okay, honey. You just get yourself better. We'll see you in a few days."

"Tell her I love her," I hear Will say in the background.

"Tell him I love him, too. And Leona, I love you."

"Aww, you know I love you more," she says, and I hear the smile in her voice.

As I set the phone down, Jen walks in and sits opposite of me. She's watching me with her concerned hazel eyes. Not wanting to deal with it, I lay my head on top of the desk.

"What am I going to do?"

I feel her pat my arm. "You are going to have to tell both of them. This isn't fair to either of them or you."

She's right, but I just can't bring myself to do it yet. I lift my head and rub my tired eyes. "I'll be over at Aunt Evie's for the night, if you need me." I stand up and follow Jen to the front counter to help power down the computers.

"Where's Dillon?" she asks as she closes the front window blinds.

"Passed out in my cabin. I think the last leg of this tour took a toll on him." I don't tell her about Mave, but I'm thinking he has been a bigger effect on Dillon than anything. The man is loyal to a fault, and I know he is taking Maverick's problems personally.

"If that fine man was in my bed, there's no way I'd leave him alone," Jen says with a smirk.

"I'm not even going to reward you with an argument on that one. I'll see you tomorrow." I head out the door and back to my cabin. I tiptoe in and find Dillon sprawled out, face down on my bed, in only his boxers. He is sound asleep and his feet are dangling off the end of the bed. I guess he is where he will be until tomorrow at least, so I grab a change of clothes before easing back over to the bed to get a better look at him. His arms are tucked under the pillow so I can't see the artwork on them. I'll have to wait on getting a good look at them. I do spot a small change to the tattoo of my name on his upper back.

Discreetly tucked under the L is the date of our last night together. Seeing this makes my throat thicken with emotion. I want to run my fingertips over those significant numbers, but I refrain myself and slip back out the door.

I walk the few streets over to Aunt Evie's and unlock her door. The floral scent of her still lingers in the air, as though she has just passed through, even though it's been five years. Everything has been left just the way she had it. I walk over to the small dinette table and set my clothes down before picking up her hymnal. I flip a few pages and see her notations every so often. She loved helping with the music in our small church, and she loved it even better when Dillon played her beloved hymns.

Too many memories haunt me all at once, sending me plopping down in her chair. Aunt Evie was my rock and I thank God for giving her to me. I just wish He would have let me keep her longer. I sure could use her advice right now. She would have told me like it is, too. One thing I always admired about that woman is she never pitied me or Kyle. She picked us up that fateful day, dusted us off, and guided us toward a better life.

She always had a way with words. One saying she had that always cracked us up was, "Don't go thinking how much greener that grass is on the other side. 'Cause just as soon as you hop over that fence, you gonna land in a big pile of cow poop." In other words, things aren't always as good as they seem. And more times than not, you discover you don't have it as bad as you thought.

Another one of her sayings that has always stuck with me is, "Always be true to God and always be true to yourself, and everything else will truly work itself out."

It's time I use this advice. It's time for me to be true, to not just me, but also to the men in my life. I'm torn between what I want to do and what I need to do. I have to figure out a way of reconciling the two before it all blows up in my face.

I get up from the small table and head to my old room, leaving this problem to sort out until tomorrow.

FIFTEEN

I wake with a start before the sun is even up, knowing he is standing over me before my eyes even open. The man has such a presence, and my skin pricks from his nearness. I just keep lying here and decide against opening them all together. His warm fingers glide over my exposed thigh, and it takes all of my willpower not to respond.

"I know you're awake. Stop pretending." His husky voice booms around the small room.

I roll over and crack an eye open, finding him staring down at me. "What are you doing here?" I ask. He is in only his boxers and the mental picture flashes through my head of this giant of a man stumbling over here, half naked, in the dark. I can just see the tabloid headlines now, if someone saw him.

ROCK LEGEND DILLON BLEU CAUGHT STREAKING!

"I think the question should be, 'What are you doing here?' I woke up alone, Jewels. I'm really tired of waking up alone," he murmurs. And he really does sound tired.

And I swear the man has just crammed himself next to me in my small bed and is cuddling me like a blame teddy bear. We lay in silence and the next thing I know he is back asleep. *Great. Now what?*

I'm about to try to squirm from underneath him, but stop. He's seeking me out because he needs me. So I try to get comfortable the best I can and hold him right back. I lay here listening to him breathe and feel his even heartbeat underneath my hand until I finally doze back off, too.

It seems my eyes just closed when I am opening them again to the sound of my phone ringing. I roll over and find myself alone. *Was it just a dream?* His cologne still lingers on my skin so maybe not. I scoop up the phone and answer it when it starts going off again.

"Hello?" I answer groggily.

"You feeling better?" Will asks.

"A little, but I think it's best for you to stay away another day. I don't want you catching it." I wander toward the front of the trailer to find my guest, but he is nowhere to be found. I rub my hands over my face. The anxiety of it all is starting to build.

"I miss you," Will nearly whispers, making me feel even worse.

"I miss you more. Just one more day. I love you." My voice breaks on the last part.

"I love you, too." He hangs up, and I wonder if he can sense something is up with me.

I can't focus on that right now. My focus has to be on figuring out what I'm going to do about Dillon. I change into a clean pair of jeans and, just for kicks, a Bleu Streak T-shirt before sliding on a pair of shoes and heading over to my cabin.

I spot Ms. Raveena in her yard, watering her little garden, and throw my hand up. "Good morning."

"Oh, yes it has been." She chuckles. "You tell that Dillon I enjoyed the little peep show he gave me this morning. He sure has grown into one *fine* looking man and can fill out a pair of boxers like no other." She's nodding her head, and you can tell she is replaying those images in her thoughts. I don't blame her. They have to be pretty spectacular.

Hotshot had to be one fine sight, walking around nearly naked. "Umm... Did anyone else get to see that show?" I ask, hesitantly.

"Just me, as far as I know, dear." She turns the hose off and wanders closer in my direction.

"How long ago was that show?" I look around for any sign of the streaking giant.

"About an hour. Tell him he can mosey on back by anytime." She's giggling like a school girl and is fanning her face with her garden gloves. The woman is in her late seventies. *Too funny!* But we are talking about Dillon Bleu. That man could get a corpse riled up.

I walk the few streets over, laughing all the way. Relief and apprehension simultaneously wash over me with finding his Harley still in the same spot as yesterday. I ease inside, but the place is abandoned. *Humph.* I glance out at the back deck. Empty.

Giving up the search, I set a pot of coffee to brewing before taking care of my tangled hair and morning breath. I'm sure he'll turn up eventually. The guy doesn't know how to sit still for very long.

After the coffee is finished brewing, I grab a cup and sit on the porch to take in the stillness of dawn. It's my favorite time of day. It's as though I have a secret with the day when we share these first private hours together. Now is normally the time I write my small weekly article for the paper. It's about whatever strikes my fancy. Writing is my creative outlet, and I'm so thankful I have this small opportunity. Thank goodness, I have already submitted it for this week. My mind is a jumbled mess, and who knows what kind of article I would end up producing.

This week's article is about a woman and her brave battle with breast cancer. I spent a few days getting to know her, and now she is my hero. She endured well over a year's worth of treatments and surgeries and hundreds of appointments and came out victorious. Ms. Spivey is celebrating her heroic accomplishment with a celebration cruise with over one hundred friends and family members. She has inspired so many along the way, never complaining openly and giving God all the praise—even through the loss of both her breasts and her hair, and close to two years of her life. But talking to her, she only feels like she has gained in that time. Her acquaintances said she was known for saying it could always be worse. She's definitely my kind of woman, and her story needed to be celebrated. I wanted the world to know about her inspiring life, so I wrote a lengthy piece, thinking it would get edited and cut down considerably. I was pretty shocked when I received a proof layout yesterday morning showing me it got the entire front page of the Lakeshore Times. I'm pretty proud of that. It's my first front page and her story is so fitting to be my first. It's not the New York Times where she should be shared, but I'm honored to do it in my town's paper all the same.

I'm going back over it all while finishing the last of my coffee. I'm about to go grab another cup when the colorful work truck takes a corner way too fast and barrels down the coquina path past me, rustling up a thick cloud of dust in its wake. The next thing I know, it does a neat one-eighty, shooting back in the opposite direction before coming to an abrupt stop in front of the cabin. I'm down the steps in one beat and am about to fire someone, when I spot Dillon trying to unfold himself from behind the driver's side of the tiny truck.

"How in the world did you get yourself in that truck, and how did you manage to steal it from Blake?" Really. Dillon has to be at least five inches past six feet, and that truck is almost too small for me. And I'm well over a foot shorter than him.

Blake wheels up behind the truck without seeing me. "Dude, that was epic! You gotta show me how to do that!" Blake is a junior in high school and helps me before school to earn gas money. He hops off the golf cart and stops dead in his tracks when he finally spots me with my hands firmly planted on my hips in frustration.

Dillon is laughing. It's obvious he's nearly giddy to see me have to be an adult. I stay silent and try to figure out how to handle this situation.

"It was my fault. I stole the truck." Dimples is trying to rein in his laughter and failing terribly.

"Liar," I say to him then turn my attention to Blake. "You need to finish the garbage collecting and we'll have a talk about this after school." He lives in the trailer park with his grandma. He's a good kid, just easily influenced. I should really try to keep him away from Dillon as much as possible.

"Dillon *Bleu* already helped me do all of it, and he helped me hose off the pool and dock walkways, too," Blake says proudly.

Oh no. He's star struck, too.

"Listen, Blake. I'll let this little incident go, if and only if, you promise to keep it to yourself that Dillon is here. We don't need a circus breaking out over him. You got it?"

"Yes ma'am," he says in agreement.

I glance over at Dillon, who is fighting a smile something awful at me just being called *ma'am*. Jerk. He gives in and chuckles, but tries to cover it with a cough, so I reach over and pop him in the gut.

Blake fist bumps Dillon before climbing in the little truck and heading slowly back to the maintenance shed. Like slow driving is going to help me forget what just transpired.

My focus shifts to the golf cart left behind.

"I did steal that. I'm sorry, *ma'am*. I promise to return it, *ma'am*," he says with a smirk on his face, making me punch him in the arm.

He holds his hands up in surrender and follows

me back into the cabin. "You still hit like a girl. You've gotta stop tucking your thumb in, *ma'am*."

I head to the kitchenette for some more coffee, hand him a cup, and lead him onto the back deck to enjoy it. I glance at the clock on the way out. It's only seven and already feels like a day's worth of mess has happened.

"Why are you up so early?" I ask as we watch the sun slowly burn off the lake's fog.

"I just had the best night's sleep in over five years. I'm good." Dillon props his feet on the rail and scans the lake. He really does seem good—refreshed even. The dark circles have all but disappeared.

"You've been back one day and are already causing mischief. What am I going to do with you?" I look at him sternly, eyes narrowed.

"Oh, I can think of a few things I would love for you to do to me," he says, showing off those darn dimples.

I can't tear my gaze away from them.

I. Am. In. Absolute. Trouble.

The black T-shirt he's wearing shows off the tattoos on his forearms. I pull his left one over to my lap and run my fingers over the intricate lettering. It is two words in a language I don't recognize. *Vita Benedetto.*

"What does that mean?" My fingers keep tracing the letters.

"It's Italian for *blessed life*," he answers, looking down at it, too.

"I should have known it was Italian. It sure is sexy."

Dillon notices my gaze has moved to his right inner forearm, so he sets his coffee cup down on the rail and places his arm in my lap. This tattoo is an elaborate cross. It reminds me of a wrought iron crucifix with scrolling medallion artwork. I trace the patterns that wind in and out.

"A cross?"

"Yeah. It's to remind me of what all God's done for me, and that no matter what, He's got my back."

I try to make a poorly timed joke. "Wow. I'm surprised you didn't leave him here with the rest of us." My teasing instantly falls flat. *I wish I could suck the stupid words back in.*

Dillon's brows pinch together as he takes a deep breath, as though he's trying to calm himself. "No. I asked Him to come along on my adventure just as I asked you." Dillon stands up and runs his hands through his hair, glaring at me. "He willingly agreed to stand by me, unlike you!" He storms back through the cabin and right out the front door.

Well, I guess I deserve that. Totally stupid. I don't know what to do, so I sit here and do nothing. Dillon is here for me, obviously, and all I seem to be able to do is try my darnedest to push him away again.

I fish my phone out and shoot Jen a text that I won't be in today, and sit out here on the deck for nearly a half hour to give Dillon time to cool off. I pick up my empty coffee cup along with his abandoned one and bring them inside. After placing the cups in the sink, I take a deep breath and set out to find Dillon and apologize. I've been debating where I want to start since he stormed out.

The search doesn't take me very far. Just to my tiny front yard, where he is kneeling by his bike, wiping the chrome down.

"I'm sorry," I blurt out.

Dillon looks over his shoulder before returning to his task at hand without saying a word.

I walk up to him and run my hand along the leather seat, admiring the gorgeous beast of a bike. "So a motorcycle is your choice of transportation," I say, trying to get him to talk to me.

He stands up and stows the rag in a side pocket. "It fits in a compartment on the tour bus. It's convenient."

"It's sexy," I murmur.

This gets him to look at me. "Take a ride with me?"

"Umm... I don't know, Dimples."

He pulls out a helmet and passes it to me. "Come on, Pretty Girl. Take a ride with me."

I take the helmet and shove it over my head as he slides on a pair of sunglasses. I walk up to the massive bike and try unsuccessfully to climb on. Dillon grabs me up by the waist and places me on the seat. He merely lifts his leg a bit and swings on in front of me.

"Sexy," I say to myself. The man oozes it.

He turns his head to the side. "What's that?"

"Nothing," I say too quickly, causing him to

chuckle. He knew what I said and I'm not repeating it.

He turns a key and the beast comes to life in a loud vivacious roar that vibrates all through my body. I've never been on the back of a bike. I'm nervous all of a sudden and place a death grip around Dillon's waist.

He pats my arms. "Relax, Jewels. I got you."

With that, he peels out of the trailer park, and it feels like we are flying. I'm too scared to open my eyes, so I keep them pinched shut for quite a while. It seems we have hit a long patch of highway, so I peek and see trees flashing by in a blur. I grab hold of him tighter and close my eyes back.

"Relax," he shouts again over his shoulder.

"Slow down and keep your eyes on the road and maybe I can," I yell back.

"You're no fun." There's laughter in his voice, but I feel the bike decelerating some, so I try to loosen my death grip on him a bit.

"Open your eyes, Jewels!" Dillon pats my arm again.

I obey and find that we are crossing a long bridge overlooking a wide river.

"Where are we going?"

"On an adventure."

I try to rein in my curiosity and just enjoy the moment. It's something I'm just starting to fully understand as I've gotten a little older. It seems in life we are too worried about what's next and we lose the gift of the present. I take in the sights and let the future wait a while longer.

Dillon's words about an adventure reminds me of a time long ago when we were just young'uns. It was late one night, when an eleven-year-old Dillon pushed into my room and demanded I go on an adventure with him.

"It's time we set out on our own, Jewels," he whispered with a backpack and his guitar slung on his back, looking all so serious.

I grabbed a bag and threw who-knows-what in it and followed him right out the door without asking one question. I didn't notice until we were outside under a nightlight that his eyes were swollen and still damp from crying.

"You okay?" I whispered.

He hitched his shoulder up before grabbing my hand to guide us on our way. As we walked down the lakeshore, he glanced back toward his trailer.

"I'm just no good for her. Cora doesn't need me. All I do is screw up. It's time I leave her," Dillon said bravely as he swiped another stray tear from his cheek.

"What happened?" I asked and held tighter to his hand.

"I happened," he said, not offering any details.

Even though I knew we would pay for the stunt later, I kept allowing him to lead us down the shore. I would have walked on fire for that boy and face the consequences. More than likely, he had probably not done something on Cora's ever-present to-do list she left him daily. And she had probably blown up at him and said hurtful words she really didn't mean, but we all know that once a word is spoken, or yelled for that matter, you cannot take it back. Cora and Dillon's life was not the one she had envisioned, and I think she hated herself most of the time for that, but ended up taking it out on him.

We walked along the small beach for what felt like hours, with Dillon telling me all about our adventure that we would never complete. He was so hopeful, and eventually his sadness had slipped away as we explored the underdeveloped shoreline of the lake in the dark and later the dawn of a new day. We walked hand in hand until I couldn't walk any farther, so Dillon pulled a sleeping bag out of his backpack, placed it on the sandy shore, and we curled up inside of it to sleep. Lying innocently with that boy felt like home, and I knew after that night I would always be homesick without him. I loved him all my life even though I didn't fall in love with him until several years past that night.

We woke midmorning with Aunt Evie standing over us. "Get home now, Dillon," she said sternly, and he obeyed immediately, without uttering one word in argument.

He spoke quickly over his shoulder as he took off down the shore. "Sorry, Jewels."

I looked at him, confused as to how abruptly our adventure had ended and him doing nothing to continue it. I had reluctantly looked back to Aunt Evie to wait for what was to come.

"Jillian, you know y'all can't do this again."

Her face looked more sorrowful than mad, and I didn't understand it at the time.

"But Dillon needed me," I said, with my own tears spilling down my cheeks.

"Honey, running away won't ever fix a problem. It will only add to it. Just be glad I found you before Cora did."

"I hate her," I said without thought.

"That's a strong word, young lady. I don't like you using it. That woman is doing the best she can. She may have a temper and her mouth gets the best of her, but you need to remember, she loves that boy with all of her being. Even though she may not know how to express it properly sometimes." Aunt Evie began making her way back down the shore with me following.

"He needs me." I only cared for Dillon's well-being. "Please, Aunt Evie. Please don't let Cora hurt him for running away."

"She won't. She feels bad for last night. She'll be relieved he is okay." She tried to soothe me because I was pretty upset. "Let's just keep it to ourselves that you were with him."

"Why does she hate *me*?" I asked through tears. I was young still, and adult actions were so confusing. Why did it matter that I was with him?

"I just think she wish she loved that boy as easily as you do." She slowed to place an arm over my shoulder, not answering my question, but I let that go.

"Dillon Bleu is the easiest to love, Aunt Evie, and

you know it," I said firmly, crossing my arms as we tracked alongside the lake, nearing the trailer park.

"I completely agree," she said as we snuck the long way back to our trailer so Cora wouldn't catch sight of us.

I was surprised that Dillon and I hadn't made it too far from home. It had felt like our adventure took us a million miles away from reality. Cora never caught that I was with Dillon, but he was still out of sight for a week after that stunt. I missed him terribly. I had no idea how awful it could feel to miss him in long stretches of years passing as I've had to do in my young adult years. It's been crippling at times.

The memory fades and all I can think about is how true my words were way back then. I ease up from cradling against his back and place a kiss on the side of his neck. He squeezes my hand in approval before placing it back on the handlebar of the bike.

Dillon Bleu is absolutely the easiest to love.

We make it down the interstate at a pretty fast rate until Dillon veers off onto a country road, passing farmland and large pastures. He pulls the bike through the open gate of a peach orchard and slows to a crawl as we pass between the rows of pink blossomed trees. The aroma is heavenly, and I'm just in awe at the beauty of this place.

Dillon stops completely and kills the engine in what feels like the very middle of the orchard, for we are surrounded by the floral landscape. He climbs off and turns around to me. He pulls the helmet off my head and runs his fingers through my tangled hair.

"Sexy," he murmurs before picking me up and slowly kissing me. It's an unrushed yet still too short kiss, and I'm surprised he ended it so fast. He steadies me on my feet and places my hand in his. "Let's take a walk," he says, so I silently follow by his side.

We walk amongst the sweet rows, leisurely. The trees are in full bloom, and I wish I had a camera. I live in Georgia and have never visited one of these luscious orchards until now. This place is heavenly and tranquil, and I wonder if it's anything close to the Garden of Eden. I can't get over how something so magnificent has been tucked so close and hidden right under my nose.

Dillon bends down during our stroll and picks up a delicate pink blossom that has drifted to the ground. He tucks it behind my ear and gazes at me. There's a palpable current pricking the air between us. It's magical. He gathers my hand and kisses my knuckles as we continue our stroll with that enchanting feeling following us.

I eventually break the silence with a question I'm not sure I want answered.

"How long will you be here?"

He glances at me before easing his gaze back to the trees. "Getting Mave healthy again is our main priority right now, so we are going on hiatus for as long as that takes. I'm guessing several months, at least."

"Where is he?"

"He's close."

I shoot him a questioning look over his vague

answer.

"Only Max and I know exactly where he's at. He's embarrassed and doesn't want anyone to know. We've got him in a facility in Atlanta. You are the only other person who knows he's in rehab." He stops us and pulls me around to face. "Jillian, it's important that no one else knows about this."

"I get it," I say with some annoyance, but then let it go. I keep forgetting how different our lives are now. I don't have to worry about the entire world knowing my business and then smearing it in a heartless way through tabloids. "I get it," I say again, but more softly this time.

"Max has rented a condo near him, so Mave's not alone," he says, and I think he is trying to reassure himself and not me. We stand in silence for a few beats as I watch the stress drain away from his features and replaced with contentment as he refocuses on me. "Dance with me, Pretty Girl." He pulls me in front of him and starts leading our bodies in a slow sway.

"We don't have any music."

Dillon chuckles softly and places my hand over his heart. "We always have music with us. Right here." He gently taps my hand and pulls me even closer until my head rests over his heart. I melt completely when he begins to hum in a melody that matches the strumming of his heartbeat. I love how the humming vibrates deeply in his chest and connects with mine. His fingertips glide along the curve of my neck, leaving a trail of goose bumps in his wake. Every so often the humming ceases with him placing whispers of kisses along my chin and the corners of my mouth.

Time passes—minutes, hours, or maybe a lifetime as this man leads me in this private dance. I just want to spend the rest of my life right here in this orchard and never return to the messy reality that needs addressing. This moment is too perfect to ruin, so I promise myself to handle it tomorrow.

I'll tell him tomorrow...

Or maybe the day after tomorrow...

We dance in this lovely orchard until the day begins winding down, but we both seem reluctant to end it. Dillon eventually pulls me back over to his bike and settles us back on before heading back onto the road.

He rolls us up to an Italian bistro. The garlic and basil aroma wafting through the air sets my mouth to watering before we even make it inside. After a star struck hostess receives Dillon's autograph, she places us in a private section near the back. Dillon is so slick, too. He promised the staff they could take as many photos with him as they wanted, as long as they allowed us to eat in peace first. He's definitely a pro at this, treating all of them as his dearest friends and them eating it up.

Luckily, the manager is a man and he has taken on the task of personally waiting on us. I was worried we would be stuck with some girl drooling over Dillon the whole time, and I just don't think I'm ready to deal with such. The chef requested that we allow him to serve up a special dinner, and so we are sitting here enjoying an antipasto platter while we await our main entrees.

I pop an olive into my mouth and eye my company. This man blows my mind. It's hard to reconcile the boy I knew with the celebrity rock star before me now. He's shoveling a chunk of fresh mozzarella and tomato into his mouth, and he doesn't seem to be any different than the Dimples I knew. But he is...

"What's on your mind, Pretty Girl?" He lifts an eyebrow and wipes his mouth with the cloth napkin.

"I'm worried I don't know you anymore," I admit.

The manager scoots back in with two monstrous plates of pasta, placing them in front of us. They are overflowing with linguine dressed in red sauce and loaded down with huge shrimp and slivers of garlic.

"Thanks, man. This looks amazing," Dillon says before taking a generous bite. I follow suit. It is so delicious. The manager seems pleased and leaves us be. "You know me. I'm still me," he says resolutely before taking another bite.

"Tell me something."

"Like what?" he asks around a mouthful of pasta.

"I want to know something about your adventure. Something epic."

Dillon wipes the corners of his mouth and takes a long swig of his tea. He seems to be deciding what to share with me when a grin sneaks along his face. It makes me impatient.

"Tell me something," I say again, nudging his leg with mine under the table.

"I met this guy named Eddie, last year," he says nonchalantly and takes another bite of his food.

Understanding strikes me instantly. I drop my fork and gasp. "No way!"

"Yes way."

"Please tell me he is as cool as I've always imagined."

"Nope. More than cool. The dude is *epic*." He smiles as he uses my word. Well, I wanted him to tell me something epic, and he sure didn't disappoint.

"Where'd you meet him?"

"We hung out after the Music Awards last year. The next thing I know, we were on a plane heading to Hawaii. We spent a week out there with him teaching me how to surf." He grabs a piece of freshly baked bread and works on sopping up the thick, red sauce with it.

"No!" I gasp again in disbelief.

"Yep," he says before cramming half the piece of bread in his mouth. "Epic."

I'm too blown away to eat anymore, so I just sit here and watch Dillon inhale his food. "You realize how jealous you just made me."

"I may have a few CD's with his name autographed on them for you." He looks up with those deep-blue eyes twinkling and a wide grin stretched out over his handsome face.

"What? Where the heck are they?"

"Waiting for you in California. Eddie really digs

my song, 'Pretty Girl on My Mind,' so I told him our history behind the song. I also told him you were in love with him." He gives me a sharp look, causing me to smirk. "He thought I should make you wait for the CD's until you came back to me." Dillon seems to slip into a somber mood. He finally pushes the nearly empty plate away and eyes me from underneath the thick fringe of eyelashes. "I'm still waiting, Jewels," he says softly.

I slide my hand over to his and entwine our fingers. "I'm right here."

"Yes. But you still feel unattainable." Dillon says this to me, but it's always felt like he is the unattainable one.

Before I can speak, the manager is back with a large square of tiramisu and two spoons, along with two coffees. We leave the conversation and politely dig in. After taking care of the bill, Dillon spends a good chunk of the next hour in the restaurant making everyone's day. It feels like hundreds of pictures have been taken and he's signed everything imaginable, before we finally slide out the door.

Dillon rides us all over the state before declaring our day done, and I have to admit I have fallen in love with his beastly bike. When we arrive back to the cabin well past sundown, we find two suitcases and Dillon's guitar on the screened-in porch.

"Ben?" I ask.

"Tate. I've promoted Ben to project manager," he says, and again my thoughts drift back to how very little I know about him anymore. That sinking feeling

I had at the restaurant has returned.

"You're making yourself right at home?" I ask as he pushes his stuff inside and unpacks some.

He glances up with all seriousness. "You're my home, Jewels. So yes, I am."

Dillon grabs the guitar and my hand, leading us to the back deck. He settles on a chair and serenades me, under the moonlight and before the welcoming lake, in an alluring spell. Oh, how I wish every day concluded in this exact manner. This man looks magical with the moonlight filtering over his handsome features as he loses himself in the lyrics of his songs. It amazes me how effortless it is for him to create such beauty in mere melodies and chords.

No matter how much I've denied myself of this man, there is no denying how much I am in love with him.

SIXTEEN

Dillon slipped into sleep almost immediately after his shower last night. Not me. I'm scared he is going to hate me. And I'm scared Will is going to hate me, too.

After the restless night, I'm having a hard time waking this morning. I'm dozing in bed, when a tickle on my face rouses me. I open my eyes and find Dillon lying beside me, leisurely tracing the contours of my face with his fingertips. I say nothing for a spell and just enjoy the moment. His dark-blue eyes look close to purple starbursts. They are exquisite and are studying me reverently. How he looks at me as though I'm so precious causes tears to prick my eyes. This man awakes all of my emotions and senses. I feel like my life went dormant while he was gone and is now reawakening.

"What are you doing, Dillon?" I ask, already knowing the answer, but wanting to hear his beautiful voice express his actions.

This is normally the other way around in the world we live in. Normally people have no trouble spurting off feelings that they have no intentions of ever backing up with actions. Not Dillon. This man's heart is on full display right on his sleeve, never hidden. Always so exposed and raw. I see it now in the firm set of his mouth and eyes that are swimming with his own unshed tears.

"I've missed this face more than I can ever express in a word." His voice is thick with sleep and sincerity. "You are my treasure. I've hated every day I've had to live without you." He continues to trace along my cheek. "You're my other half, Pretty Girl. I've lived too long not being whole."

These are words that Aunt Evie shared with me all those sad years ago, and they finish the job of spilling my trapped tears. Dillon wipes them away with the pad of his thumb. I grab hold of his hand and place a kiss on his palm. Then I place it on my cheek.

Giving him a wobbly smile, I say, "Good things come to those who wait."

"I'm over the waiting." Dillon pulls me closer to him so there's no space between our bodies, forcing me to wrap my arms around his neck.

"I agree."

Dillon leans in to brush a faint kiss over my lips, but seems to think better of it and returns to deepen it. We become lost in it, and all I want is to have the power to pause time. Because in this moment, in this man's comforting arms, I never want to leave. Dillon Bleu is my home and I've been homesick for way too long.

Dillon cocoons us with my quilt, and we eventually drift back off to sleep for a little bit longer.

I leave Dillon in bed later this morning and sneak

off to see Will. I miss him too, and I needed to relieve some of my guilt. I have breakfast with Will and saw him off for his day before making my way to the office. This is the most time we have ever been apart since he entered my life and he seems to be not taking too kindly to it.

Today is Friday, so I need to make sure all the weekend bookings are squared away. I have the paperwork set before me, but I'm having a hard time focusing on it.

The morning drags by with me booking sites over the phone and helping Jen figure out the schedule. We have moved on to writing up late notices that she'll hand deliver later today. There are quite a few, and it's disheartening. I've even been helping some of the residents find jobs. I can't tell you how many single moms I have hooked up with condo cleaning on the other side of the lake. It's hard work, but it pays well and the poor women don't have to work crazy late hours. I help out where I can with babysitting and being lenient on rent, but there's only so much I can do myself. It's a hard time to be living in this country. People are hurting all around, and it can feel right hopeless.

I'm lost in these hopeless thoughts when the door is yanked open all of a sudden with Dillon storming in. My stomach plummets with fear that he has found out about Will on his own. He braces his hands against the counter and leans toward me with a glowering stare. Steeling myself for what's about to come, my shoulders stiffen and my breath becomes trapped in my lungs. I can't even swallow.

"Where are they, Jillian? What did you do with our sheds?" He's called me Jillian, making it clear he means business.

Relief washes over me as laughter falls from my lips. Jen joins in, and this is rubbing Dillon wrong something fierce.

"It. Ain't. Funny," he slowly says.

"Did you really think this place would stand still while you were off living your life?" I put away the paperwork before returning my attention to our angry guest.

"But those were our sheds!" he snaps, losing his patience and slapping a palm against the counter. He looks close to tears.

I grab a set of golf cart keys and pull him out the door. "I'll be back later, Jen."

"No worries," she says before the door closes.

I escort this brokenhearted rock star to the cart and drive him into the back of the woods, to a new clearing where two new storage buildings sit hidden. I stop in front of them. "All you had to do was nose around a little bit more and you would have found them, busy breeches."

"What happened to the other ones? And why is there a big cabin in their place?" He still doesn't sound happy with the changes, each question sharp with accusation.

"I wanted a bigger place, and where the sheds sat was the only place the county would approve it to be built." I climb off the cart seat and open the shed door. "All of the old stuff has been moved here. I couldn't fathom not having a place to treasure hunt." We look around at the packed space, brimming with the craziest assortment of stuff. "I even hired some guys to move most of it so I wouldn't discover all the treasures." I smile and glance over at my sulking man. "The old sheds were also rotting down, Dillon. It all had to be moved regardless."

Dillon trails behind me and seems to be calming down a bit, so I reward him with a treasure I found for him last year. "I got a treasure for you," I say as reach in a trunk and then hand the ukulele to him that was tucked under a towel inside.

He takes it and studies it with an awed expression. "This is from the mid-nineteen hundreds," he says reverently as he inspects it.

"I had it polished up and restrung before I hid it back in here. How can you tell?" I ask as we both eye the honey-toned instrument. It looks so tiny in his large grasp.

"I've taken some music history lessons online and I've had a private music teacher who didn't mind tagging along on the tour. I finished high school that first year through private tutors and completed my Masters in music." He says this as though it's no big deal, but my mouth gapes open. He begins strumming and stops to adjust the strings until they sound just right.

"Dillon, that's really impressive." Pride tightens my chest.

He shrugs his shoulders. "The twins ended up

graduating, too." He's still trying to downplay how remarkable his accomplishment is.

"I really thought you were done with school the day you left this place. I'm totally proud of you, Dimples."

He starts strumming a song that sounds like it should be heard on a Hawaiian beach and grins. "I'm really digging my treasure. Thanks."

"Why are you grinning so big?" I ask, watching him bring the petite instrument to life.

"You've been waiting for me to come back." He holds the ukulele up as evidence and then returns to strumming the strings. "I knew you still loved me."

I lean against a wooden totem pole and grin back at him. Don't ask me how this eclectic collection came to be. It's the oddest bunch of stuff I have ever seen, but it sure is fun to sift through.

"Loving you was never the issue," I admit.

The whimsical song cuts off as he knits his brows together. "Then what was? Why did you leave me?"

"We've already been over this, Dillon. I would have held you back. We were too young and stupid." I hold my hair off my neck as this space starts growing warmer by the minute.

Dillon takes advantage of this and runs his fingertips along the dewy length of my neck, leaving a trail of tingles. "Well, I'm older and wiser now, and I still don't see your reasoning."

"Music was your dream and I didn't want to hold you back in any way." His fingers leave my skin, so I drop my hair back down.

"Music has never been my dream, Jewels. It's my adventure, sure. But you have always been my dream. I've loved you all my life, Pretty Girl." He shakes his head and releases a long, gruffly sigh. "Like I said yesterday, all I wanted was for you to go on my adventure with me just as God did. He never got in the way of it. He only helped to keep me on the right path."

"God also knew I needed to stay here. Aunt Evie... She would have died alone if I had gone with you." My lips tremble as Dillon wraps me in his arms and holds me gently.

"I'm sorry. I know," he whispers while slowly rocking us in place, the motion soothing.

There's more than just the loss of Aunt Evie that has glued me here, and I should be apologizing to him. We've both lost things we can never get back, and I worry we may not be allotted a second chance. *Only time will tell...*

He sets the ukulele down and eases me over to the couch that was just delivered yesterday. It's wrapped in moving blankets. The floors in the cabin will be completely dried by tomorrow I'm told, so things can start being moved in by the start of the week.

Dillon sits down and straddles me over his lap while pulling my head to his chest. He is so much bigger than me, and I fit quite nicely in his embrace. I feel so safe and protected in his arms.

Eventually the holding moves to caressing and continues to accelerate from there until we are back to kissing and losing ourselves into one another in this moment. It's like we can't get close enough. The easiest thing I have ever done is love this man. It comes so naturally, even when I fight so hard against it. I don't realize how incomplete I am until he shows back up and makes me whole again with his unconditional love. The way he loves is uninhibited and with abandon and makes me come alive.

"You're mine," he says in a growl against my lips.

"Yes," I declare back. *I am completely his.*

• ♫ • ♫ • ♫ •

We drift asleep, wrapped around each other on the couch for a while as the day moves forward without us. Eventually we rouse back up and spend more alone time together, not wanting to leave the bubble we've formed while hidden away in this treasure trove.

A little later I have no choice but to leave Dillon to treasure hunt while I go back to work. The overwhelming need to clear my head hits me as soon as my feet step outside the shed, so I leave him the golf cart and walk back. It takes me fifteen minutes to get back to the office and another fifteen to snap out of the funk I'm in.

"You need to straighten up or go away," Jen demands after she catches me staring off into space.

"Sorry," I mutter, blinking back to where we're propped at the front counter.

"Oh shoot. Here comes some more pizazz." Jen

points to the front gate as a large truck comes creeping through, hauling a massive Formula Sun Sport boat and two Yamaha Waverunners. These babies are custom built and are all sleek with the same paintjob. Black and silver dominates with sharp blues.

I'm thinking this delivery is on the wrong side of the lake, but after a closer look, Bleu Streak's custom band logo embedded near the rear of each toy catch my attention. The logo itself would make a killer tattoo with the words in an edgy font. There are all sorts of scrolling lines blazing in and out around the words, and if you study the logo long enough, you will see hidden art. The T in Streak is actually a cross and each band member's name is camouflaged in a scrolling line. The well thought-out creativity in the logo alone is just mind blowing. When the truck turns the corner, I see that the boat's name is painted across the back of it. *My Jewel*, of course.

"Good grief. We might as well send out a full-blown invite for the media now," I gripe. "This place is going to be swarming with chaos."

"Should I book some security guards?" Jen asks as we walk over to the computer to look them up. We are about to pick up the phone when a super-cute guy with auburn hair walks in. He's probably just twenty, if that. I look over at Jen and notice she is enjoying the view.

"Hello ladies. I'm Tate O'Ferrell." He extends his hand, so we use our southern manners and shake it.

I'd rather strangle him and his boss at the

225

moment.

"I'm Jen," she says, almost purring her introduction.

Before I can introduce myself, Tate beats me to it. "It's a pleasure to finally meet Dillon's Jewel." He smiles widely.

I smirk at this. *Mr. O'Ferrell thinks of himself as a lady's man.* "Okay, buddy, what can we do you for?" I ask.

"Well, you see, it's my job to see after Dillon's best interests, and I hope you don't mind if we bring in our personal security crew."

This man has just made my day. So now I'm over the whole strangling idea. "Okay. What does that entail?"

"A guard at each gate and one to patrol the grounds should do it." He's scrolling through his smartphone as he talks. "They're on their way." He looks up from his phone with another flashy smile.

"Who's gonna keep the daredevil safe with all those toys you just hauled in?" I point outside. Tate laughs like I just made a joke. "I'm not joking," I clarify, just as the daredevil in question zooms up on the golf cart.

He jumps off before the cart completely stops, climbs the side of the trailer, and hops into the boat. I can see the dimples from here as he checks things out. He disappears below deck for a few minutes and then bolts over the side quickly to exchange some words with the driver. The driver pulls a CD case out of the cab and hands it to Dillon to sign with a Sharpie.

After Dillon autographs it, he shakes the driver's hand with a manly slap to his back and jets inside where we are all watching him.

"Jewels is mine," Dillon declares as he eyes me, excitement radiating from his sparkly peeps. *He likes saying that, I do believe.* "Tate, my man, you need to help Jen for the rest of the day." He's already pulling me toward the door before I can protest.

"The pleasure will be all mine, boss," Tate says with Jen giggling.

Good grief.

"What are you doing, Dillon?" I ask as he leads me over to my cabin.

"Today is our day and we are celebrating." He looks down at me with a bit of apprehension. "You didn't forget, did you?"

"No, Dimples. I didn't forget."

He leans over and kisses my cheek. "Good. Because we got a lot of celebrating to catch up on, Pretty Girl." The eagerness laces back into his tone, making me giddy as well.

Once we are inside the cabin, he points to my small armoire. "Bathing suit, preferably a bikini." The man is a ball of energy as he hastily rummages through a shopping bag I hadn't noticed before and pulls out a pair of board shorts. Without thinking twice about it, he is naked and redressed before I can tear my eyes away. And there is nothing *boy* about that body anymore. Just let me tell you. I feel my face grow red from the peep show. "You like what you see, Pretty Girl?" he asks as he pushes his long bangs

227

out of his eyes and stares at me. The heat in his gaze is enough cause my entire body to go up in flames.

I let out the breath I was holding and shuffle over to the armoire to grab a bathing suit. I scurry off to the bathroom without answering him. The man can totally fluster me, even after all of this time.

"No need to be shy now," I hear him say with a chuckle before I close the door.

I change into the suit and make a quick call to Leona. "I need some more time."

"Okay. Will's going to start wondering what's going on. It's getting hard to keep him distracted enough to not want to head over there to see you," she says.

"I know," I whisper. "I just need one more day. If I can, I'll break away later and go see him." I end the call and shake off my guilt before heading out of the bathroom to see what the plans are for the day. It's been a hot spring, so a day on the lake sounds heavenly. I am a bit excited about the boat ride. It looked pretty impressive from afar.

Within thirty minutes, we are cruising along the lake in style. Dillon can drive anything with an engine and is at the helm like he was born to be. He is wearing only the dark-blue board shorts and a tattered hat low on his head. His dazzling eyes are masked behind a pair of designer sunglasses. With his tattoos on full display, he looks tough and untouchable and most definitely drool-worthy.

People are gawking as we pass. Some have been trailing us and taking photos. I nudge Dillon.

"Dimples, you know you are broadcasting with this boat. Why would you want to put your brand all over it?"

"I've worked hard, Jewels. I should be able to enjoy it all I want." He grins and those darn dimples take my breath. "I owed my woman a boat, and I want no one doubting who she belongs to."

"But, what about the photos?" I look out over the shore and spot a few professional looking cameras aimed our way.

"Let them have their pics. There's nothing I want to hide. I want the world to know you're mine," he says proudly, but it makes me nervous.

There he goes with the whole *you're mine* caveman attitude again. If he wanted me to be his so badly, then why on earth did it take him so long to come home and lay claim to me? I want to ask him this, but I keep quiet. I'm not ready to stir up the trouble the both of us will have to face soon enough.

I keep my sunhat pulled low and don't take off my own designer sunglasses Dillon gifted me earlier. I definitely do not take off my bathing suit cover-up either.

As the day strolls along, Dillon drops anchor right in the middle of the lake and heads below deck. He reemerges carrying a picnic basket. I'm instantly impressed. Or I am until he starts pulling out a tub of pimento cheese, pork rinds, a loaf of white bread, and RC colas. I have to laugh as he sets up our white-trash picnic. He's grinning, too.

"I really missed this stuff," he says as he spoons

some pimento cheese in his mouth, before assembling us a sandwich.

"I'm surprised you don't have it shipped to you in California," I say before taking my first tangy bite. It is really good stuff.

Dillon just shakes his head and gives me a knowing look. "Some things are worth waiting for, Jewels." And I believe those words.

My throat thickens at this statement. "What took you so long?" I whisper and am thankful he didn't hear me.

Dillon eats two sandwiches, and then uses the pork rinds to dip out the rest of the pimento cheese from the tub. He then digs us each out a double-stuffed moon pie. The gooey, chocolaty, marshmallow goodness is heavenly with the icy cold cola.

We stretch out and snooze in the late afternoon sun afterwards. Dillon has been stroking my finger on my left hand for quite some time. He has taken his hat and glasses off so I watch him stare at my bare finger.

"You need to put your ring back on where it belongs."

"You're such a caveman." I laugh, causing him to growl. He sounds like one too.

He leans over and starts tickling me. "You. Mine. Ring. On. Finger." He is now mimicking a caveman and I'm laughing so hard my sides ache. I've missed him so much.

I laugh until an image of Will trying to tickle me in the same manner pops in my head and my stomach flip flops. I stiffen all of a sudden and am baffled by how easy it has been to forget all about my troubles.

Dillon senses my sudden change and pulls me close to his side. He skims his nose along my neck and stops at my ear to places a kiss there. "What's on your mind, Pretty Girl?"

I should probably protest him calling me this, but I don't. He's either called me Jewels or Pretty Girl all my life. I like his little names for me. I like it even better because just last year his band released a ballad that won them a Grammy for song of the year. The song is titled "Pretty Girl on My Mind," and I cried off and on for a month after its release. Will thought I was losing my mind.

"We are going to need to have a serious talk. It doesn't have to be today. Today can be our day. But there are things we need to discuss soon."

He peels my shades off. "You're worrying me." His brows are pinched with concern.

I pull him close and kiss him with all the longing and regret I can pour into it. "Tomorrow. Not today. Love me completely today," I murmur against his lips. I take his words that he spoke to me all those years ago and give them back to him.

He takes them willingly. "Tomorrow," he says, and doesn't ask about it for the remainder of our day.

We try to sunbathe with boats constantly passing and passengers calling out to Dillon. He's a good sport and waves at all of them. He seems to know just how much attention to give the fans as well as making his boundaries clear at the same time. The man is a pro. With the sun setting, Dillon glides the boat back to the dock. When we arrive, Tate is there waiting to take over the task of tying the boat down for the night.

We stroll back into my cabin, and I feel pleasantly sun-kissed and groggy. It's been an amazing day. A day I can hold on to after I mess everything up with Dillon.

SEVENTEEN

Midday on Saturday, I stroll back into the small cabin to find it empty. There's a note on the counter. It makes my stomach cringe, and man has my stomach been on a roller coaster ride ever since Dillon returned.

Jewels,
Spent better part of the night looking for you. What gives? Mave and Max need me so I'm heading out. Call me. I want that ring on your finger by the time I get back.

Love, Dillon
BTW—Yesterday was incredible. I could write a song about it.

After reading the note, I head right back out the door. I promised Dillon the day and gave him every minute of it. But as soon as he was out for the count, I headed over to Will. This double life is getting exhausting.

For now, I have some making up to do with Will. I find Will on the couch at the townhouse, zoned into some movie on the large flat-screen. I sneak up behind him and playfully place my hands over his eyes.

"Guess who?" I whisper in his ear. His cheeks turn up in a smile against my palms and that makes my day. He grabs ahold of my hands, so I drop them and give him a hug from behind. "How 'bout you come home with me?"

He nods his head and we are out the door in the next beat.

As we ease back through the gates of the trailer park, Will's eyes land on the luxury boat and jets skis tied off at the dock where they stick out like a sore thumb.

"Man, those are tough. Why are they on the wrong side of the lake?" He may not have been a local for very long, but Will already knows the way things are around here.

"Someone got lost," I say, trying to quickly dismiss this by going straight to our new cabin. We pull up and I look over to see the question along his features. "Welcome home!"

"Really?" I see the excitement has now replaced the questioning look.

"Yep. It's ready for us to move in!"

We hurry out of the car. Will grabs hold of my hand and pulls us inside to inspect our new home. It's gorgeous too. The walls are cedar wood paneling that rises and covers the ceiling as well. The smell, mixed with the freshly lacquered wood floors, is heavenly. The living room is to the front with a cozy kitchen in the back. The upstairs is made up of two very roomy bedrooms, each with their own bathroom. It's not an extravagant house, but it is to me and Will, and that's all that matters. I just wish Aunt Evie was here to enjoy it with us. I wish she could have met Will too. I know she would have approved of him.

We spend our day moving into our home, only stopping long enough for a pizza. Leona and Jen stop in to help and to cut up with Will. He is such a charmer and women just gravitate toward him. And believe me, he seems to not mind one bit. I catch myself laughing as he animatedly tells the two some long tale. I definitely have a certain type of man for sure. *Charismatic with dimples.*

We spend our first night in our new home and head to church this morning, a bit sore from all of the moving but totally happy. We make it just in time for the opening song. Will heads over to the small fellowship hall where he promised to help Brina, our neighbor, with children's class.

Brina has become another close friend of mine over the years. She is my age, but has her hands full with three rambunctious boys. They remind me of the twins and Kyle so much. I help her out as much as I can so she can work. Her husband left her a few months back and has yet to return. Good riddance. He's a mean man, and I have seen him be pretty violent toward her. I have already warned her if he returns they will all have to go. I'm not allowing such chaos around here.

I ease into a back pew beside Leona and am taken

aback when I spot Dillon at the piano. My happy-go-lucky mood evaporates instantly with him being in the same vicinity as Will. *This could be really bad.*

The preacher stands behind the podium to read the select scripture for the day and briefly speaks. I'm ashamed to say I couldn't tell you what he has said, because all of my focus is on Dillon. He sits patiently behind the piano, wearing a pair of black dress slacks and a grey dress shirt. The sleeves are rolled up with his tattoos exposed.

I lean over and whisper to Leona, "What is Dillon doing?"

"He arrived here before you and the entire church begged him to play," she whispers back as she rubs her beautiful baby bump. She is due in only a few weeks, and I'm pretty excited to have a baby girl I get to help spoil. Her sweet husband, Grant, sits on her other side while holding her hand attentively.

"Now I know that was a short message, but I feel God has us a message waiting through song today," Preacher Floyd says, drawing my attention back to him. With this he has a seat on the front pew and all eyes fall on Dillon.

Dillon's hands move over the piano and the sanctuary comes to life with the melody so sweet. His head is bowed toward the keys and his eyes are closed. The small space has just been transformed into a cathedral with the fluid tunes Dillon beckons from the piano keys. His hands glide gracefully over the instrument. He plays for a while before adding the lyrics to "Amazing Grace." This rendition is slow and sends chills all over me. He sings quietly and you know he's not singing to us, but only for God. He is worshiping Him with this marvelous gift he has been blessed with, and the entire sanctuary is swept away in awe. Amens are breaking out all over and the spirit keeps growing sweeter and sweeter. I don't even realize I'm crying until Leona hands me a tissue.

The next song Dillon brings forth from the piano is "Cry Out to Jesus." He plays a few keys before saying, "This is for Aunt Evie." This song is about grief over a loved one lost long before their time, and how you just didn't feel like you had the opportunity to say goodbye. In times like that, all you can do is cry out to Jesus. I have done plenty of that, and feel like doing more now. Dillon wipes at his eyes a few times during the song and it chokes me up even more.

There's not a dry eye in the room by the time Dillon plays the last note. He plays through several of Aunt Evie's favorite hymns—"Love Lifted Me," "I Surrender All," "The Solid Rock," and "Just as I Am."

As he continues to play, I sit in this pew and mourn over the mess I've made. And for being in love with Dillon and not being able to stop it. I don't know how to reconcile the wrong I've done to Dillon and the wrong I'm doing now to Will. Sensing Dillon drawing to a close, I scoot out and head home before he can stop me.

• ♫ • ♫ • ♫ •

Everyone has decided that this Sunday's meal is at my

place, so I hustle over to town and grab a bucket of fried chicken with all of our favorite sides along with two gallons of sweet tea. I haven't set the kitchen up yet, so the beggars aren't allowed to be choosers today.

Once everyone is content with a generous plate of food, I slide out the back door and scoot over to my small cabin. I didn't eat; worrying Dillon was going to come to the new cabin looking for me. The Harley is parked beside it just as I had suspected. Before I open the door, mellow guitar riffs float outside to welcome me. I nearly lose my nerve, but push on through the door anyway. It's time to come clean with him about Will.

He smiles up at me from the couch and sets the guitar down. He's changed into T-shirt and jeans and is casually barefooted.

"You and your disappearing acts are starting to bug me, Jewels." His dimples disappear when he takes in my expression. I'm sure it's a mixture of guilt and regret. "Just drop it on me and get it over with," he says brusquely. He's a lot like me in this sense. Just rip the Band-Aid off in one quick snatch. No poking around it.

I can't look at him, so I study my hands. "There's someone I need to tell you about." It comes out in a choked whisper, so I look up to make sure he has heard me. His brows are deeply furrowed in anger. Yep. He heard me. The hurt is etched all over his face.

Dillon is off the couch in an instant and is towering over me. "Who is he and where is he?"

He's scaring me, so I take a step back with my hands

in front of me. "Leave Will out of it. This is just between you and me." I'm shaking a bit and try to calm down.

"You can't marry him! He can't have you!" Dillon shouts.

"I know this." I begin to cry. "I'm messing this up. I mean, he is—"

"Oh, so you're just going to shack up with him? God don't think too highly of that crap!"

I think it's Dillon who doesn't think too highly of this. I'm getting this all wrong. "Wait! You don't understand—"

"You're *my* wife, Jillian!" He's called me Jillian and I think I'm going to throw up. He kicks the toy basket, launching it across the room. I've never seen him so upset. It's scaring me.

"I know I'm your wife. I was there when we said the *I do's!*" I shout back at him.

"Well. I'm starting to wonder if you didn't get the whole reason for those vows. You ran off on me the very next morning." Dillon is running his hands through his hair aggressively. "Does Will even know you're married?"

I shake my head because it's the truth. I've never told anyone but Leona that I married Dillon five years ago. Yesterday was the first anniversary I actually spent with him. This has to have been the longest long-distance marriage in the history of marriages. And maybe the most screwed up.

"He's a special part of my life," I try to explain but I'm getting it all wrong.

"But you're mine." He is still glowering over me.

239

"If you're so keen on wanting me as your wife, then why on earth did you stay away for so long?" I'm getting mad now. Hot tears spill down my cheeks.

"I let you push me away. I was broken at first. Then I got good and pissed with you. I figured I needed to prove myself worthy, so I set out to becoming a man worthy enough." He stops to drag in a jagged breath. "You've took care of me all my life. I was determined to fix it so I could take care of you for the rest of yours." His voice goes hoarse, so he stops to clear his throat. "Then the next thing I know, I'm on tour, then in the studio recording another album. Another year escapes me and then the international tour got underway. I blinked my eyes and lost five years, but I gained so much in that time."

"Dillon..."

Even though he's fuming, Dillon wraps his arms around me. "I'm not that boy who blindly ran off into the world nearly a decade ago. I've done a lot of living since then. I've seen a lot of life that I needed you there for. My life ain't right without you. I'm lost without you." He runs his hand through my hair. "Even before things started going down with Mave, I knew it was time to come home. You're my home, Jewels. Please tell me it's not too late." His eyes redden with hurt.

I don't know how to explain. *Yes, I do, but I'm a chicken.* So much a coward that my lips grow mute.

A bit defeated, he releases me and starts packing his bag. "I'm spending the week with Max," he says between sniffs. "Mave is going through some brutal withdrawals."

He's shaking his head in frustration. "I got to focus on that right now. Mave has to be my top priority." He shoves his wallet and keys into his pockets, and then pulls on his boots. Once his bag is packed, Dillon faces me. "You've got one week to let the dude know you have a husband. Put your wedding ring back on," he says vehemently, pointing at my ring finger. "Or be ready to sign some divorce papers." The last part is only a hoarse whisper. He slams the door on the way out, and moments later he is peeling out on his bike.

I watch him disappear through the gates and realize I have just screwed up big time. That was not how I envisioned that going at all. I stumble over to the rocking chair and cry it all out as memories of my wedding keeps me company.

That night five years ago, Dillon pulled a marriage license out of his guitar case, beaming with hope and had asked me to commit to being his wife that very night. He said he couldn't wait any longer, and he needed me by his side. I was shocked at first by the unexpected request, but quickly agreed anyway. How could I not? My best friend, my first and only love wanted to keep me forever. Of course, I agreed. With Ben's help, Dillon had everything already arranged by the time we arrived at our little home church.

I pledged my life to him in a simple ceremony that spring. It was nearing midnight by the time we were secretly tucked inside our church. Midnight has always held a special time for us, always using that significant hour as a symbolic testament to the importance for each of our loved ones. Although this time it was chosen for privacy concerns, it still made the event that more sacred to me. This was also the very place where Dillon first admitted his feelings for me, making it so fitting to be the place he chose for us to commit to those feelings.

The quaint sanctuary had been illuminated with warm glowing candles and lent an intimate feel to the evening. It was simple, yet breathtaking. As I walked down that short aisle, my heart beat wildly in my chest, not from fear, but with pure joy and excitement. Leona lent me a vintage lace gown she unearthed on that treasure hunt all those years ago in our shed. Dillon wore simple black jeans and a white button-down shirt, but looked priceless. We vowed to love one another completely that night before only God and our three guests, who only included Leona, Ben, and the pastor.

Nothing fancy by the world's standards, but it was perfect to me.

Dillon pulled me out the back door of the church after excusing our guests that night and placed us in the very spot we had shared our first kiss. He held me and whispered how incredible it would be to finally love me the way he had wanted to for so long.

He tilted my head back, and while skimming his fingers along my cheek, he whispered, "I want that kiss back now."

We kissed and then danced in the moonlight of that abandoned church parking lot. He sang as we danced and then not being able to get close enough, decided it was time for the honeymoon. A night I carry with me daily. To be loved by Dillon Bleu is such a divine treasure.

I was so excited that I was finally going to get to keep Dillon forever, after years of coming to terms of him not being attainable. He wanted me and that was all I focused on until the next morning when Cora showed up to serve me up a healthy serving of reality. Yes, she forced my hand to let him go, but we both had only wanted the best for her son. I don't think Dillon thought the decision to marry me that night all the way through, anyway. We were so naïve, and I'm still facing the consequences of that.

I walk over to the armoire and pull out the small keepsake box that holds two treasures dear to my heart— my wedding ring and our wedding certificate. I open the lid, pull out the emerald and diamond ring, and place a kiss on the cool, smooth stone before slipping it on my finger for the first time since the wedding. It still fits perfectly. More tears trickle down my face as I try unsuccessfully to figure out how to fix everything. With no answer to that to be found, I slip the ring back off and put it back away for now.

EIGHTEEN

So I'm married...

With an estranged husband. Only months after mine and Cora's final spat, a lawyer showed up at my door. I thought for sure it was for an annulment, but ended up being a confidentiality agreement for me to sign. It stated that I was not allowed to share any personal information pertaining to any member of Bleu Streak. Those papers had Cora written all over them. I would never share anything about them, so I agreed to sign the papers without any qualms to prove it.

Everything stinks. Things can't get any worse. Right? Wrong. Things can always be worse.

Even though Dillon has not been here this week, the media thinks differently. I've been trying to convince them otherwise, but they ain't having it. Luckily, Dillon left the guards on duty while he's been gone.

We've only had minimal intruders to kick out. The headlines vary from ROCKER DILLON BLEU HIDES OUT IN NONE OTHER THAN A TRAILER PARK to THE WORLD IS BLEU WITH DILLON HIDING. Pictures of his empty boat are normally paired with these headlines. To my embarrassment, photos of us getting cozy on his boat are also floating around. ROCK LEGEND BLEU SPOTTED WITH A MYSTERY WOMAN. I laugh at being called a mystery. I'm sure with some more digging they will find out I'm just an ordinary nobody who's far from mysterious.

Boy, am I glad Will hasn't got wind of it. He knows about the uproar around town about the celebrity hanging out. He just doesn't know the celebrity has been hanging out with me and the celebrity in question is none other than my husband. Things are going to get worse! I'm still trying to decide how to break it to him about Dillon.

The trailer park has had an uproar, too—white-trash style. Tuesday night, Brina's own estranged husband, Bubba, decides to show up, drunk as a skunk. Before he even made it to her, the idiot crashed a golf cart in the pool, taking out some of my lounge chairs along the way. How he got ahold of it is still a little unclear. Somehow he entered the back gate on foot. I guess he got tired of walking and stole the cart from one of the RV residences. The drunken fool ended up getting over to her and commenced to beating the daylights out of her sister, thinking it was Brina. That's how wasted he was. So Brina jumped him from behind, and the next thing I know, I'm in the midst of it, and all three of us going redneck style on him and beating him with anything we could get our hands on. The old trailer rocked in protest as we bounced around the small space. I ended up cracking him over the head with a beer bottle to bring the fiasco to an end.

Luckily, all the kids were down at the pier for s'mores night with Jen.

The cops eventually showed up to haul him away and actually looked the other way when it came to our bruised knuckles. That is definitely a first in these parts. It was dawn by the time we had Brina's small trailer squared back away from the broken glass and overturned furniture. All the kids spent the following day and night with me and Will, while she got her bearings back.

The golf cart got fished out of the pool the next morning, but drowned completely. Fortunately, my insurance covered it and a new cart was delivered to the campers this morning. It has been one heck of a time around here the past two weeks.

Jen wanted some *pizazz*. Well, girlfriend surely got it!

The entire week passes with no word from Dillon. I'm worried about Mave. Feeling helpless, I called Kyle yesterday to see what he knows. We talk in code for a while with him deciphering. He only told me what I already knew about Mave, but then he wanted to know about me and Dillon.

"Did he meet Will yet?" Kyle asked and I wish he didn't.

"No. Not yet," I answered hesitantly.

"It's time to clear the air, Jillian, and you know it."

"I know. I'm just scared how it's going to turn out." I fidgeted at my desk while we were on the phone, unraveling several paperclips in a nervous fit. "I sure wish you were here."

Leave it to Kyle to say the wrong thing. "Me too. I'd love to see the crap hit the fan!" he said while laughing.

"It ain't funny!" I can't believe he was actually joking about it.

"On this side of the phone, it's hilarious. Jillian and her little soap opera. I never thought you to be the drama type." He tsked and continued laughing, so I hung up on him. *Jerk.* Typical little brother *jerk.* I guess success in the Capital doesn't get rid of that.

I head back to the new cabin this afternoon with the last load of odds and ends, and am putting things away in the kitchen when I hear the door open and close. My skin pricks with awareness as the sound of his heavy boots tap against the wood floor.

Dillon wanders into the kitchen moments later, his demeanor a bit distant and weary. He's a few days past needing a shave, and his clothes look as though he might have slept in them.

"How's Mave?" I want to demand Dillon to take me to see him so I can check on him myself, but I know that's not a good idea at the moment.

"Some better," he says evenly as he leans a hip against the counter.

I wipe my hands on my ratty jeans and face him. I want to give him a hug, but think better of it and stay put. He eyes my bare hand and a shadow crosses his face. He takes this as my decision and I literally watch him crumble. Tears swell in his eyes and his shoulders droop.

"I can't live without you," he whispers.

"You deserve better than me. I'm a nobody." I hold my bruised up knuckles as evidence. "White trash."

He grabs hold of my hand and places kisses on my knuckles. "No. You're the one that deserves better, Jewels. And I've worked hard so I can give it to you. Please. You deserve better than this trailer park."

"I can't just walk away like you did. Everyone got an opportunity—you, the twins, Leona, and even Kyle. Not me!" I clutch my chest as the words heave out. I don't know why I immediately go on the defense. Guilt, I guess.

"You get it now. Put this place behind you and give our marriage a chance. Please," he begs as he grips my shoulders.

"You think I could ever live with myself, if I put all of these people on the streets?" I motion in the direction of the trailers. "If I walk away, that's what's going to happen."

I try to turn away, but Dillon pulls me back to face him. "Then find someone to manage it. I'm not leaving this time without you. And I'm not taking no for an answer."

It's getting dangerously close to Will's arrival. I need to figure out how to get Dillon to leave. "I need to think things through... I need some time... I need you to leave. Now." I nudge him toward the living room. "Please."

I leave him standing in the living room and head back to the kitchen. I'm silently begging him to leave and hold my breath until I hear the front door open and close.

The breath rushes out that I was holding in before hearing Will shout out playfully, "Honey, I'm home!"

A loud thud hits the floor in the living room as Will lets out a surprised squeal.

Rushing in the room, I find Dillon on his knees, clutching his stomach as he stares down at Will. Will stares curiously back at him. Brina shifts by the door, catching my attention, and is taking in the scene. She glances at me with a look of sympathy before scurrying away.

The world is on some morbid pause as the guys continue with their stare-down. The only thing moving is my chest as each intake of air hiccups in and then back out of me in a panicked rhythm.

Will finally gives in first and scoots over to me. He holds his little arms out to me and I scoop him up and place him on my hip. I look at my little boy, trying to gauge his reaction. He takes my face in his tiny hands and directs my attention back to the man kneeling on the floor in a frozen state.

"Mommy, that man has my eyes," Will whispers loudly. My little guy doesn't miss much.

I watch those deep-blue eyes fill with tears and shock. "No baby. You have his eyes," I correct. Dillon looks to be at his breaking point. He's pale and still clutching his stomach. "I'm um... Will, do you want to go play at Ms. Brina's for a while?"

"Yay!" he cheers, oblivious to the storm I've deliberately kicked up.

I rush out the front door still holding him, not knowing what else to do. I drop him off to Brina and rush back to the cabin, finding Dillon in the exact same spot.

Only now he is weeping. I kneel in front of him and wait.

Several long minutes pass before his hoarse voice cuts the anxious silence in a harsh bite. "How could you, Jillian?" He's called me Jillian and it punches me in the stomach. The magnitude of my mistake is making me nauseous.

"How could I?" I ask back. "How could I not, Dillon?" My words come out harsh as well. "I couldn't be the ruin of your career." I place my hands on his knees.

"But he's my son." He abruptly stands, sending me tumbling backwards. "I've lost years I can never get back." He scrubs his hands over his tense face.

"You were just starting out! I couldn't let you be trapped here with me, working at the tire factory or something and growing bitter along the way. I would have ruined you."

"You did ruin me!" he says. His deep voice booms around the room as angry, thick tears plop onto his shirt. "I made vows to you before God. You were all I wanted and then you treated me as you've always hated being treated. You threw me away like I was trash!"

He has it all wrong. I shake my head vigorously. "No—"

Dillon cuts into my explanation. "Now I find out you've kept my child, my son, from me for close to five years?"

"I tried to tell you, but you kept interrupting and my words kept coming out wrong."

"No! Not now. Way back then. You knew how to

reach me... Not one time!" He pauses and shakes his index finger in the air. "Not one time did you try! What? Am I not good enough for y'all?" Dillon is irate and is falling apart quickly. The tension is excruciating with him pacing the room in tight circles, his hands grasping his hips.

When he passes near, I grab his arm to get him to focus on me. "No. Listen to me, Dillon. I swear to you. It's me! All me! I'm not good enough! And I thought a baby would have just gotten in your way more. All I ever wanted, and will ever want, is you. I just didn't know how to make it work. You deserve better than me." My voice is hoarse and I can barely squeak the words out.

He shakes his head. "You just don't get it, do you? A measure of a man's worth ain't by his wallet size. A measure of a man's worth is what's in his heart." He steps closer and places his hand over my heart. It's hammering away so vigorously that my ears are ringing.

"Please—"

He shakes his head. "You've thought all this time you were gifting, but all you've done is rob me of the biggest treasures of my life. You stole my heart and robbed me of my own son."

"I didn't mean to. Please Dillon. I just want to make this right..."

He pulls his arm out of my grasp. "I can't even think right now... I just don't know if there's a way to right this." Without another word, Dillon stalks out of the house and slams the door so fiercely the frame protests.

I bow my head to the floor and beg God to help me

make this right, crying until I can cry no more.

Oh, how I wish Aunt Evie was here to help me clean up this mess I have made. Life without her anchoring me has been excruciating. It's stinging so bad at this moment that I can hardly breathe. My mind plays back in a quick reel of the last five difficult years that were barely survivable.

I hid my pregnancy for as long as I could, but Will seemed to be growing straight out, and so at only six months in there was no hiding it. Jen did all my business outside of the trailer park so I could hide out. The residents here were more sympathetic than judgmental. I guess in their minds I was just another trailer park statistic.

If Aunt Evie would have been here, she would have told me to hold my head high, but as it was, most days I didn't see no farther than my shoes.

Kyle came home and was by my side the morning my son was born into this world. With school, he was only able to stay a few days until I was released from the hospital. Jen and Leona stepped in and kept a close eye on me and Will. The short spells that I found myself alone, I spent that time crying. I don't know if it was postpartum depression, or me mourning the loss of Dillon and Aunt Evie and wanting so badly for them to still be a part of my life. I was so scared and had no idea what to do with a baby.

But loving Will ended up being as easy as loving Dillon. It all felt natural after I got over the first mom jitters.

Eventually I ran out of tears and grew a thicker skin for my child's sake.

• ♪ • ♪ • ♪ •

Nearly an hour later, I shuffle to the bathroom to wash the hurt off my face so I can go get Will and try to fix things.

I ride my golf cart over and knock on Brina's door. She opens it and looks at me curiously.

"Thanks for watching Will. Can you tell him it's time to go?" My words are all nasally and fatigued.

"He's not here. Dillon picked him up."

"Brina! How could you just hand my son over to someone without my permission?"

"Hello! Dillon Bleu!" She says this like that's supposed to make it okay.

I don't say another word, just storm off before I punch her. The pit of my stomach is on fire with anxiety. I head over to the office in a mad sprint, not knowing exactly what to do. I round the corner and hear them before I see them. Relief floods over me when I spot Dillon and Will hunkered down underneath our favorite willow tree with Dillon playing the theme song to *SpongeBob SquarePants* on his guitar. Will is grinning as he claps his hands to the beat. I stop dead in my tracks and watch.

As the song ends, Will begs, "Play another one, please!" Dillon obliges and starts playing one of his hit songs.

When Will starts singing along Dillon stops playing and looks at our son in amazement. "How do you know this song, little man?"

"My mommy has a crush on the band. Her listens to them *all* the time," he says.

This makes Dillon chuckle. He musses Will's hair and starts playing again, but this time he is playing "My Jewel."

Will jumps up and down. "That's her favoritest!"

Dillon glances over to where I'm standing, aware of my presence. He points at me and Will looks in my direction, too. This seems like an invitation to join them, so I walk over and sit.

"Mommy, he can really play that guitar good," Will says in awe. This makes Dillon and I laugh.

"Will, run over to the ice cream hut and get yourself a Popsicle."

He hops up and scurries over to the little stand at the edge of the pier. This is something new I just recently added. We watch as he climbs onto one of the stools and asks for cherry limeade.

"You always knew how hard it was on me to not have my dad," Dillon whispers, his eyes trained on Will. "How could you do that to our son?" He has no intentions of letting me off easy on this. I don't blame him either.

"I'm sorry. I never thought it would take so long for you to come back. It's like you said, life got busy and time slipped by."

He shakes his head in disbelief. "Will?" he asks. He

glances over at me sideways before shifting his focus back to our son.

"I named him that because he gave me the will to keep it together."

Dillon scoffs at this.

"You were gone... Then I lost Aunt Evie and became a mom all in one year. So yes, our son gave me the will to go on."

"Jewels, you didn't have to go through any of that alone. You made that choice."

We grow quiet, both our statements placing us into a somber spell.

Will giggles about something, snapping us back to him.

Dillon runs his hands through his hair and smiles weakly. "A honeymoon baby. That's a special gift."

I can barely swallow from all of the emotions whirling around me. "I've always thought so. I thought that maybe... Maybe if I couldn't ever get you back, I would at least always have a part of you." I look over at the spitting image of him. The little guy is swinging his legs as he enjoys his Popsicle.

"We need to tell my mom. She has a right to know, too."

I snort at this and he glares at me questionably. "She already knows, Dillon. Who do you think talked me into letting you go?"

"How? Why?" His eyebrows are pinched in confusion. Then acute anger takes over his features.

I shake my head, knowing it will only make things worse.

"Tell me." He growls under his breath, close to losing his cool again.

"Cora showed up that morning after we got married and told me to give you a chance with your career. Said I would only get in the way of that. And you know what Dillon? She was absolutely right." He recoils, so I reach over and grab his hand. "She came back for Aunt Evie's funeral and knew right away. I tried hiding it under a frumpy dress." I feel Dillon's eyes boring into me, but can't bring myself to look at him. "She did what she knew was right for her son. I understand that now. Please don't be mad at her. Just be mad at me."

"You're stronger willed than that, Jillian. What did my mother do?" He eyes me and is beckoning the truth out of me.

I clear my throat. "She said the papers wouldn't take too kindly to our romance. Especially the part where it began with you a minor and me already a legal adult."

He rubs his face roughly with his free hand. "I can't believe this." He shakes his head at the absurdity of it. "We never did anything inappropriate."

"Cora said the media wouldn't see it that way," I whisper. We sit silently for a while before I speak again. "I promise I wanted nothing more than to be your wife and to go with you. But everything, and I mean everything, was against it. First Cora, then I found out I was pregnant, and then Aunt Evie died. No matter how badly I wanted you, it seemed to not be in God's favor."

Dillon lets out a long frustrated breath. "Mave is being moved to another facility. Word has leaked out, so I've got to go take care of some business out of town." He grabs hold of my arm. "Look at me, Jillian." I look up. "Will is mine and I've got a lot of time to make up for with my son. You need to decide if you're going to be on board with that. 'Cause it's happening with or without you." With the stern warning, he gets up and walks over to Will.

He perches on a stool and shares a Popsicle with our son. I watch until their treats are gone and Dillon is swooping Will up and is carrying him over to me. This giant of a man carrying our bundle of a treasure in his strong arms—it's an image I never want to forget. It's a beautiful sight. He hugs the little guy tightly before handing him over to me.

"What's your name?" Will asks him.

"Daddy. Please call me Daddy," he says proudly. "I'll see you soon, buddy." Dillon barely glances at me before heading over to the small cabin to grab his bags, I'm guessing. For the last time, I worry.

"When will you be back?" I yell over at him. He keeps walking and just shrugs his shoulders. And with that, Dillon Bleu walks back out of my life.

NINETEEN

Okay... So in all of one afternoon, I totally earned the worst wife as well as the worst mom in the world award.

I've defended my decisions adamantly over the years, sure that they were the right ones. I couldn't let me be the ruin of Dillon's musical dreams. There's no way I could have lived with myself. But I'm now realizing how much those decisions have cost each one of us.

I've set out in the last two months to reconcile this. I've done my best to give Will a detailed history of his daddy. I told him I had kept him a surprise from Dillon, which is absolutely true. I try to help Will understand why Dillon can't be with us by explaining to him that our dear friend Mave is sick and really needs his daddy right now.

I've cost my son a lot. Four years to be exact.

We've spent many afternoons under the willow tree with me rambling on about growing up with Dillon as my best friend and about some of the mischief we got into along the way. He loved that his daddy actually blew a boat up—even though it was by accident. I share about the treasure hunts and promise him one soon. We visit Leona and her new baby girl, Phoebe, every afternoon. Leona shares stories about Dillon with Will while I love on that sweet baby. She talks about how Dillon serenaded the trailer park all those years and how Aunt Evie would beg him to play her favorite hymns.

I enjoy telling Will all about his daddy's magical talent of music. I finally let him watch the Bleu Streak YouTube concert videos. My child is hooked on the band now just as much as I am. It's hilarious to watch a four-year-old rocking out, just let me tell you. It's in his blood, so what can I say?

I don't know if I've lost Dillon. When he calls, he asks immediately to speak to Will. So I have no choice but to hand over the phone and be ignored. I try asking him about Mave and I only get vague answers. He states evenly that Mave is making progress and then shuts me out. I ask him about when he is returning, but he always says he's not sure. I deserve this, I know. It still doesn't make it any easier. Dillon has always treated me with love and compassion and this coldness really stings. I know one thing for sure. He will be back for his son, if nothing else.

A week after he left abruptly, a massive delivery came for Will. It included a child-sized set of drums, a children's guitar that is the exact replica of Dillon's electric-blue one, and an upright black piano. Fingers crossed, Will took after his daddy in the music department and not his momma. A laptop was also included with the instructions on how to set up Skype. Dillon video chats with Will every night and prays with him before saying good night. It shows me that we could have made this work all along.

Again, Dillon never asks to speak with me.

That delivery had a note with it that simply stated, *just because*. Now that didn't make too much sense to me, until a few weeks after that another delivery was made. Each package was labeled for each birthday Dillon missed. Four birthdays I stole from him.

The first birthday package was a Bible. The rich leather cover is embossed with Will Bleu and the inside is dated for the first birthday. A card tucked inside was scrawled in Dillon's handwriting. It stated: *These are the words to live by, my son. The Bible is your road map. Keep it close to your heart and you'll never be lost. ~Proverbs 4:4.*

The second package was a humongous set of Legos. Those suckers are strung and strode all over my living room at the moment. The card with this gift stated: *You can build any life you want as long as you have the right foundation ~Matthew 7:24.*

The third birthday gift was a bicycle that resembled a mini Harley with the same paintjob as Dillon's. It is the coolest bike I have ever seen, even with training wheels. All of the neighbor kids beg Will to let them take a spin. My sweet boy shares, too. He knows this is not the land of good and plenty already. The note attached to the bike stated: *This life is a journey. Always keep your wheels on the right path and nothing will be out of reach. ~Psalm 119:34.*

The man is such a poet with his words. I've taken the cards and tucked them into Will's baby book for safe keeping. I hope to share this book with Dillon someday, if he ever speaks to me again.

The fourth birthday gift totally blew my mind. It is a framed copy of the lyrics to a song written by Dillon entitled "My Will." The note tucked with it told us that all money from this song goes directly into a college account for Will. The note attached stated: *The will of our lives is in God's hands and I'm a blessed man that He saw fit for you to be my Will. ~Ephesians 1:5.*

There was a lot of thought put into these gifts, and it makes my heart squeeze. Each of these verses is marked in Will's Bible and has comments scribbled in the margin from his daddy. Will is a blessed boy to have Dillon Bleu for his daddy. I've never seen someone with such a loyal heart as that man.

I got the funniest text from Dillon just this week. *My son needs a haircut. Get him one.* I laughed and came close to texting back that he was a fine one to talk, but I thought better of it. Will has always worn his hair on the long, shaggy side. It broke my heart to have his hair cut, and he felt the same way.

"I want my hair like Daddy's," he said. After I told him it was his daddy's request, Will got over it instantly. Good grief. I can already see who gets to be the good guy, and it ain't Momma.

Another delivery followed the hair text. It was an entire new wardrobe for Will. It was all high-end designers, but tasteful. It's basically designer jeans and T-shirts with every brand of shoes you could think of. The note he scribbled stated: *Please dress my son better.* I thought I was already doing a decent job of that. I didn't let him wear the secondhand clothes like I wore. I have always searched diligently on the clearance racks at the outlet stores for his outfits. I guess Dillon only has his childhood to go off of, and I'm guessing he is determined to make his son's better. Again, I keep my snide comments about the subject to myself. Dillon also has no clue how our boy's body is growing with a blink of an eye. I seriously doubt Will gets the chance to try out each pair of shoes before he outgrows them. There's plenty of kids around here to share them with, though.

Speaking of which, there was also several packages for Brina's young'uns. Dillon scribbled a note saying: *Brina's kids look to be in need of some clothes.* That man's heart is bigger than anyone's I know. So me and my little boy snuck over to Brina's late that very night and left the clothes on her tiny porch.

Dillon won't speak to me, so I have texted an apology. *I can never apologize enough for my mistakes. I swear to you I have loved you more than God expects a wife to love her husband. My love for you is so far beyond that. Not a day has ever gone by that I have not physically ached for you. I love you.* It has gone unanswered and it breaks my heart. I never weighed the impact of those choices I made for Dillon and me—and Will for that matter.

I received a letter from Cora apologizing last week, to my surprise. I can only begin to imagine how Dillon probably laid into her. She said she had no business ordering me to stay away from Dillon and she was sorry for all of the time lost. I'm not crazy about forgiving her.

But if I want Dillon to forgive me, then there's really no other choice. She wants to meet Will and this rubs me wrong something awful. Cora knew he existed all of these years and now wants to show interest. My baby has never had a grandparent and I think he has done just well without one. I just don't know about this one. I guess we will cross that bridge when we get to it. From the sounds of things, Dillon won't be pushing that any time soon.

It did make me feel better that Dillon isn't talking to her at the moment either. Kyle called last night and filled me in some.

"Dillon told Cora it was in her best interest to leave him alone for a while. He also told her she best get busy with apologizing to you," Kyle said.

"Great. Now she's going to bug me. Just great!"

"I still can't believe you two have been married all these years behind my back. Both of you really suck for keeping it from me."

"But you knew I had his child."

"Yeah. I just thought you were following in the footsteps of half the residents of Shimmer Lakes Trailer Park," he said with a laugh.

"That ain't funny, Kyle, and you know it. Things happen and these poor people don't need you casting your humorous stones at them."

"I was just kidding around, Jillian. Don't get so defensive."

"Come home," I said, barely able to choke the words out. Boy, did I need him right now.

"No way. I done missed the crap hitting the fan. All the fun is over. You are boring again!" He was laughing at me again, so I hung up on him *again*.

There's been plenty to keep me busy around here. I let Jen have my small cabin as a promotion. I need more time to figure out the new life that will be taking place once Dillon finally figures out how spend time with Will, so I promoted her to manager of Shimmer Lakes.

I finally called Hudson, and we have come up with an amicable plan on partnering. He promises to leave the trailer park section, if I agree to take no new occupants. Once he has a good bit of vacant trailers, the plan is to move them out and build more cabins. I like that idea, because no one will be put on the streets this way. The game room is also being revamped into an arcade and small snack bar. I like this too, because it will create some jobs and be great revenue.

The contract is very clear on not kicking out any resident and that no condos or hotels can ever be built. Hudson promises to keep things the way he knows that Aunt Evie would have given her blessings. He's so excited that I've finally agreed to let him pave the roads. That took a month to talk me into, but I know it will be a good move. He's footing the bill for the new renovations as his pay for the partnering.

● ♫ ● ♫ ● ♫ ●

"Blake, I won't tell you again about not being allowed

to do the one-eighty maneuver with the truck. Do it one more time and I'm going to have to fire you." I eye him sternly and watch him fidget.

"Yes, ma'am. I'm sorry, Ms. Jillian," Blake says, making me want to punch him more for making me feel old than for taking out a few of Mr. Wayne's rose bushes with his little stunt.

"Please head over to the arcade and help the guys unload the new games," I say and dismiss the teenage boy from my office. Ugh. I hate having to act all grown.

"Yes, ma'am," he says remorsefully and heads out of my office.

I look down at the damage estimates and shake my head in aggravation. Hudson demanded I fire Blake immediately, but Hudson has some learning to do about this side of the lake. This isn't just some nonsense job for this teenager. He has to help his grandma make ends meet. I finally talked him into giving Blake one more chance. Hudson also assumes the damages will be taken out of the guy's paycheck. I told him I agreed that should be done, but I never said I would. So I'm writing Mr. Wayne a personal check and Blake has promised to help him clean and replant the damaged portion of the yard.

My phone starts coming to life as I sign my name at the bottom of the check. I drop the pen and answer it. "Hello?"

"Hey. Ms. Raveena said she just saw a strange man climb into the back window of Aunt Evie's trailer," Jen says.

"Great. Just what I need."

"You want me to call the cops?" Jen asks.

I'm already heading out the door. "No. Let me go check it out first. Can you grab Will from preschool and drop him off with Brina just in case this takes more time than I have?" I ask, climbing on the golf cart.

"Sure. No problem. Be careful."

"I'll call you back as soon as I figure out what's going on," I promise before hanging up. It only takes two minutes at the most to zoom up to the trailer. I hop off the cart to walk around the back to peep in my old room's window. Lying on my bed is a rail thin man with his back toward me. He clothes are good quality but are rumpled, and his long brown hair is seriously tangled. His tatted up arms are shielding his face from me, but does nothing to hide his identity.

For old time's sake, I ease the window open, crawl in beside him, and sit on the edge of the bed. I rub his bony shoulder and he slowly rolls over in the small space and stares at me blankly. I get a good look at him and it rips my heart out. He looks like a ghost of himself, with pale skin that makes the dark circles under his tired eyes much more prominent.

"You okay?" I whisper, worried I may scare him. He looks so frail.

He nods his head slightly for an answer.

I pull his hand in mine and hold it tightly. "Are you clean?" I ask in another whisper.

"Yeah. Just needed to come home... Please don't make

me leave," Mave whispers back. His exhausted eyes convey a plea before sliding back shut.

"Of course not." I release his hand and pull my phone out. I shoot Dillon a text. *Got Mave. He's straight. Just leave him here for now. Call u later.*

Dillon texts back immediately. *Thank God. Keep a close eye on him.*

I put the phone back in my pocket and go back to holding Mave's hand. He drifts off to sleep for a while, but I don't leave him. It seems this is what he needs at the moment.

Dillon didn't let on that it was this bad. By the looks of Mave, he got himself into some pretty bad stuff. No wonder Dillon was so broke up about it. Guilt slices through me once again, for not being there for both Mave and the rest of the band. They are my family and I shut them out, too. I'm right ashamed of myself. I might have been able to prevent this for Mave, if I was there by their sides being the mother hen they obviously needed. But I guess that's neither here nor there now. What's done is done and all I can do now is try to make up for the lost time.

Mave eventually wakes with a start and seems to have forgotten where he is at. His entire body trembles even though he's washed down with sweat.

"It's okay," I murmur, hoping to soothe him. "You're home."

His eyes dart around the room in a wild, skittish manner for a few moments before they focus on me. He scoots up in the bed and wipes his hands over his gaunt face.

"Sorry," he mumbles.

We do another quiet spell as we watch each other. His gaze cagey and my stare cautious from being scared I'm going to spook him.

This frail shadow of Mave is a stranger, but I think I know how to reach the old one.

"I still think you have worms," I say, causing a slight smile to pull at his lips. I reach over and squeeze his barely there waist, before pulling my phone out and dialing Jen. "Hey. I'm still at the trailer. I need you to head over to Momma May's and pick up a large bucket of fried chicken with all the fixings and a gallon of tea." As I say this Mave holds up two fingers. "Make that two gallons of tea and a peach cobbler." I'm about to hang up when Mave mouths, *ice cream.* Yep. I've reached my Mave. "And can you stop by the store and grab a container of vanilla ice cream?"

"Sure," Jen says.

I put the phone away and continue to sit with my dear friend. He's like a brother to me, even after all these years of separation. I hate that he got mixed up with such and now has to fight his way out of it.

"I've been praying for you," I whisper.

Tears well up in his eyes. Before they spill, he flings his arm up to hide his face. I know he's ashamed of himself.

"Mave, we all make mistakes. Just promise you won't let this beat you," I say through my own tears. He has had to fight to survive all of his life and I just can't fathom this being the ending to his story.

"I'm working on it. I'm clean. It just hurts a lot," he says hoarsely.

I have no clue as to what it feels like to come off drugs, but seeing him in this shape, it's definitely something I never want to experience. Mave seems to fold in on himself as he curls up in a ball on his side while sobs break from his trembling lips. They come from deep within and shake the tiny bed.

"I'm here..." I rub his back, but barely contain the cringe when my hand meets nothing but skin and bones.

Dillon texted back while Mave slept, letting me know that Mave went missing early yesterday morning and they had been searching for him. I reassured him it was best to stay put for the time being and that I would keep him posted. It wouldn't surprise me if the whole cavalry shows up by nightfall. I just hope the guys hold off and give Mave some space.

"I'm sorry I wasn't there for you," I say quietly. I'm so mad at myself.

"This is on me. No one else," he says, voice muffled by his arm.

"I'm here for you now, Mave. Whatever you need. Promise." I sniffle. Seeing him like this is killing me.

"This is what I need right now. Please let me stay," he begs, breaking my heart.

I pull his arm down from his head so I can see his eyes. "We got this, okay?" He simply nods in agreement.

A loud creaking pop from the front door lets me know the food is here, so I scurry to the front of the trailer and meet Jen.

"Let's eat," she says as she unloads the bags onto the table.

"I need you to leave. Sorry." I shrug and give her my best apologetic face.

"Well, I'm taking a chicken leg at least." Jen narrows her eyes, but grabs a piece of chicken along with a roll and heads back out the door without giving me any more lip.

I texted her back earlier and told her an old friend of mine needed me. I didn't tell her it was Maverick King. She would have gone all fan-freak on me. She's a pretty big fan of the Bleu Streak twins.

As soon as the door slams, I feel the trailer rock slightly with Mave walking toward the small kitchen. I pile him a plate with three pieces of chicken and a pile of mash potatoes and coleslaw as he takes a seat beside me. He digs into it likes he's not eaten in ages. He looks like he hasn't, too. He uncaps the jug of tea and drinks greedily straight from it before sitting it down by his plate

"So I guess you don't need a glass." I hitch a brow up at him.

"I'm good," he garbles out around a mouthful of coleslaw.

By the time I'm done nibbling on a chicken thigh, Mave has made his second plate and has chugged half a gallon of tea. It blows my mind how him and Max have always been able to eat such large quantities of food without getting sick. Really. Where do they put it? These two could be competitive eaters, without a doubt.

I inhale deeply as Mave peels the lid off the tin pan and the aroma of baked peaches fills the space. He looks at the dessert lustfully while licking his greasy lips. It would be comical if he didn't look so pitiful.

"Ice cream?" I ask.

"Please," he mumbles, nodding his head.

I reach behind me, grabbing the carton off the counter and pass it to him. He pops the lid off and sets out to dumping all of it on top of the cobbler. He seems on a mission so I don't fuss at him about it. Instead, I just grab us two spoons and we dig into the rich dessert without a word. He makes fast work of it. I barely get four good bites before the tin container is scraped clean.

"Worms. You have worms." I nod my head at my certainty on the matter, making him laugh. That one thing melts my heart. It's a rich happy laugh and it gives me hope that Mave just might make it through this.

He sits back in his chair and pats his protruding belly with satisfaction. His red rimmed eyes seem to grow quite heavy at the same time.

"Why don't you stretch out in Aunt Evie's bed? There's more room," I suggest.

He sits, thinking about it for a while. "If it's okay, I would rather crash in your bed. I don't think Aunt Evie would be too happy with me right now." He averts his eyes as that haunted expression slips back over his handsome face.

I place my hand over his shaky one, hoping to offer some comfort. "Aunt Evie would be proud that you are fighting to get better."

Mave nods his head and lets out a long sigh as he stands and heads back to my room. I listen to the groaning of the small bed as he lies back down and ask a silent prayer for his healing. By the time I clean the table, his soft snores echo from the back and offer me a little peace, knowing he's getting some rest. I don't want to leave Mave alone, so I ask Brina to let Will spend the night with her, and then I climb into Aunt Evie's bed.

• ♫ • ♫ • ♫ •

Worried that Mave would disappear in the middle of the night, sleep was elusive and my mind was a raging lunatic of *what-if's*. I kept checking on him, but the only time he moved all night was one trip to the bathroom and then right back to bed.

It's already midmorning. I've drunk an entire pot of coffee while waiting on him to wake up and now have a bad case of the jitters. With one knee bouncing uncontrollably, I eye the bag of sausage biscuits Jen grabbed up for me. They are cold now, but I'm sure he will eat them all the same.

While waiting for Mave to rouse, I text Dillon an update. *Mave inhaled a large quantity of food last night and has been in a sleep coma ever since.*

He texts back. *Good. That's exactly what he needs.*

My eyes flick down the hall, then back to the phone screen. *Please let him stay.*

There's a punctuated pause before he responds. *For a few more days, but he's got to go back to treatment soon.*

Before I can reply, Dillon sends another text. *What do you need?*

My first response is instant, but I don't send it. *You.* Instead, I text—*We're good for now.*

I have only a few days to help out the best I can. My sole duty is to feed him constantly and to let him rest. Hopefully, both will be manageable.

After about another hour slowly goes by, Mave shuffles out looking worse for wear, and his hair needs combing in a bad way. He sits by me and without a word I hand him the bag of biscuits and the quart of orange juice. After the five biscuits are gone and the juice chugged, he rewards me with another smile, although it's a weak one.

"What happened, Mave?" I ask, needing the answer.

He shrugs his shoulders. "Curiosity nearly killed this cat," he says. He looks at me and gives me a sad smile that doesn't make it to his bloodshot eyes. "I sure wish I could go back and stay on that dang path Preacher Floyd introduced me to. That dude was so right."

"It's not too late. You're still here. God's giving you a second chance," I say to reassure him.

"I know. I'm not gonna squander it." He shivers and looks lost in thought. "I've been scared straight," he murmurs.

"I need you to get healthy." Then I lay it on him.

"You're an uncle now and I need you to be a good one." I know he's not blood kin, but he might as well be.

"What?" he asks, his confused gaze dropping to my belly. "You don't look pregnant." His eyebrows pinched together as he scratches at the side of his head.

I laugh at the hilarity of his statement. "Me and Dillon have a four-year-old son," I say, and his jaw nearly hits the floor. I have his full attention now.

"Does Dillon know?"

"He just found out and that's why he's not speaking to me at the moment." I pause before finishing my confession, thinking it might do Mave good to focus on something other than his personal demons at the moment. "Dillon and I got married that night before y'all left for that first tour."

"Holy *sh*...crap!" He bolts out of his chair, looking like he's about to laugh or bolt. "You're joking!"

I jump up too and stand in front of the door just in case he tries making a run for it. "No. No joke, Mave. That's why I really need you to focus on getting better. We need you. Will needs you."

"Will?" he asks.

"Yes. He gave me the will I needed to get through these years without Dillon and Aunt Evie. And I bet if you allow it, he can give you the will to get better, too."

He's laughing now, and although it's not the best timing, it sounds like music to my ears. "No wonder our man acted so weird all these years. You wouldn't believe the number of babes that have thrown themselves at him.

All the time." Mave's eyes round for emphasis I don't need.

"I can just imagine." I scoff and cross my arms. Those are images I could live a lifetime without.

Mave laughs some more. "No. The dude wouldn't even look at 'em. We called him Saint Bleu." He rubs the side of his neck, chuckling once more before growing serious. "Me and Max figured you must have broke the dude from all females. Jewels, that man has loved you all his life." He shakes his head and narrows his eyes. "It all makes sense now... You both are creeps for keeping it from us, though."

Mave grabs me up in a fierce hug and I hold him tight right back until I get a good whiff of him.

"Whew. Okay, buddy. Let's head over to my cabin. Dillon left some clothes and I think we can make do with them. You gotta wash your hide." I release him and Mave follows me out to the golf cart. The sun seems to hurt his eyes so he shields them the entire ride. He really looks rough and it's got me seriously worried.

We pull up at my new place and I see the confusion in his features. I quickly reassure him the treasure trove still exists, and as we push through the front he eyes all of the toys scattered around.

"This is gonna be fun. I can't wait to meet the little dude." He smiles over at me, a flicker of excitement in his brown eyes.

I get him set up in Will's bathroom and head to the kitchen to figure out if I have enough food to keep him fed.

I seriously have my doubts. I hate to bother Jen, but she is going to have to do a grocery run for me. I'm making the list out when there's a knock at the door. I hurry through the house to open it and find Tate standing there, with an overnight bag, and wearing his usual warm smile.

"What are you doing here?" Fear hits me that Dillon has sent him to collect Mave already.

"Dillon says I'm to help you in any way needed," he says.

This is a relief to me so I move out of the doorway and welcome him in. "Perfect. I need you to grab groceries first thing." Thank goodness for personal assistants, even if mine is only on loan.

"Sure thing." Tate looks around, placing his bag by the couch. "How is he?"

"Showering at the moment. You might want to pick him up some clothes, too." I pause, trying not to get emotional because Tate is still waiting for me to answer. "He's in bad shape, but please don't worry Dillon about it right now. I just feel like I need some time with Mave. If he doesn't seem any better by tomorrow, I promise I will call Dillon myself."

"Okay," Tate says, looking around again. "Can you make me a list?"

"I'm on it." I finish writing out the shopping list and he heads back out for the groceries. I know Tate gets paid to do this, but the dude is just so pleasantly accommodating.

Mave reemerges later on, looking a bit more human

with his long, wet hair tangle free and clean. Dillon's clothes are way too big with the shirt nearly hanging off Mave's bony shoulder, but they are going to have to work for the time being. The bottoms of the pants are dragging past his bare feet, but Mave seems to not mind. I notice he has to keep hitching the pants back onto his bony hips. I would offer him one of my belts, but I don't think he would accept it.

He places a kiss on my cheek, as he passes me. I know that's his way of saying *thank you.* A few memories of Mave doing that very gesture to Aunt Evie flicker through my mind. I tamp the sentimental emotions it stirs back down and follow after him.

He shuffles into the kitchen without a word and grabs two family-sized bags of chips off the counter and a container of dip out of my fridge, along with the other gallon of tea I brought over from the trailer. He then sets up shop in the hammock on my back deck. After the chip bags are empty and the tea drained, he is out like a light again.

Tate makes it back and after he helps me put everything away, we stand by the sliding glass doors and watched Mave sleep.

"Mave's been going through a pretty rough spell of insomnia." Tate sighs. "Him finally resting is great news."

"Did Mave overdose?"

He nods his head and frowns. "Yeah. Talk about a wakeup call. Dillon found him backstage after the London concert and thought he was dead."

I gulp for air and brace a hand against the doorframe as the room tilts.

Tate seems lost in his own dark reverie and doesn't notice me falling apart. "He was close, too... I saw something in Dillon break that night."

The seriousness of it all clamps down on me, sending the rest of my questions to bolt. My nerves can't take any more answers, so I leave Tate to watch over him and busy myself with fixing Mave a home-cooked meal.

He sleeps until Will gets home from preschool and starts worrying him to no end. The afternoon is filled with Mave going to town on Will's little drum set. The set is so small that he has to kneel in front of them in order to play. It's quite comical to watch.

I snag a picture of Mave playing the drums with Will watching on, both wearing huge grins. I send it to Dillon along with a text. *Mave is going to break your son's drums.* I keep checking my phone, but he doesn't reply.

Before supper, a van pulls up and unloads a full set of drums.

"How does Dillon make these things happen so quickly?" I mutter in astonishment.

"Money talks," is all Tate says before helping Mave set the drums up beside Will's tiny kit.

So, for the next several days, I feed Mave abundantly with Will in awe at how much food the scrawny man can consume. When he's awake, Mave spends most of his time cramming food into his mouth and beating away on those darn drums until my ears won't stop ringing.

I text Dillon my concerns about the loudness of the drums, worrying about Will's eardrums. Again, no reply, but protective headphones show up for Will. The cutie pie wears them while playing his drums alongside Mave.

I keep sending Dillon lots of pictures and videos. Still with no replies. Mave has shared a few video chats with Will and Dillon. Admittedly, I've eavesdropped and have not liked what I've overheard. Mave has had a field day, ragging Dillon on our little secrets. I can tell by Dillon's tone, he's not taking too kindly to it either. I beg Mave to stop adding fuel to the fire. I desperately need Dillon to forgive me and Mave smearing it in his face isn't helping my cause at all. The guy has been relentless.

Mave is definitely acting like his old self, albeit a puny one. He still sleeps a lot. Maybe it's his body's way of repairing the drug damage and giving him a break from the withdrawals. I'm thankful he gets those reprieves because I've seen his demons sneak up and attack him. He'll break out in a cold sweat from out of nowhere and will wander off outside until the episode passes.

All in all, the last several days have been great. We talked Dillon into stretching the visit for two weeks, much to my relief. I'm not ready to let my friend go just yet. Mave is looking healthier and like his old self, but still has a ways to go in his recovery.

We snuck the boat out at sunset last night, with Tate captaining, for a cruise around the lake. It was a peacefully clear night, and Mave really enjoyed it. He also gave Will a more animated version of the whole boat explosion incident. He even included the arrest part, which I had omitted from my version.

But all things have to come to an end, it seems. So this morning after I got Will off to school, Tate sat us down and said the rehab center is requiring Mave to return for another month. He also said that the band thought that it is in Mave's best interest to finish out the program. Mave nodded his head solemnly in agreement.

With a heavy heart, we said goodbye an hour ago. I hate goodbyes, feeling like I have spent my life telling people this too much.

TWENTY

I've been sick to my stomach with worry for the past week ever since Mave left. Dillon is keeping quiet and I'm becoming unnerved by that. I'm back in my office at the computer, trying to dig up anything on the band. Word is the band is back in the studio, recording a new album. I haven't the faintest clue if this is true or not. Dillon won't speak to me still. It's been two and a half months and I'm getting right tired of it.

A knock at the door draws me out of my depressing thoughts.

"Come in," I call out and close my laptop. I'm not expecting the gentleman that enters. He's in a perfectly tailored suit and is wearing horn-rimmed glasses. My stomach gets queasy at the sight of a fancy briefcase in his manicured hand.

He heads over with his free hand stretched in my direction. I take it as he introduces himself. "I'm Bernard Rivers."

"Jillian Whitman," I say just as Jen wanders toward the door like a fly to the bug zapper. I ease over and close the door in her face.

GOODBYES & SECOND CHANCES

"Well now. That's just flat-out rude," Jen sasses from the other side.

I ignore her and head back to my desk. "How can I help you?" I motion for him to have a seat as I do the same.

"I represent Bleu Streak, and I have just a small matter of business to take care of that involves you."

My stomach plummets completely and the room takes on a hazy aura.

"Okay," I say, nervously, blinking several times with hopes my eyes will focus. It doesn't work.

He pulls out a thick set of papers from his briefcase and hands them over to me. "The band would like to compensate you for the songs you have written for previous albums." He then passes over a check with more zeros than I have ever seen on a check with my name on it.

My songs have made their way on albums throughout the last several years, and I always thought it an honor they continued to use my lyrics.

"What?" I look at the check in disbelief as my ears start to ring.

"You realize your songs have been a major contributor to the success of Bleu Streak. It's only fair business for you to be compensated. You will also begin receiving monthly royalty checks based on sales. This was decided upon by Dillon Bleu, and each band member has signed legally binding contracts in agreement to Mr. Bleu's request. Your name is already on the albums, indicating you are the songwriter of the songs... Mr. Bleu wanted to settle this matter sooner rather than later."

I can barely swallow at this point. It's like Dillon is getting all of his ducks in a row. My bleary eyes struggle to focus as the lawyer shows me where to sign on the documents. I should probably have my own lawyer look these over, but I'm in shock, and to be honest, I don't care. The check sitting on my desk is much greater than my last five years' worth of paychecks combined. I really never thought twice about ever making money off of Bleu Streak. This one definitely took me by surprise.

"You have any other papers with you that need my signature?" Unable to meet his eyes, the question comes out just over a whisper.

"No. I only handle legal matters pertaining to the band. Not personal matters of Mr. Bleu." Mr. Rivers answers without meeting my eyes either. It's like we are playing *don't catch the eye* game and it's making me even more uncomfortable. So I guess he knows more papers are on the way.

The lawyer stuffs the papers back into his briefcase. "I represent other bands as well, Ms. Whitman. You are one talented songwriter. I would be happy to get you in contact with them." He hands me a business card.

"I appreciate that, sir, but there's no way I could ever write for another band." I try to hand him the card back, but he won't accept it.

"Keep it in case you ever change your mind. You never know what the future holds," he says with one more handshake before heading out.

I stare at the check for the remainder of the afternoon with a feeling of pure dread. My future is probably holding divorce papers and my last goodbye from Dillon Bleu.

Another week passes with no other lawyers turning up. But I'm still waiting. I just know it's coming. I don't want it to happen, but I'm just ready for it to be over with, all the same. I'm back in my office, trying to focus on work, but my focus is fuzzy. My mind is in a constant haze lately.

"Hello, sunshine," Jen says as she enters my office carrying her usual coffee cup along with a thick package. She plops the package down and sits opposite of me. "It came certified. I had to sign for it." She points to the label with a California address on it.

She's waiting for me to open it but I can't bring myself to do it just yet. I push it to the side and ask her to go check on the pool guy. Jen eyes the package suspiciously once more, but heads out the door without one word of comment.

Later this afternoon, Jen is about to climb the walls. "Open that dang package right now or I'm going to do it for you!" She lunges for it, but I snatch it away before she can get ahold of it good.

"Your freaky nosiness is not healthy," I bicker.

As it is, I can't put it off any longer. I want the sting of it over with before Will gets home from preschool. I take a deep breath and tear into it, confused and then shocked at what I find.

"This was nowhere near what I thought would be in

this envelope," I mumble.

There are two first class plane tickets to California and two tickets to a private Bleu Streak performance, along with hotel reservation details. A scribbled note in Dillon's handwriting is tucked between the tickets. *It's time my son knows who I am. I expect you to be there.* I want to call and yell at him that I've been working on that, but there's no use. He won't answer.

Jen leans over my shoulder and studies the tickets. "Hot dang!"

"So I guess me and little man fly out in two days." I rise from my desk on unsteady legs and set out to get everything ready for this unexpected trip. Feelings of relief and apprehension wash over me at the same time.

It is both literally and figuratively time to face the music.

By the time the plane lands in California, Will is overjoyed and I'm overwhelmed. My nausea got the best of me twice during the flight. I'm a bundle of nerves, but feel a bit better when I spot Tate waiting for us in the terminal. He takes care of loading our luggage, and we set off toward our hotel in record time. This guy is quite efficient. I'm starting to see the true value of having a personal assistant. I wish I could steal him away from Dillon. But Tate is a smart young man, and I think this is just a pit stop along his way to success.

"Dillon said to get you settled in and then escort you to the auditorium later," Tate says as he opens the door to the luxurious hotel suite.

"Okay," I mumble in awe while taking in the lovely space. Everything is plush in creams and light greys. Will spots a massive welcome basket, full of baked treats, and beelines straight to it. I follow behind him and rummage around for some plain crackers. I still don't feel so good after my first-ever flight. I grab a ginger ale from the fridge that is conveniently stocked and plop down on the super-soft couch. Tate goes right to work on putting the luggage away in the bedrooms. Then he grabs Will a juice box and is leading him out to the balcony before I have enough wits about me to say anything.

"Tate," I call weakly after him. "You don't have to do all this, but thank you." I lean my head back on the couch and shut my eyes, but open them again when Tate speaks.

"You don't seem to be doing too well. Was the flight rocky?" he asks as he pauses by the French doors.

"First time flying, so I don't know," I mumble.

Tate quietly chuckles. "You've got a good hour before we need to get ready. How about you rest while this little dude and I hang out."

I whisper, "Okay," and doze off immediately.

• ♫ • ♫ • ♫ •

The auditorium is only a few miles from the hotel, and we are there in a flash. I'm feeling a lot better after the nap and a soak in the massive tub. I'm wearing a simple white maxi dress that Leona dropped off while I was packing. She demanded I wear it to the concert. Will is sporting a

Bleu Streak T-shirt that Dillon sent him with his jeans. He looks so handsome with his shorter hairdo. I styled it with some gel. He's just so darn cute.

We enter through a side door and Tate escorts us to the front row. The place is already packed, and the crowd is murmuring away. I can't help but be nervous and make no eye contact as we take our seats. The person sitting next to me clears his throat, and it's all I can do not to cry. I look up through a watery sheen and see Kyle sitting beside me.

"Surprise," he whispers and gives me a sideways hug.

Will bounces in Kyle's lap and flings his arms around my brother's neck. We've not seen my brother in almost six months. "Uncle Kyle, I missed you!"

"I missed you too, buddy."

Before I can find my voice, the house lights go down. The crowd erupts in applause when the stage lights come up and reveal Bleu Streak minus the drummer, perched on top of stools with Dillon in the middle and mics before them. First thing I notice is he has cut his long locks off and is now sporting a short messy do that is wildly similar to his son's new hairstyle. I've never seen him with short hair. It's stunning. His face is completely opened now and his features are so well defined. His square jaw, with the normal bit of stubble, is such a gorgeous sight with no shield of hair. I don't notice the other change until he starts working the chords of his guitar. There's new ink on his wedding-ring finger, but I can't make out what it is from here.

Without a word of welcome, the band launches into a

mellow acoustic rendition of Creed's "With Arms Wide Open." Dillon parts those lips and the words just flow out, velvety. He only looks at Will and me for the entire song. Clearly, this performance is just for us and no one else here tonight. This is one of the most beautifully written songs I have ever heard. The lyrics speak about lives changing in a mighty way, full of hope and joy. He sings about a man and woman creating life and how that life changes everything. The desire for a future and a man praying for a blessed life for his family.

I'm finally able to take a deep, easy breath for the first time since Dillon left almost three months ago.

As they reach the middle of the song, the other band members stop playing and Dillon takes over with the guitar break before he begins to sing so achingly sweet again. The man's voice is absolutely brilliant, and I can't control the emotions he summons out of me.

The crowd erupts as Dillon eases the song to a close. He gazes out over the audience as though it's the first time he's noticed they are here. It takes forever for them to settle down enough so that Dillon can speak. The band waves and smiles, and then try to quiet the crowd by turning their attention to the band leader perched in the middle of them. I see the respect he has so graciously earned over the years as head of this extraordinary group. The impression they display is a united family, and I am a blessed woman to get another opportunity to be a part of it. I know the look Dillon is giving me. It's the look of absolute love and adoration. And most importantly, forgiveness.

"Welcome to this private gig, tonight. Hope you don't mind if we keep it keyed down. My son is in the audience, and I want him to still be able to hear when he walks out of here later." The crowd laughs and I nudge Will's leg. He is grinning ear to ear and his own little dimples are on display.

A stagehand takes Dillon's guitar and hands him the ukulele I gave him. "This next song is new, and it's for my son. It's titled "My Will." The single acoustic version drops tonight." The crowd cheers at this.

He takes the ukulele in his long graceful hands and begins to strum the little instrument and the place fills with a jovial sound. Trace has maracas and begins to shake them to the rhythm Dillon is creating with the ukulele. Max and Logan join next with hushed guitar chords. It sounds like a celebration, and quickly becomes one when Dillon adds the sweet lyrics. Everybody claps along.

My Will...My Will...My Will
I am yours and you are mine
And everything else is gonna be just fine

My Will...My Will...My Will
I got you and you got me
We're rooted together in this family tree

My Will...My Will...My Will
I got my Will
I'm well on my way`
Living this life
Day by day

My Will...My Will...My Will
You got me and I got you
Come on now
Our dreams are about to come true

Be my Will
Always my Will
Stay with me my Will

The cheery song repeats back through after a quicker beat bridge. It's a lively song and I absolutely love it. Will does too. He's bouncing up and down in Kyle's lap and clapping along. It doesn't get past my attention that my son is keeping the exact beat to the song.

After the song concludes, a stagehand reappears to retrieve the ukulele from Dillon. He grabs the mic and stands. "Tonight is a night of celebration and I got a lot to make up for."

At this point a bodyguard escorts me and Will to the stage. The big guy sits Will in a movie director's chair that has been placed beside Max. Max fist bumps with Will's tiny one. Dillon walks over as he places the mic in his back pocket and gives Will a kiss, and then musses the little guy's hair.

Then, Dillon grabs my hand and walks us to the center of the stage. All I want to do is kiss him. He must sense this or wants the same, because the next thing I know he has wrapped his arms around me and claims my lips in front of this packed house.

"It's about time you put that ring back on your finger, where it belongs," he murmurs against my lips. He holds up my hand and places a kiss on top of my wedding ring. The place erupts in whistles and more applause.

I grab up his hand to inspect the ink. On the top of his finger is a cursive *J*. It's so elegant, but I love it even more when Dillon flips his hand over and exposes a cursive *W* that connects to the *J* underneath. "It's not so bad being by my side is it, Pretty Girl?"

"Not at all. It's where I belong," I admit, my voice finally finding a steadiness.

"It's about time you realized it. I love you and we'll work things out. Promise."

I'm crying again, so all I can do is nod my head in agreement. Dillon wipes my face gently, and then looks over his shoulder. A stool is brought out and Dillon gently sets me on it.

Dillon pulls the mic from his pocket, brings it to those full lips, and announces, "Ladies and dudes, this is my gorgeous wife, Jewels." He points over to Will. "And that good looking guy is my son, Will." More applause breaks out. Dillon squeezes my hand and waits for the crowd to settle back down. "My Pretty Girl and I recently celebrated our fifth wedding anniversary." The crowd erupts again with applause. They seem to be as overjoyed as I feel. He patiently waits for them to calm before continuing. "And that got me to thinking about the traditional wedding anniversary gifts." He pauses and nods his head toward Will. "I already gave her the best gift I could ever give her on our wedding night." He winks at me. "I gave her a son," he says smugly, causing more whistles to erupt.

"The fifth anniversary gift is wood. We had ourselves a sweet boat when we were kids. It was a wood sports boat." Dillon cuts his eyes over to my brother in the audience. "But I blew that sucker up." He shrugs his shoulders. Kyle and Max are howling with laughter at the memory. "So I gave my lady a new boat."

Tate walks out on stage and hands Dillon a thick leather journal. Dillon nods his head at him in thanks, and then hands it to me. "The fourth anniversary is leather. All the pages in this leather journal are blank, and I want us to write our future together in it." This gorgeous poet is bringing me to tears in front of all of these strangers.

Dillon kisses an escaped tear away before he opens the journal to the back page and pulls out a paper that's tucked there. "The third anniversary is fruit." As he hands me the paper, I'm racking my brains at what he could possibly be giving me that is related to fruit. I nearly drop the paper in shock when I read it. "Jewels and I danced the day away in a peach orchard not too long ago. It was one of the best moments in my life. Just me and my girl and all those peach trees. I want to be able to relive that moment any time I see fit, so I bought it for her." My hand shakes as I stare in awe at the bill of sale for the orchard. How romantic can he get? Women in the audience are swooning at his sentiment.

"The second anniversary is cotton and the first is paper," he states these two together as Tate carries out a very simple, yet very exquisite, wedding gown and hands me a marriage renewal certificate. "Let's renew those vows we took before God so we can get to work on our ever after."

I sniffle some and try to clear my throat. I shake my head no and Dillon looks at me with concern furrowing his brow. "We're gonna have to do it soon or I won't be able to fit into that dress," I finally mutter out around more sniffling.

"What was that?" he asks, but I know he heard me. Those dimples are on full display.

He eases the mic closer to my lips. He wants everyone to hear what I just announced. "I said we are gonna have to say those I do's soon, or I won't be able to fit into that beautiful gown." Whistles and clapping erupts across the crowd as I run a sweaty palm over my belly.

A smirk crosses Dillon's face as he puts the mic back to his lips. "Man, I'm good." He growls playfully and places the mic behind his back and whispers in my ear, "We created our own treasure in that shed." He is grinning in such a way that is absolutely stunning. His purplish-blue eyes sparkle with unshed tears of joy and he is nearly glowing with pride.

I like that he thinks so much like me. I had already come to the same conclusion about our own treasure over a month ago when I found out I was pregnant.

"Yes, Dimples. We did."

Dillon drops the mic and kisses me like his very life depended on it. After we are both breathless, he pulls back and looks at me sternly. "No more goodbyes."

"No more goodbyes," I promise.

EPILOGUE

Wow. All I can say is wow!

Me and Dimples have stuck to our promise and have not said goodbye since that night on that stage six years ago. A smile eases on my face from just thinking about that magical night. The crowd started chanting after a while for more songs, so eventually Dillon tore his lips from mine and Bleu Streak rocked that place out.

Dillon moved us over to his hillside mansion after that concert, and I finally got my autographed CD's!

I asked him later that night as he held me in his king-sized bed, why had it taken him well over two months to send for me and Will. I was worried he had second-guessed wanting to be with me during those silent months. He chuckled at my nervous question, making me want to pinch him.

"Buying a peach orchard was no easy feat. That ornery owner didn't want to come off it, so I ended up paying a small fortune." We both laughed at this. My husband was held up buying me gifts while I fretted our marriage was over.

Every spring he whisks me away to our orchard

and we spend the day dancing among the pink-flowered trees. We picnic there quite often during the summer. There's nothing better than hand-picking your sweet dessert right from the tree.

Kyle flew back with us after the California concert so he could walk me down the aisle in my second wedding to Dillon Bleu. Will was the best man and Leona was my maid of honor, with Jen as my matron of honor. Trace played the piano, of course. Logan and Max were groomsmen. Mave flew in with Dillon and had asked just to be a guest. He was still pretty weak.

The ceremony was held in our small church, which was so packed, people had to stand outside. We had Momma May's cater the reception that was set up on the lakeshore. A country feast of fried chicken and all the fixings that led to Max and Mave having an eating contest. You can only imagine how that went. Needless to say, we had no leftovers.

The band set up on the dock and serenaded the crowd off and on throughout the night when Dillon wasn't busy dancing with me. The other side of the lake was packed with spectators trying to get a glimpse of the rock stars through binoculars and high-powered cameras. How do I know this? Because our wedding and reception pictures were plastered all over the Internet the very next day. Dillon joked that we threw our money away on a private photographer when we could have gotten all we wanted for free online. Some were quite good, so we did swipe some a few.

The paparazzi bugged us to no end that first year, but Dillon always allowed them have the pics they wanted. He assured me it was pointless to fight against them. I guess we were too nice, and eventually too boring, because the numbers trickled down to only a rare few popping up occasionally.

A month after the wedding, Dillon pulled up in a custom black Cadillac Escalade. The sides are slashed with intricate blue and silver streaks and the windows are tinted super dark. The interior has black, buttery-soft leather and every electronic gadget you can imagine. It's totally tricked out.

I questioned the purchase and he shrugged his shoulders and answered, "We need family wheels."

I nodded my head in understanding. "Family wheels, Dillon Bleu style."

He produced those dimples and replied, "Of course."

Dillon didn't leave my side the entire pregnancy, saying he would not miss a moment of his baby growing in his bride's body. He was fascinated with my ever-changing body and couldn't keep his hands off me. And just let me tell you, the most precious vision I have ever witnessed was the day my husband held our baby girl in his arms for the first time and openly wept at the sight of her. Our Grace has her own hit song, "My Amazing Grace," and at only age five is already set for college and life after because of it.

I have filled four leather journals so far with this treasure of a life with my family. I've been approached to turn them into a memoir for Bleu Streak. I hesitantly told the agent, maybe one day, but as for now the answer is no. I'm not ready to let those treasures be discovered yet. I want them all to myself.

The band is doing better than ever. They only commit to one performance a month so we can all tag along. Trace ran off with Jen last month and got married. They are still honeymooning in Jen's small cabin at the moment. They are quite the lively couple, with both of them always having an abundance of energy. I'm surprised it took them this long to figure out they belonged together.

Oh, I almost forgot to tell you that Mr. Wayne and Ms. Raveena went all Dillon and Jillian style. Those two got secretly married a few years back. We put two and two together after catching them sneaking out of each other's trailer several times before dawn. We threw them a surprise wedding reception and pretty much forced them to admit it. They are quite the cute couple.

Max, Mave, and Logan went in together and purchased a bachelor pad a few miles from here. It's a lake house closer to our side than the rich side of the lake. So all of my family is close, except for Kyle. He makes more trips home now than what he used to, which makes me happy. His life isn't here, but I'm glad he still visits often. I think it's because Grace has him wrapped around her little finger.

The first row of new cabins has just been completed, and we gave Tate the one closest to the lake. He is working on his business degree through an online college, and Dillon is planning on bumping him up to the Bleu Streak management team after Tate graduates. So he is sticking around, too. I like that. He is a great help, and more importantly, a great friend.

A recording studio was constructed in record time behind our cabin. We also added a master suite to the bottom floor of our home. In interviews, a popular question they like to ask Dillon is, "You're a rock star with millions in the bank. Why on earth do you live in a trailer park?"

He always shrugs his shoulder and looks at the interviewer as though the answer should already be so obvious. "Because it's home," he simply answers each time.

You still have to keep on your toes around this crowd. A few months into us getting settled in, Max made the mistake of wanting to spend the weekend with us before they had their place ready. Max was bragging on and on about staying up days upon days at a time during the tours. He was stretching the truth quite a bit, so Dillon challenged him to see just how long Max could actually go straight without any sleep and promised to pay him a thousand dollars if he could stay awake until the sun came up the third morning. Never one to back down from a challenge, no matter how stupid it is, Max said he would kick butt. The guys took turns staying up with him, and Max actually made it a little over forty-eight hours before passing out. Now maybe this sounds like a pretty lame challenge, but Dimples had an ulterior motive. Max woke up the next morning, stumbled into the kitchen, and just about scared me to death. I thought a stranger was robbing me or something. I had to take a second good look and found it to be a very bald Max.

He ran his hand over his slick scalp and declared, "Dillon is going down for this."

When he turned to walk back out, I was barely able to restrain myself. Written on the back of his bald head in permanent marker was, *Dillon was here*. No one, not even Will, told Max about it either. So the poor idiot walked around for close to a week oblivious.

People would asked, "So, you close to Dillon?" or "You and Dillon tight?"

The doofus would carry on and tell them, "Yes, Dillon is my man." Or he would declare, "Dude always has my back." It was hilarious. The boys had a field day with Max until the ink eventually wore off.

Mave came home a few weeks after that and set out to cutting his own hair off when he took in Dillon and Max's transformations. Logan followed suit and trimmed his afro way down. So Trace felt left out, of course. He cut all of his fluffy blond hair off, too. I always liked their long hair, but those dudes got even more handsome once you could actually see their faces.

The only new ink Dillon has is a cursive G he had his tattoo artist add to his ring finger tattoo. He's such a sentimental old soul. I fall in love with him more each day. Really. How could I not?

Music is a constant in this house. Now my son does not have the divine gift as his daddy has been blessed with—the gift Dillon has is a rarity—but this doesn't deter Will. He just can't figure out what instrument he wants to commit to entirely. One month he is dead-set on the guitar and plays nothing but it, and the next month he is back to being obsessed with the drums. This delights Mave. He has spent many an hour working with Will on his technique. I personally think Will is born to be a drummer. I guess only time will tell on that.

My little Grace is all about the piano. She plays duets with Dillon in church every third Sunday. The girl has an ear for music and this tickles her daddy. You should see him all lit up as they sit on the piano bench in the small sanctuary—Dillon looking larger than life beside our dainty little girl. It's precious.

Mave is doing great, by the way. He's still too curious for his own good. He set out to showing Blake what that little work truck could really do one afternoon and ended up pushing the truck on to its demise. Mave earned a crushed foot in the accident, but was adamant about only taking over-the-counter pain meds. The poor guy suffered until his foot was healed. He spent a lot of time asking to be alone. The pain would escalate and he wouldn't be able to tolerate being around people. His doctor and drug counselor reassured him there were choices for pain management for him, but he was scared he would relapse, so he suffered it out. Whatever he got caught up in really scared him straight. He now has Psalm

46:1 tattooed on top of his right hand as his reminder. *God is our refuge and strength, a very present help in trouble.*

As for our poor truck, Dillon had a metal worker salvage as many pieces of the body as possible, and then he had it professionally cabled and attached from the ceiling in the larger shed. We call it our redneck chandelier. A hidden message was discovered underneath the frame too. Painted in neon green on the backside of one of the fenders is *Dimples Loves His Jewel*. I asked Dillon about when the message came to be and was astonished by his answer.

"I painted that the winter before the boat blew up," he admitted. Of course that earned him a lot of love that night. I thought that confession was the sweetest thing—him loving me long before admitting it.

Hudson replaced the truck with a John Deere Gator with a dump bed. He had a custom bumper sticker made and placed across the back that says, *Maverick King is NOT Allowed to Drive Me!!* The Gator is actually bigger than the truck. Blake was pretty stoked about it. He is graduating college soon. Dillon rode him pretty hard and the kid has been receiving straight A's all the way.

Dillon even made the arrangements for Brina to go back to school. She is now an RN, I'm proud to say. She can afford to live outside of the trailer park, but has no desire to live anywhere else. Brina says this is home and I couldn't agree with her more. Last year she got permission from me and Hudson to replace her old trailer with a brand new one that is bigger but can still fit on her lot.

There have been other instances of Dillon helping others get a better shot at life throughout the last few years. I teased him a while back, saying, "You can't save the entire world, Dimples."

He gave me a glance at those dimples and rebuked, "No, but as long as God puts them in my path I will never stop trying."

Oh, how I love that man!

I'm in the midst of putting away some dishes, lost in my thoughts, as my crowd busts through the kitchen. Dillon picks me up and kisses me, before setting me down and grabbing a bottle of water. My babies shadow behind him. "We're going on a treasure hunt, Mommy," Grace squeals in delight.

I look down at my baby girl. She has long, wavy hair in the same black hue as her daddy, but has striking green eyes. She makes me smile just by looking at her. She smiles back and rewards me with a showing of her sweet dimples. Will stands behind her. He's working on being taller than me already at only the age of ten. He looks more and more like his daddy the older he gets, too. Besides Grace's eyes, it seems I had no part in the making of my own young'uns.

Dillon walks over to Grace and swoops her up in his arm. There is nothing sexier than seeing that tough-looking giant of a man charmingly carry his daughter around like the princess she is. He places a kiss on her temple and swipes both of them a strawberry from the bowl Will is munching through.

"Find me something pretty," I say as they head out the back door. Dillon turns and gives me a wink before disappearing. Treasure hunts are a tradition around here. I've taken to hitting up flea markets and thrift shops for the oddest things I can find and secretly tuck them into the sheds without anyone knowing I do this.

I love it when Dillon discovers something and shakes his head. "I thought I knew everything in this place by now, but new stuff just seems to appear from out of nowhere."

Now that's just between me and you. Let me have my fun!

This life, minus the occasional concert or music awards show, may seem pretty bland or too ordinary to some. But simple can be quite satisfying. I have a gift that many in this world will never taste. I know what it feels like to be truly loved and adored. And it's not based on my social status or size of my wallet or what I can give. I'm simply loved for being me.

My simple life is beyond extraordinary. It's my treasure.

Goodbyes & Second Chances Playlist

"Best Day of My Life" by American Authors
"Daylight" by Maroon 5
"Tower" by Skylar Grey
"Waiting on Superman" by Daughtry
"Don't Follow" by Alice in Chains
"Here without You" by 3 Doors Down
"Rise" by Eddie Vedder
"Future Days" by Pearl Jam
Any and Every song by Pearl Jam!!
"Slip on By" by Finding Favour
"With Arms Wide Open" by Creed
"Hard Sun" by Eddie Vedder
"Back Home" by Andy Grammer

ABOUT THE AUTHOR

Bestselling author T.I. Lowe sees herself as an ordinary country girl who loves to tell extraordinary stories. She knows she's just getting started and has many more stories to tell. A wife and mother and active in her church community, she resides in coastal South Carolina with her family.

For a complete list of Lowe's published books, biography, upcoming events, and other information, visit tilowe.com and be sure to check out her blog, COFFEE CUP, while you're there!

She would love to hear from you!!
ti.lowe@yahoo.com
twitter: TiLowe
facebook: T.I. Lowe

Made in United States
Orlando, FL
20 April 2024

46013785R10173